LOVE IN VENICE

ADAM WYE

Anchor Mill Publishing

Love in Venice

All rights reserved. Copyright ©Adam Wye 2016

Anchor Mill Publishing

4/04 Anchor Mill

Paisley PA1 1JR

SCOTLAND

anchormillpublishing@gmail.com

The individual depicted in the cover artwork is a model. No inference in regard to his sexual orientation may be drawn from the content of the book.

Adam Wye

For Steve Gee

Love in Venice

Adam Wye

ONE

The taxi reversed into the milling traffic. Then the driver opened the throttle and we were off. The bow reared up and our stern wake grew turbulent and thick. We left the shelter of the airport canal after a minute and the lagoon opened out ahead of us, the city at the centre of it seeming to float upon the water a mile or so distant like a long, long ship. Its masts were the Campanile of the Piazza San Marco and the towers and spires of the city's hundred other churches.

There were six of us in the passenger cabin, all bound for different hotels but for the moment all sitting knee to knee in the cramped, low-roofed space. By chance we were all of us young men. Young or youngish. I took the opportunity to press my thigh against the thigh of the guy next to me. Because we were crammed so close together he could think it was a necessity or an accidental bit of carelessness. He seemed to be about the same age as I was – twenty-one – and like me he had flown out from London wearing shorts.

I enjoyed the warm contact of his bare thigh, his light fuzz of dark hair brushing the even lighter blond fuzz that grew on my own legs. I gazed at his shorts, at his crotch, where the material gathered tightly. He displayed a sizeable mound there. I tried to guess which bit of it was which. I wasn't going to be able to find out for sure though. Not in the public space of a water taxi.

Love in Venice

The going was smooth, though fast. The motor churned the water into a little tower astern, whose summit divided into a V that spread behind us, met and overpowered our bow-wave and turned the road we'd travelled into glistening diamond shapes. When we met another speedboat coming the other way between the marker posts we leapt across its bow and stern waves like a racehorse clearing a couple of fences, and the spray rose on all sides in curtains a dozen feet in height.

Six young men, knee to knee in the cramped space… I'd never done anything involving six people, though I'd seen such things in videos. But I couldn't help thinking, at that moment, that the idea was rather nice.

At last the landmass that was Venice loomed close. We seemed to be aiming straight for the mid-point of the main island's northern waterfront. Then, just as we looked to be set on a collision course for the shore a narrow canal, with an elegant low bridge across its entrance, opened up ahead of us. The driver slowed suddenly and we glided into it.

It was my first time in Venice, my first sight of the place. Our little winding backwater, lovely in its own romantic way, opened out after a few minutes into the glory that was the Grand Canal. Its double row of palaces stood like lines of chocolate boxes in a shiny airport shop, each competing with its neighbour in size and prettiness.

One by one my temporary companions were disembarked – given a steadying hand by the boatman as they climbed out of the rocking craft – at the various waterfront hotels we passed. Mine was the last hotel. I was the last to leave the boat. My arrival along the vistas of the Grand Canal was the longest and dreamiest of any of the passengers'. Drifting beneath the unmistakeable profile of the Rialto Bridge, and heading around the canal's famous S-curve, palazzo-lined, I found I had no objection to that.

*

I'd never checked into a hotel on my own before. I'd never come to Italy before. I only had a few words of Italian, and those that I did have were mostly the instructions used in the performance of classical music: things like *allegro ma non troppo* and *con sordini* (don't use the right pedal) which were not much use in everyday life. Still, I managed it, and was soon installed – for my one night's stay – in a pretty little pink-painted building at the waterfront end of Via Garibaldi. The front door was in the wide pedestrian street (though even this solid walkway had been a canal once) while the back door led to a landing-stage and a mooring post. The windows of my room looked out onto the wide sweep of water where the Grand Canal and the Giudecca Canal met the lagoon's open space in the San Marco basin. Two magnificent churches were in full view across a half mile of water. San Giorgio Maggiore, its campanile standing beside it and pointing skywards like a sharpened pencil – the church had a whole island to itself – and the equally prominently sited, grey domed Salute church. In the far distance the line of the Lido formed the horizon and protected the calm waters of the lagoon from the unpredictable rages of the Adriatic. I had never had a room with a view that was anything like this.

I ate that evening in a nearby restaurant, dining on a plate of lightly battered fried mixed fish. After that it was still too early to go straight to bed. I walked around the area a little, while the lights began to come on in the summer dusk and gave the water in the canals and lagoon a new, polished look. Then I picked a bar at random and went into it.

Fortunately, among the Italian words I did know – among the *tema con variazione* and *largo con gran espressione* prhrases, were the more practical, *birra, vino* and *spritz*. I ordered a beer, found an empty stool and, glass in hand, sat on it.

The internal space of the bar was narrow. The bar ran along one long wall and the stools were ranged opposite it. Behind the stools was a long narrow shelf on which you could perch your drink if you were happy to keep reaching behind your head for it when you wanted to take a gulp or sip. As you sat on your stool there was just enough room for people to squeeze past between your knees and the bar counter. I wasn't yet sure whether *Scusi* corresponded more closely to Excuse me or Sorry, but that was the word on everyone's lips as they squeaked past.

I was content to sit and watch the world for a bit. An elderly woman, smartly dressed, came in with a tiny dog on a lead, ordered herself a Campari and soda and, after nodding to me graciously, sat down a couple of stools away. Then something beautiful happened. A lovely guy – he looked about eighteen – entered the bar, looked around him, saw no empty seats but went to the counter and ordered a drink anyway. There was space to stand, in the corners at each end of the bar, and he could have shouldered his way among the other standing locals if he'd wanted to, or taken his drink out onto the pavement.

But just as he'd got his drink and turned away from the bar with it the man next to me got down from his stool and with a call of, *Ciao, grazie,* made his way out. The young guy saw his chance of a seat, took the necessary three steps towards it and quickly sat on it before anyone else could. I nodded a smile at him but he ignored that.

We sat knee to knee for a bit. We were both wearing shorts and from time to time our bare knees touched. He didn't greet anybody else in the bar. Nobody there was quite as young as he was. I got the impression he was a little ill at ease or anxious. After a few minutes he got his phone out.

From where I sat I could see what he was looking at on it. I saw him check for missed calls, then texts, then emails. There were none. My heart went out to him. It had been the same for me when I'd checked my own phone in the restaurant earlier.

He began to thumb through his apps. I looked carefully – while trying not to look like I was – to see if he had Grind'r or other gay things among his stuff. As far as I could see he did not. He had Google Earth or something similar, though, because after a while I watched him begin to take a tour around the world in his imagination. Starting from Venice he quickly hopped across the Adriatic and headed down the island-studded coasts of Albania and Greece. Was he visualising an exciting sailing trip? Or in his imagination flying a fighter jet? He threaded his way among the islands of the Peleponnese, then headed off towards Crete.

When I could I stole a glance at his profile. At his charming stubby nose and fullish lips. At his eyes… They were hazel, I thought. As far as I could make out, but the angle was difficult. His cheeks still had the soft plumpness of adolescence, while his eyelashes were adorably long, curled and thick. His skin was on the fair side and his hair was the colour of rope. Not everyone in Italy is black-haired and olive-skinned, I was beginning to realise. Especially in the north. Timidly, bravely, I rubbed my knee against his for a moment. Hoping that he wouldn't notice. Hoping that he would.

A man came into the bar, in old clothes and wellington boots. In each hand he carried a bag of clear plastic. The bags contained – were crammed full of – small green shore crabs, about two kilogrammes of them in each bag. The crabs, alive alive-o, were wriggling and flexing their claws, trying unsuccessfully to get comfortable in the uncongenial place in which they found themselves. Their captor held them up at the bar counter, offering them for sale to the bar's staff.

Although small snacks were on sale – slices of cheese and various types of salami and preserved peppers – the menu did not run to crabs of that sort and the staff, though smiling, shook their heads.

The crab catcher turned his attention to the customers at that point. One by one they turned him down… Who would want to stand chatting over a drink with a sack of live crabs in their hand? At last he came to where I and the guy next to me sat. Because we were the two youngest people there and were sitting knee to knee he probably assumed that we were together, and looked into out two faces alternately as, in words I didn't know, he offered his wares to the pair of us.

Paying no attention to me the guy on my right said what was clearly a polite No thanks. It then crossed the man's mind that we might not be together so he looked straight at me and said something I didn't catch.

I took a leaf out of my neighbour's book. *'No, grazie,'* I said.

That was enough for him, fortunately. With a gracious nod he moved away and went to try somebody else. But my *No grazie,* delivered in what must have been a recognizably English accent caused the guy beside me to turn and look at me for the first time. To my great relief he smiled at me as he did so. It was a cracker of a smile, a beauty of a smile, and instinctively I smiled back.

'You English?' he asked – in English.

'Yes,' I said.

The next thing he said was ... and remember that our nearside knees were pressed up against each other's as if by accident ... 'You're nice.'

He hadn't said I looked nice, only that I was nice, and nice can mean anything you want it to mean and – if English isn't your native language it can mean all sorts of things you perhaps didn't want. However, I decided not to be cautious. Instead I took one of the bigger risks in my life up to that date. I rubbed my knee quite unmistakeably up and down against his. 'So are you,' I said.

And, while I hardly dared to believe this was happening, his own bare knee rubbed mine back.

'Holiday?' he asked me.

'Just tonight,' I said. 'Tomorrow I start a job.' I wondered if his English would be up to understanding that.

He nodded anyway, whether he'd understood or not. But he didn't ask me what the job was, and I was glad of that. He probably wouldn't have understood if I'd told him, and even more likely would not have been impressed or interested if I had.

'You live in Venice?' I asked.

He nodded in reply. I didn't pursue him with a nosey, pointless, *Whereabouts?* Instead I clapped my hand on his bare thigh, halfway between his knee and the hem of his shorts. I did this in a fairly butch and manly way; the way I'd seen other Italian men do with their friends; there was nothing tentative about it. I gave him an interested-looking grin, though. It was a combination of signals that he could interpret in whatever way he wished.

His response was first to grin back at me and then to look very obviously down at my crotch. I looked there too, and saw the makings of an erection in my shorts. I glanced across at his crotch and saw something similar, if on a slightly smaller scale, taking shape in his own shorts.

He looked back up at my face. His own was more serious now. He said, in English and in a very deliberate tone of voice, 'I worked in this bar once. In school holidays. There is a place we can go. At the back.' He looked anxious for a moment, afraid that he'd said too much. More doubtfully he added, 'If you want.'

'Yeah,' I said.

He hopped down from his stool. 'Leave your beer,' he said. 'Come after me.'

'OK,' I said.

I followed him between the row of knees and glasses and the bar counter. Ducking our heads we walked beneath the arch that led to the unisex toilet. Next to it was a door with a no-go sign on it, which my new friend unlatched and pushed open with an insider's confidence. We found ourselves in the open air, on a tiny water-lapped platform among stacked crates of bottles and with a view across the light-flashed water to the floodlit churches a half mile opposite.

We turned towards each other and without thinking about it embraced. Then within seconds our hands strayed down to each other's shorts. We unclasped each other's waistbands and yanked downwards till our shorts were round our knees and our cocks had popped up. Neither of us was wearing underpants.

I briefly tickled his balls first. Only then did I grasp his dick.

He was doing the same to me. 'You are big,' he said. I wasn't really, I thought, but still it was nice to be told I was

I fondled his foreskin and helped it to retract. 'You're not so small yourself. How old are you?'

'Eighteen,' he said. 'You?'

'Twenty-one,' I said. Spontaneously we kissed. 'What's your name?'

'Tomassio,' he said.

'You're beautiful,' I said.

'And your name? You too are beautiful.'

'You're just being nice,' I said. 'I'm Ben. Short for Benjamin, not Benedict.' I've no idea why that last detail should have seemed important at such a moment.

Tomassio was now beginning to engage with my dick. He held it loosely, confidently, allowing the skin to slip back and forth. The same thing was happening to Tomassio's cock, I noticed. 'I'm going to shoot,' he suddenly said. He turned his body half away from me, though allowing me to continue to rub his cock. Then I saw his semen arc out from him, landing a couple of feet out in the water of the lagoon as if in some ancient ceremony. Within seconds my own cock had shot its load, its white line of sperm following my new friend's into the dark water whose high-lit wavelets lapped around our feet.

TWO

I woke up in a room full of light, wondering where I was. I peered towards the window, saw that I'd left the curtains open overnight and simultaneously realised why I had.

The sun was playing on the water's surface all across the lagoon. Reflected upwards it bathed the distant churches in light and rippled across my own ceiling, making the space I'd woken into pulse with light. It was as if I'd woken up in paradise.

I had the best part of the day in which to do as I liked. I was due to meet the Dragonetti family – or one of them – at the water taxi stop at five o'clock. My little white lie to my new employers was that I was arriving today from the airport. The truth was that I'd wanted a twenty-four hour experience of freedom in Venice before I entered the captivity that was the price I would inevitably pay for being a rich Venetian family's house guest for three months.

So far my plan had paid dividends. My little adventure with Tomassio last night would be difficult to repeat, I thought. I was delighted that it had happened as it did, on my first – and only free – night in the city. After we had both come into the lagoon we had buttoned up our shorts, given each other another quick kiss, then gone back inside the bar, hoping we looked as if butter wouldn't melt in our mouths and that people would think we'd just been for a companionable piss.

We'd returned to our stools to find them occupied by other people. We'd retrieved the remains of our drinks from behind their heads and, standing by the bar, drunk them up. Then Tomassio looked ready to depart. I asked him for his contact details but he shook his head. I was disappointed but not really surprised. Eighteen he may have been but he was Italian and he still lived, no doubt, under the eagle eyes of his parents and probably shouldn't have been out late, trolling among the canals and back streets. I'd told him the name of the hotel I was spending that one night at, though I didn't expect anything would come of that and indeed it had not. I'd watched his speedy departure; I'd stood in the doorway and watched his receding buttocks till they melted into the crowd. Then I'd returned inside and consoled myself with a second, final drink.

Now, this morning, I was looking at some seven hours of freedom in Venice. I reckoned that the Dragonettis would at some point introduce me to the major sights – the Doge's Palace, St Mark's Basilica, the Accademia – and, quite importantly, at their expense. So I decided to give those tourist must-sees a miss today. I took the waterbus up the S-shaped Grand Canal instead and looked at the outside of every building we passed with eyes full of wonder and childlike happiness.

*

I've referred to my imminent captivity. But I don't want to sound ungrateful for what was about to happen to me. Perhaps it's time to explain how my summer in Venice – the summer that was just beginning – had come about.

We final year students at Trinity College London had given a concert in the Painted Hall just after Easter. I'd played a Beethoven piano sonata – the late one in E, Opus 109. Not quite the most difficult of the thirty-two, but very far from being one of the easiest. A woman came up to me after the concert and introduced herself. 'I liked the way you played the one-oh-nine,' she said. She was an Englishwoman, very well-spoken, and in her mid-forties, I guessed, and still very beautiful, as well as smartly dressed. She gave me her hand to shake. 'My name's Annabelle,' she said. She could equally truthfully have given her name as Signora Dragonetti and told me that she was married to one of the wealthiest men in Venice, but she did not. That all came out later, drip by drip.

Instead she told me that she had studied at Trinity College over twenty years earlier. Not piano, she explained, but violin. She asked me what other composers I liked to play. I told her lightly that in addition to Beethoven I was especially fond of Mozart and Schubert. She didn't let it go at that. She wanted to know which individual works of those composers I played, or liked best. This was quite a big subject to open up and we talked for some time and in some detail about particular impromptus, sonatas and so forth. I began to wonder where this conversation was leading. I didn't wonder for very long, though. 'I don't suppose you're in the market for a summer job in Venice?' she said.

Her elder son Matteo was due to start at Trinity College in the autumn, following in his mother's footsteps, except in the matter of the instrument. He was not a violinist but, like me, a piano student. She spelled the offer out, and it got better and better with every detail she told me about. She was afraid that going to college in a foreign country, among strangers and in a foreign language, would put her son at a disadvantage. She wanted Matteo to have intensive coaching between mid-June and mid-September so that he would at least be confident when it came to the music.

I – or whoever took up the temporary post – would live with the family in their palazzo and be treated in every way as a family member. Coaching Matteo wouldn't take up all of every day; there would be plenty of free time. But I might also be able to help Matteo – and his younger brother Marco – with their English. Nothing too formal in this department, Annabelle clarified quickly. Just a little help here and there with idiomatic conversation...

Half an hour later, by which time I'd introduced Annabelle to my professor, and we'd swapped addresses and names of referees, I'd provisionally accepted the post. We would confirm things in a few days' time by letter. It was only after Annabelle had gone and I was left knowing that I'd just experienced a life-changing moment, that I realised I had no idea whether Matteo was any good at playing the piano or whether he was simply a rich kid no-hoper. But at that moment it was a detail that didn't seem to matter very much.

*

I made sure I arrived at the water taxi stop well ahead of time. That was in order to sustain my little deception: that I'd arrived just minutes earlier from the airport. I was glad I'd taken the trouble to get there early, because Annabelle and someone I presumed was one of her sons turned up just a few minutes later, also a good while before the time we'd arranged to meet.

The son – it was the elder one, Matteo, my pupil for the duration – was drop-dead handsome. He had a look about him that at moments reminded me of my last-night's one-off, Tomassio. But he was a year or so older than Tomassio was. He gave me a generous smile as soon as we were introduced and I knew that I was going to like him, whether he could play the piano or whether he couldn't.

'We can walk from here,' Annabelle said. 'It's only round the corner.'

Round the corners of two narrow alleyways to the back door of a Venetian palazzo. Arriving at the house I'd be staying in for the next three months... I'd never had an experience quite like this.

The alleys got narrower, darker and more claustrophobic. High up in one wall a sculpted stone head glowered down at us. The final alley ended in an iron grille, which Matteo unlocked and pushed open.

Beyond it a forbidding, dark-painted door led into my new palace.

We entered the ground-floor space, the water floor, of the building. It was enormous, like a warehouse, with mote-filled daylight streaming in bleakly through grimy windows. People fill their garages with all kinds of stuff, and if they had twenty times as much garage space they would probably easily fill that. So it was here. There were old and broken boats, piled in corners. Disused furniture, chairs and wardrobes, stood indecisively on pallets. Also raised up from the liable-to-flood floor on pallets were a washing-machine and a large freezer... I won't go on with this inventory. It would take the next two pages. Enough to say, there was an awful lot of it. We climbed the broad staircase... And on opening the door at the top of it we entered a different world.

Light flooded into the room we found ourselves in. Light from a row of tall Gothic windows, ogee-arched and traceried, at one end of the long space, and from another identical set of windows at the other end of it. The room – which I would soon learn to call the *portego* – must have been forty feet long and nearly twenty wide ... and fifteen feet high at least. Persian carpets overlaid the parquet floor and the two concert-size grand pianos that it contained didn't overcrowd it. The walls were hung with tapestries and lined with glass-fronted bookshelves as if in a library. The ceiling was panelled – coffered, I think is the right word – with carved and gilded cedar. Swagged curtains softened the outline of the huge and ancient windows, their colour-scheme the traditional Venetian one of blue and gold.

'Matteo,' said his mother, 'Why don't you show Benjamin his room and bathroom? Then bring him down for a cup of tea. Show him the rest of the house after that.'

My bedroom was up two more staircases. It was one of a line of bedrooms that ran along the front of the palazzo, looking onto the Grand Canal a long way below. Next to my room was Matteo's and next to that – Matteo let me peep through the door of it – the bedroom of his younger brother Marco. The only other occupants of that huge floor of bedrooms, Matteo told me, were a middle-aged couple who worked for the family: the wife was cook and housekeeper, the husband managed to be handyman, boatman and occasionally butler, when there were guests. 'They have the big suite at the back,' Matteo said. 'It's like a separate apartment actually. They will not trouble us.' I liked the sound of that. I liked the little hint of complicity in the way he said it.

Tea was served in the vast *portego*, at a relaxing distance from the two pianos. I looked up at the huge chandeliers above me, and the coffered ceiling and – mainly because I was already falling in love with Matteo, with whom I had quickly bonded – felt that I had arrived in heaven... Whatever heaven was.

I hesitate to describe the geography of that house in too much detail. Such descriptions tend to make boring books. But this place was so exceptional, so unlike any other house I'd lived in, that I'm going to risk it...

The house was roughly square in ground plan and was on four storeys. The water floor has already been dealt with. So has the top floor, with its warren of modest-sized rooms where I would live alongside the two brothers. The glories of the house were the two high-ceilinged floors between them: the *piani nobili*. Each of those floors had its central space, the grand windowed *portego*, and smaller rooms led off from the sides of it. On the lower of those two floors – where we'd had tea and where the pianos were – the side rooms were dining-room and kitchen on one side, while on the other side were a smaller, more intimate, drawing-room, and Signor Dragonetti's study. The layout of the upper *piano nobile* was identical to the lower one, though the rooms were given over to different uses. Up here the huge portego was not dedicated to books and music but to paintings. A collection of old masters and some more modern works crowded the walls. There was a painting of the palazzo itself that had been done by Canaletto, no less, and the vast room had a painted ceiling. Not just any painted ceiling. It had been painted by Tiepolo in the 1740s... The rooms that led off this light-swamped space were the bedrooms and other private quarters of my new friend's parents, and there were also two quite elaborate guestrooms, which Matteo showed me.

Unpacking in my simpler room above this lot I thought it would all take a bit of getting used to. I would be sleeping above what was in essence a small art gallery, which was itself set over a small concert hall – and that above a boathouse...

'I like your house,' I said to Matteo when I rejoined him in the lower portego some half an hour later. I hoped he was sophisticated enough to recognise an example of British understatement.

He was. He grinned at me and his eyes twinkled mischievously. 'Me too,' he said. 'Which is lucky. Because I do not have another.'

That made me laugh. And that in turn made him laugh. I was over the moon then. I knew for certain that we liked each other.

Matteo was about an inch taller than I was. He was also a looker, and I was pleased about that. Young classical musicians are sometimes rather weedy physical specimens, geeky in appearance and nerdy in the way they behave. They've spent their teen years nurturing their talent with hours of difficult practice on their instruments or voices. That often means they've had little time left over to chase a football around a pitch or to build up their muscles on the tennis court. I'd been lucky in that respect. I had a well-developed body: good enough at any rate to give people the impression I spent hours in a gym toning it even though in fact I didn't do that and never had done. Matteo was another young musician who was lucky in that respect. He might or might not spend hours in the gym or on the tennis court: the key thing was that he looked as if he did.

He was wearing chinos; as I was, out of respect for the occasion: meeting new employers, starting a new job. But I was able to get a reasonable impression, even through his trousers, of what his legs were like. I'd had years of practice at this and was now something of an expert. As far as his physique was concerned – well, I was already impressed by it. As for his face…

His ice-blue eyes and sun-blond hair would not have looked out of place on a Swede or a Norwegian. His nose was neat, not too big, and straight. He had high cheekbones and full, well-coloured lips. His smile was full of radiant though not enormous teeth. He had another feature, though, that to my own taste was the icing on the cake. His slender eyebrows and thick eyelashes were dark. He was clean-shaven, but a careful scrutiny of his cheeks and chin – I always scrutinised such things carefully – showed me that had he chosen to wear a beard that too would be nearly black.

As we walked around the palazzo – Matteo showing me this and pointing out that – and as we talked of many things (carefully avoiding the subjects of music and pianos for the moment, I noticed) I began to suspect that Matteo was appraising my appearance in the same way as I was appraising his. I tried not to think too much about that, or to try to imagine any possible reason for it. I didn't want to get my hopes up only to have them dashed.

'You will meet my father and my brother at dinner,' Matteo said.

Hmm. Yes, I had been wondering about that. Then Matteo looked at me in a particular way that I thought I recognised. 'In the meantime,' he said, 'would you like to go out and have beer? Escape for a bit?'

I had interpreted his look correctly. I grinned gratefully at him. 'I'd like that very much,' I said.

We made our way out through the grubby back door that we'd arrived through, squeezed down the alley way and after a few disorienting twists and turns came to a small hole-in-the-wall type of bar. The sort of bar you would only ever find if you weren't looking for it.

We took our small glasses of beer out onto the narrow pavement, and stood drinking them beside the lapping water six inches below our feet. I couldn't help remembering the last time, less than twenty-four hours ago, that I'd stood outside a bar on a similarly narrow ledge with somebody else…

Still we avoided the subject of music. We talked casually about items in the news, about sport; Matteo asked me if I thought Andy Murray would win this year's Wimbledon. I had no idea, of course. 'About time,' I said.

As we drained our glasses Matteo glanced quickly at his watch. 'It is now dinner time,' he said. Then he shot me a very charmingly teenage look. 'Are you OK with that?'

'Of course,' I said.

The family was gathered in the portego when we got back. There were Annabelle, and her husband, to whom I was about to be introduced. Also there was Matteo's younger brother Marco. Seeing him I got the most enormous shock. It was a shock that Marco shared equally. I could see it in his face. He was introduced to me as Marco, so obviously that was his name. His parents and his brother thought it was and there was no arguing with that. But I knew him already. I'd met him the previous night. I still thought of him by the name he'd given me then. Tomassio.

I took his hand and shook it. 'A pleasure to meet you, Marco,' I said.

THREE

What's in a name? that which we call a rose

By any other name would smell as sweet.

So Romeo would were he not Romeo called.

It was strange the power that names had, I thought. I looked across the table at Marco from time to time during that extraordinary dinnertime, though trying not to catch his eye. I knew I wouldn't know what to do with it if I did catch it. I knew the same went for Marco also.

Marco. Workaday, serviceable, two-syllable Marco. I couldn't help still wanting to think of his as Tomassio. Tomassio Dragonetti... He'd been Tomassio when we'd held each other on the landing stage, he'd been Tomassio when he projected his sperm a metre out into the water. He'd been Tomassio when I'd brought him vividly to my mind as I masturbated in my hotel bed before getting up this morning. Tomassio... Perhaps he'd let me go on calling him Tomassio when we were alone together. It would be a private thing. Our little secret...

I had to stop thinking like this, I told myself. But my mind was in a whirl. Did Tomassio – sorry, Marco – make a habit of wanking off with other boys? Or had I been a one-off, an aberration? Was he gay? Lots of eighteen-year-olds behaved the way Marco had done (I knew because I'd been one of them) but that didn't mean they were all gay. It often meant no more than that they were highly sexed.

Then there was Matteo. Sitting next to me, twirling pasta. Did he know the things his little brother got up to? Was he in on the secret? Was Matteo…? Did Matteo…? I could hardly bring my thought processes to complete the questions. I'd read somewhere that the homosexual disposition ran in families. If one of a pair of brothers was gay, then often the other was too. OK, I knew many sets of siblings that didn't apply to – pairs of brothers of which one was definitely gay and the other definitely wasn't – but I also knew a good few families in which that rule of thumb held good.

But the big question was the one that only time would answer. What was going to happen? Between me and Marco? Between me and Matteo? I sighed involuntarily into my forkful of twisted pasta. Probably nothing would happen. All the same I could feel myself getting excited in my chinos. Experimentally I touched my knee against Matteo's. Accidentally on purpose.

Dinner had been served by Artemia, the wifely half of the couple that lived on 'my' bedroom floor. I'd been introduced to her and to her beaming husband Albano. I was relieved to find that they were not dour and surly; it seemed that chips on the shoulder were not a necessary attribute of servant status in a house as big and elegant as the Dragonettis'. Signor Dragonetti himself had turned out to be approachable and unintimidating: a youthful fifty-something. He spoke excellent English and, as soon as we were introduced, asked me to call him by his first name, Domenico. It seemed a good start.

When dinner was over Marco excused himself politely then scuttled up to his room, presumably to watch television or to do something on his computer. I didn't blame him. It was exactly what I'd have done in his position.

Matteo, though, was taking on the responsibility that went with having a house guest. He clearly saw me by now as *his* guest and had gracefully shouldered the burden. He wasn't going to run away to his TV or computer, but was going to entertain me for the evening. I loved the discovery that he was going to do that. I loved him for being prepared to do it.

His conversational opener, once we were left alone together, will read as banal and flat to anyone who is not in love with music. They will have to take my word – with my apologies – for the fact that to me it was magical. Matteo said, 'Would you like to see the pianos?'

My heart leapt. 'Yes,' I said.

Lovingly he opened them up. They were both full-size concert instruments – that is nine feet long – but neither of them was a boring shiny ebonised black, like you'd see in a concert hall. One was veneered in glowing walnut, the other in luminous rosewood. The walnut one was a Fazioli make. Italian, and the most expensive model, these days, on the planet. It was spanking new. The other was an old but re-conditioned Bechstein.

We looked at each other, standing at opposite ends of the Bechstein's keyboard. One of us had to say it. Turned out it was Matteo. 'You first.' He smiled mischievously. 'You're the expert.'

'Shit, man,' I said. 'I've had wine with dinner…'

'Something slow, then. Something easy.'

I sat at the Bechstein, fingered a chord softly… I played the slow movement of a Schubert sonata. I'd freshly learnt it and it was still clear in my head: every note and every nuance, everything I knew I wanted to do with it. It was a reasonably easy piece, for the fingers at any rate, and shortish. I knew it had gone well as soon as I'd finished. Shyly I looked up at Matteo.

His face was radiant. I could see and feel his response to my 'performance' without his having to find words for it. It made my heart hurt; I was awed by it. But then he did find words. Actually just once word. 'Beautiful,' he said.

'Grazie,' I answered. Then, reverting to my mother tongue, 'Now it's your turn.'

He groaned theatrically. 'Oh no,' he said. 'After that? Do I have to?'

'You're only pretending,' I said. 'You know you want to.'

He chose the other piano, the Fazioli. I found I was holding my breath. This was the moment I'd been putting off, the moment I'd dreaded: the moment when I would find out if he was any good at playing the piano or if he was hopeless.

To my surprise big C-minor chords rang out, slow and solemn, glittering, under his fingers. It was the grandiose opening of Bach's second Partita. Matteo too had had wine at dinner. I had studied the piece myself, but after two glasses of wine wouldn't have attempted it. Perhaps he would stop at the end of the introduction. Before the fast bit…

He didn't stop. He played the whole of the first movement, including the virtuosic final section, which he did very fast and very staccato, without dropping a stitch. I was more than impressed. He stopped at the end of that, though. I was rather relieved in a way. Had he gone on and played the other five dance movements – still without the music in front of him – I might have felt intimidated. As it was I found myself experiencing a mixture of feelings. I was greatly relieved to discover that he could play not only beautifully but with great technical assurance. But I did wonder now what on earth, in the three months that lay ahead of us, I would be able to teach him.

I'd been sitting on the stool in front of the keyboard of the other piano. Now I got up and walked to where he still sat at the other one. I put my hand on his right shoulder. 'That was wonderful,' I said quietly. I kept my hand on his shoulder while he laid his own left hand on top of it.

I might have leant in towards him, pressed my chest against his back and then, if he didn't flinch away, leaned down and kissed the side of his head... I thought about this for a second. Wanting to. But I didn't. Didn't dare to. If the advance were to prove unwelcome, if I'd misread the signals... The consequences of that – three months of painful awkwardness between us as we worked together in a physical proximity that would of necessity be very close – would be too hideously embarrassing even to contemplate.

Instead I took half a pace back, allowing our hands to slip apart naturally without haste or fuss. He turned and smiled at me then, his relief at my approval of his playing written all over his handsome face. I decided to tell the truth. 'You're very accomplished,' I said. 'You've got a solid technique already, plus you play with sensitivity and spirit.' I smiled at him a bit awkwardly. 'To be honest, I don't know what I'm going to be able to teach you over the next three months.'

His smile became roguish. 'I'm sure we'll think of something,' he said.

I told myself to be careful. To be careful not to read too much into that.

The sexual static between us – if there even was any – would have to remain unresolved for the moment, but at least in the area of music the ice was well and truly broken. We began to have fun at the two pianos. We played the Mozart sonata for two pianos, which we both knew, from the music. Then we sat at the same piano, our two butts on the same seat and romped through a four-hand arrangement of The Arrival of the Queen of Sheba, with some collisions of fingers and much laughter.

When we had finished it I became aware that something in the room had changed. I looked up and saw that the door to the stairs, which had been closed, now stood open. In the doorway, looking at us, stood Marco.

With a jerk of my head I beckoned him over, and was reassured when he unselfconsciously walked towards us. 'You have found each other,' he said cryptically when he arrived beside us.

'Yes,' I said. 'We're friends already.' Then I added, 'I hope you and I will be.' He would know what I was getting at, while it would sound an innocuous enough remark in the ears of Matteo.

'Yes,' Marco said very earnestly. 'I want that.' There was a second's awkward silence. I think we were both wondering if Matteo had found that last remark puzzling: a bit intense for the situation. Then Marco said brightly, to me, 'I like your playing. You're brilliant.'

'Hey, whoa,' I said. 'Don't put your brother's nose out of joint. It's actually he that's brilliant. Anyway, both of us played. How do you know which one of us you were hearing if you weren't watching us?'

'You played the Schubert,' said Marco matter-of-factly. 'I know that because Matteo doesn't play it. He did the Bach. He always plays that when he wants to show off to people.' He smiled and chuckled.

'Don't be horrible,' I said, laughing. I felt we were on easy enough terms for me to say that.

So Marco had recognised a piece by Schubert that wasn't regularly played in the household... I wondered if he too played the piano, or some other instrument. I didn't ask him at that moment. I had three months in which to find out.

We chatted, the three of us, about other things, lounging about in the big space of the portego. Then suddenly it was bedtime. We went to our separate rooms, in which we each had our individual bathrooms. There was no need for our paths to cross again before morning – a circumstance I couldn't help regretting.

I lay in bed for quite a long time before doing it. Matteo's room was next to mine and Marco's was on the other side of Matteo's. I certainly wasn't brave enough to tiptoe past Matteo's door and call speculatively on his younger brother. I did wonder whether Marco might come and call on me; that was why I waited before going for it. Eventually I gave him up, though. Either he didn't want sex with me again or else he was no braver than I was.

So at last I got down to it. My very full erection must have been wondering why I hadn't attended to it earlier. I made the most of it anyway, though I kept my handkerchief prudently handy. The Dragonettis' fresh clean sheets were monogrammed and beautiful. I didn't want to mess them. Not on my first night in them anyway.

I wondered, as I pulled myself towards the inevitable climax, whether the other two were doing exactly the same as I was in their two next-door bedrooms. The thought of that helped spur me on a bit, I must admit, and it wasn't long before I'd emptied myself comfortingly into my un-monogrammed and not especially clean handkerchief.

*

I was woken by the sound of someone practising the piano two floors below me. I groped for my watch. It was after nine o'clock. I was horrified. I was here to do a job of work, and I was late on my first morning. I dived into my clothes and dashed down the big staircase. I made my entrance – it really was like walking onto the stage of a theatre or an opera house – into the portego. There was Matteo, alone in the huge space, sitting at the Fazioli in bare feet, very short shorts and a T-shirt. He looked absolutely gorgeous. He was working on a difficult passage – I knew it well – in a piece by Chopin. He stopped and stood up when he saw me.

I walked towards him. 'I'm awfully sorry,' I said, extremely flustered. 'You should have woken me…'

'Don't be sorry,' he said. He put his two hands reassuringly on my upper arms. 'Mama said to leave you. And, hey, look, there's no timetable. No stress.'

I remembered then that in addition to coaching him on

the piano I was supposed to be helping him with his idiomatic English. I seemed to be doubly redundant.

'Marco's gone to school already,' Matteo said. 'Unlike me his holidays don't start till tomorrow. He said to say *buona giornata.*' I knew that *Buongiorno* was good day or good morning. *Buona giornata* must mean have a good day. Enjoy your day. I decided I was going to.

'Hey...' A new thought seemed to have struck Matteo. 'Shall we go out for breakfast?'

I liked the sound of that and said so. Waves of relief were breaking over me. Matteo looked down at my chinos. 'Want to put shorts on? Then it wouldn't feel so much like we were working.'

Ten minutes later, with both of us in shorts (Matteo had prudently added trainers) we had arrived at the café-bar where we'd had a beer yesterday and were again sitting outside it on the narrow strip of pavement that bordered the side-canal. 'One day the parents will take us to Florian's and other places. Promise you. It's fun to go to them, but the food is just the same, and so is the coffee.' We were drinking *latti* and eating jam-filled croissants.

Then Matteo looked at me very intently, intensely even, across the little table. It was a look he hadn't given me before. There was interest, a residue of surprise, and a lot of amusement in it.

'You know!' I blurted.

Matteo nodded. 'Marco told me. Or should I say… Tomassio…?'

I burst out laughing. From relief as much as anything. So did Matteo. Probably for the same reason. It was wonderful, I discovered, to find us sharing that particular secret.

'When did he tell you…?'

'In the kitchen. Just as he was leaving for school. There was no-one else there. No-one heard us, I promise.'

'Does he always tell you about his exploits?' I asked, curious.

Matteo thought for a second. 'I wouldn't know about *always*,' he answered sensibly. 'I mean, how could I? But he tells me quite a lot to be going on with.'

I wanted to ask, was it reciprocal? Did Matteo tell his kid brother about his own sexual adventures – if he had them? And if he did have them, then were they hetero- or homosexual? I really, really wanted to know the answers but couldn't summon up the nerve just yet to ask the questions. I mean, over breakfast…?

But I did find the nerve to ask a different, related question. 'Did he tell you the details?'

Matteo nodded slowly. 'A bar. Your knee alerting him… Like you did with me last night at dinner…'

'Oh God!' I said, though inside I was delightedly

squirming. 'Then you both...' he looked around quickly to check no-one was listening. Even then he lowered his voice considerably to tell me, *'Sega* into the canal together.'

'Wow,' I said. I found I was leaning back in my seat, like a pilot propelled backwards by G-force. 'You seem to know everything about me.'

'Hmm,' he said thoughtfully and paused. Then he looked at me rather shyly. 'I'd like to know quite a bit more actually.'

FOUR

There wasn't much to know, I thought. I didn't have much, I hadn't done much. And – except for when it came to playing the piano – I didn't think I amounted to very much either.

I was born, my parents' only child, in a suburban semi-detached house on the outskirts of the London commuter-belt town of Redhill. A few miles away lay London's Gatwick airport, paradoxically in deep countryside. From where we lived the incoming and departing planes could be seen clearly but, like good Victorian children, rarely heard.

From my earliest years I was enthralled by the planes. My parents took me, when I was about three, to watch them closer at hand from a convenient bit of high ground just off the eastern approach path to the field. That was such an exciting experience for me that over the next few years I would beg to be taken there again and again. When I was old enough to ride a bicycle and be allowed out on my own I would cycle there by myself and spend hours just watching the incoming planes. When it was clear I could see them lining up in the sky, one behind the other, each pair separated – I had learnt – by a distance of about five miles. They came from the south to join that queue: that was standard procedure; I learnt that too. Where had they come from before I spotted them, though? That was something I could only dream.

They would pass overhead with a satisfying roar, then float down towards the tarmac like eagles – or giant moths: it depended on my mood. A few seconds later – the delay was due to my mile's distance and the slow speed of sound – would come a new, more distant roar as the pilots selected reverse thrust to slow the landed aircraft down.

I'd watch the take-offs too. When the wind blew from the east these would come my way. Some would continue eastward, others swing north or south. Some doubled back completely, heading I could only guess where. America, north or south? The Mediterranean holiday spots? Scandinavia? Moscow?

I wanted to be up there, to join them on their mysterious travels through thin air. I wanted to be a pilot, I need hardly say. But slowly I came to realise that pilots needed a few special qualities that were not handed out to everyone. They had to be good at maths and science. I was not. They had to be quick-witted and capable of making the right decision very fast indeed. It took me ages to make up my mind about anything. They needed fantastic eye-brain-hand co-ordination. I could scarcely hit a cricket-ball.

By the time I was in my mid-teens I had concluded reluctantly that piloting jet aeroplanes was something I was not cut out to do. Fortunately by then I had another string to my bow.

Well, not to my bow exactly. I never learnt the violin. But there were strings attached to the upright piano in my parents' living-room. I discovered them for myself, long before I was expected to learn to play. I reached up, if the lid was left open, and pushed down random keys. Soon I was making up my own chords. I guess they must have been pretty weird.

My mother played the piano sometimes. At first I didn't really process the sounds she made. They didn't speak to me. Then one day something did. She played the Rondo alla Turca from Mozart's piano sonata in A. Da-da-da-da-Dum, Da-da-da-da-Dum... The notes arranged themselves in my head, coming together the way the pieces of a kit model join up to make something solid, three-dimensional and real. When she finished playing the model stayed together in my head: it didn't fall apart, disappear or dissolve. All the same I asked my mother to play it again.

And again and again.

A few days later I still had the Rondo alla Turca in my head, real as a headache but unlike a headache a thing of delight. It hammered to get out. I realised there was only one thing to do. I climbed onto the piano stool...

No, I didn't get as far as the fast bit in the middle. Torrents of rapid semiquavers were beyond the powers of my brain or the soft little fingers of my four-year-old hands. Even so, I managed to work my way slowly but reasonably accurately through most of the first page using my aural memory alone. My performance brought both my parents to the door of the living-room – from the kitchen, where they'd been washing up after a meal.

They didn't tell me I was a genius – to their credit – and neither did anyone else … to theirs. But within a week they'd found a teacher for me and I was having lessons.

So while other kids played football or computer games I sat at the piano and played. That might sound sad. It would have been sad if I'd had no talent. And if I hadn't enjoyed what I was doing. But I did have talent. And I loved my practice. I lapped up all the music I was given as eagerly and quickly as if it had been ice-cream. And when I wanted exercise and fresh air … then I got on my bike and rode like the wind to the place from which I liked to watch the planes.

*

I wasn't paraded around the capital cities of Europe, an infant prodigy, the way Mozart was. I wasn't a Mozart. I wasn't a genius. I wasn't even a prodigy. But I was good. I played at music festivals throughout the south-east of England as a child and as a teenager. I had notched up Distinctions at the Associated Board's grades seven and eight by the time I was fourteen and soon after that began attending Trinity College as an out-patient (actually they use a different expression) before starting to study there full-time after I left school.

I loved the deep emotionality of serious music. My schoolmates couldn't see that. They found emotion enough in the lighter stuff of today, in hip-hop, rap or techno. I couldn't see that at all. Well, perhaps I could, but it seemed a bit lacking in depth to me. There was nothing like the primal scream I heard in the A-minor sonata of Mozart, written after the death of his mother left him a lone, bereaved foreigner in Paris when he was just twenty-two. Nothing like the grieving for lost opportunities in love that I found in the late works of Brahms. Nothing like the jubilation, planted proudly on the surface of his violin sonata by César Franck when he had fallen in love with a woman who was not his wife. Nothing like the back-from-the-grave exhilaration that Beethoven expressed in his late A-flat piano sonata, written after a bout of illness – syphilis – from which he'd nearly died...

All that I found in the music I was learning and playing, or learning by hearing, and coming to love. But for the time being I found no such emotions inside myself. I was a late developer physically, and the same went for my emotions too.

OK, those things came to me late, but they came in time.

I wasn't particularly attracted to the girls at my school. Perhaps that would come later, I thought. Or when I met a different set of girls. If I was attracted to some of the boys... Well, I was, but I didn't give that too much thought at first. There wasn't much point, anyway, as none of them seemed attracted to me.

Until my final year, that was. Then a guy called Daniel, whom I'd sort of known forever, started taking an interest in me. Quite by accident, I thought at first, he'd find himself sitting next to me on the bus. We started to chat. Then we started chatting in the breaks between classes at school. We swapped numbers so we could text and WhatsApp each other at home.

One day we were walking together towards the bus stop near the school. 'Do you?' Daniel said suddenly, a-propos of nothing.

'Do I what?' I asked him, genuinely confused.

'Oh, I don't know,' he answered casually. 'Not quite sure what I meant there.' Then to my astonishment I saw that he'd started to blush heavily.

I made the next move, I now realise. At the time I had no idea that I was making a move. I just wanted to change the subject and spare him that inexplicable blush. 'Want to come round my place sometime and see some videos?'

From then on we were round at each other's houses most evenings every week. In my room or in his. Watching videos or playing computer games. One of us in the chair, the other sprawled on the bed. Sometimes we both sprawled on the bed.

On one of those occasions Dan (as I called him now) looked me straight in the eye, although a bit diffidently, and said, 'Can I kiss you?'

'Yes,' I said.

And we took it from there. Even my beloved piano practice began to take second place to Dan. We never told each other that we loved each other; that would have made what was already frighteningly difficult to deal with ten times harder to manage; but looking back I realise that we did. But then came the end of our last term at school and the end of the holidays that followed on… And I went to college at Greenwich while Dan moved lock, stock and barrel to university at Nottingham. We continued to text and email for a while but then that dried up. We never saw each other again.

*

Going to college was liberating. I lived away from home, sharing a flat in Woolwich with five other students. Where our studies were concerned we did this, that and the other at our different colleges: we weren't all musicians. Going to college was not just a liberating experience but also an eye-opening one. Some of my fellow students were – shock, awe and wonder – openly gay.

I wasn't openly gay. At least I wasn't when I started there. But in my first term I had furtive masturbatory sex with a trombonist. In my second term with a viola player. Somebody once said that in order to appreciate chamber music you needed to fall in love with two violinists, a viola player and a cellist. Well, for a first-year student I wasn't doing too badly. Except that I wasn't falling in love. Just wanking my fellow students off. Perhaps that was just as well. I was only eighteen. And falling in love, with all that it entails in the way of heartache, is a pretty daunting, pretty adult thing to do.

Adam Wye

It happened to me in my third and final year. I'd just turned twenty. He (it was, it goes without saying, a he) was in the same year as I was but, as is often the way of things, we'd never really noticed each other before. He played the violin. We were thrown together by our chamber-music coach, a man called Martin. 'You two,' he said to us, picking us out like army cadets on parade, 'Find something to play for us next time. Beethoven, Mozart... Something that's fun.'

'There's a Mozart violin sonata I've always wanted to do,' I said to the other guy immediately we started to talk about what we were going to do. We should have been negotiating this politely but I came in like a steamroller. 'The late one in A. Are you up for it, Jake?' This was the first time I'd called him by his name.

'I know the one you mean...' he said cautiously. 'I've never...'

'Want to try crash it now?' I asked eagerly. Urgently somehow.

We got a copy of the score from the college library and read it through in the Painted Hall. Jake at the music stand and me on an old Steinway grand that was going slightly out of tune. The piece is a total joy. Even the meditative slow movement reeks of joy. While the outer movements... Mozart at his most witty and carefree, writing in the sunniest of all keys. We played the finale at a death-defying speed, ignoring all the rules about sight-reading at a safe pace. Our occasional wrong notes ricocheted around the college like misfired bullets, and brought other students to the door of the Painted Hall – where, actually, we weren't supposed to be.

When we'd finished we turned to each other in delighted astonishment. We gaped at each other open-mouthed, and then we vented our surprise in gales of shared guffaws. We knew that we could work the piece up within a week or two and bowl our chamber-music colleagues over with it. I also knew, as I looked Jake squarely in the eye, that I wanted to take him to bed with me. I knew too, inexperienced as I was in judging such things, that he wanted to go to bed with me.

That night we did just that. Jake lived with his parents, but they were conveniently away, while his sister turned a benevolently blind eye to my presence in the house and in her brother's bedroom. Jake was a handsome, dark-haired boy and once he was undressed I thought him the loveliest sight I'd ever seen. His cock was long and tapering, with a pronounced leftward curve. I took it to bed with me and masturbated it until it came, and Jake did exactly the same with mine.

When the two of us played the sunny Mozart piece at our chamber group a fortnight later we dazzled everyone. I couldn't believe that all present wouldn't see at once that we were in the throes of a passionate fling. Perhaps they did all see it but were too polite to say so.

Jake had had a girlfriend, he told me, but they'd recently split up. He was more gay than straight, he'd realised. Our passionate liaison lived on beyond our spirited public rendition of the Mozart. It lasted several months. We slept together as often as we could. Usually at my place, if his parents weren't away. If I'd been secretive about my orientation where my flatmates were concerned, that all changed now. I threw caution to the winds. I discovered how much easier it was to come out as gay when you were bringing a drop-dead gorgeous boyfriend home to bed with you.

I loved Jake, and Jake loved me. But we never told each other so, never uttered those irretrievable three words. In hindsight I'm glad we didn't. I wanted our thing together to last for ever. I was ready to tell my parents about Jake – come out to them at last – move with Jake into a place that would be just ours. I wanted to marry him.

Jake's girlfriend came back onto the scene. I met her. She was nice, I had to admit. But little by little she pulled him back into her orbit and out of mine. Jake had the unenviable task, eventually, of telling me the score. He'd fallen in love with the way I played the piano, he said. He'd been blinded by that. Result – he'd fallen a bit in love with me. But it couldn't have lasted, could it? He invited me to share that view and to make it easier for him I said, no, that was true. The fact remained, he went on, that he was more straight than gay. Always had been, really. All the same, the thing we'd had together had been wonderfully good, hadn't it? It had, and I wasn't just being nice when I said most vehemently that I agreed. Agreed even as I was breaking up inside.

By the time I came to play Beethoven at that final concert – the concert that Annabelle had come to hear –

it was all over. I was on my own again and – hope springing eternal in my breast – ready to fall in love with the first reasonably nice and good-looking male I saw.

Fate had brought me Annabelle and her job offer. That had brought me to Venice and to Matteo. Perfect, wonderful Matteo. Matteo, who was now sitting at a café table opposite me, clad in shorts, and telling me he wanted to know more about me. I'd tell him in due course. About Dan. About Jake... He, Matteo, would be number three. Third time lucky, I hoped. And yet... I'd been badly bruised just months ago. I was going to be more wary now. I was ready to fall in love with Matteo this very afternoon. But the wisdom I'd learned so recently, learned the hard way, cautioned me. Enjoy, a voice advised inside me. Enjoy the moment, but don't fall. Or not too soon, anyway.

FIVE

I came back to the present. 'I think *sega* means wank in English,' I said. 'Both as a verb and as a noun.'

'I know it does,' said Matteo. 'I just couldn't remember the word for the moment.' He sounded a little annoyed with himself for his lapse of memory.

'Sorry,' I said. 'It's just that your mother said I was to help you with your idiomatic English. Which to me already sounds perfect. I was just trying to earn my wages for a moment.'

Matteo turned towards me and grinned. 'Thank you for your diligence,' he said.

We were walking back from the café through the maze of alleys that led to the back door of the palazzo – the land door, they called it. It would take me a few days to learn the routes through this local labyrinth, I thought. We passed beneath the carved stone head that glowered down from a wall about nine feet up. It was a useful landmark. I would remember that. Matteo unlocked the grille that closed the end of the alley, then the land door itself. Even when there were other people inside the house you had to be punctilious about keeping doors locked. With a collection of old masters on the second floor you couldn't be too careful. Matteo would probably have called it due diligence.

Once inside, on the water floor, Matteo re-locked the

door behind us. What happened next unfolded then as gracefully and inexorably as a flower opening at the touch of spring. After a very quick look round, to check that Artemia wasn't down here rummaging in the deep-freeze or Albano repairing something at the work-bench, Matteo leaned his face towards mine and our lips met.

My arms were around his back. I don't remember putting them there. Then his encircled mine. I do remember that.

We started to kiss. And having started, didn't seem to want to stop. One of my hands pried its way down the back of Matteo's shorts. Easily my middle finger found its way down the smooth warm cleft. He didn't seem to be wearing underpants. Like somebody using a tin-opener I worked my hand around to the front. My fingers encountered his springy pubes and then the base of his downward pressed but rigid cock. It felt positively hot to my touch. And he definitely wasn't wearing underpants.

Matteo was by now fiddling with the fastening of my shorts. Seconds later both pairs of shorts were down, around our thighs and Matteo had discovered what I already knew: that I too was unencumbered by underpants.

Matteo's dick was bigger than his little brother's, as was fitting. It was also slightly bigger than mine. As I was two years his senior I might have had a problem with that but I found in all the excitement that I did not.

We began to masturbate each other. Standing up, front to front. Alternately crushing our cocks towards each other's bellies and pulling back a few inches so we could watch. Matteo came first, twisting quickly sideways just in time to project his arc of semen, aided by my busy hand, across the floor rather than all over my clean shorts. That hurried me towards my own climax of course and it duly came in less than another minute. I too managed to twist sideways but my ejaculate simply spooled downwards onto the bricks rather than arcing across them. I was mildly disappointed at not being able to show off on this first time with Matteo as spectacularly as he had done, or as I had done with his brother two nights back. But it was a minor flaw in a beautiful experience. I would have other opportunities to impress Matteo I hoped.

As our physical tension wound down we embraced each other again, clamping our two wet dicks together between our warm bellies. Then after a couple of minutes we gently disengaged and pulled our shorts up. Involuntarily I glance down at our two messes on the floor. 'Don't worry,' said Matteo. 'It has all happened before down here. I am sure it will again.'

'I hope so,' I said banally, and laughed. Then I said, 'And now I suppose we ought to go and do some work. Or we'll be talked about.'

Matteo laughed. I had a point. Marco had gone to school and Annabelle and Domenico had gone to work. But you could never be entirely alone in a house in which there were servants. It was one of the things I was just realising – among so much else along what was becoming one of the steepest, fastest learning curves of my life.

Still in shorts and still a little bit damp inside them we sat down at the two pianos. I didn't have to ask what Matteo was going to play me today. His practising it had woken me up an hour and a half earlier. It was one of the mightier steeds among the warhorses of the piano repertoire. Chopin's Scherzo in B flat minor – the one whose opening has been compared to the sound of someone starting a motor-bike. I had learnt the piece at college: an experience for which I was thanking my stars at this particular moment.

Now I sat with the score in my hands while Matteo, after a shrug and a grimace in my direction, launched into it without the music. He played it from start to finish, without interruption either from me or from himself. He worked it up into a hair-raising speed for the last tempestuous page, the left-hand chords flashing like lightning as the galloping horses of the right-hand thundered past. At last he brought the fiery thing to a stop. Then he turned and looked at me, like a dog that is trying to read the expression on its master's face.

'I don't know what to say,' I said when at last I was able to speak. 'You play that far better than I ever did. Apart from anything else … do you realise you played the whole thing without one single fucking wrong note?'

'I didn't know I had,' he said, in a wondering tone of voice.

'I don't know what I can possibly teach you,' I said. For an awful moment I was afraid I was going to cry. 'I don't know what I'm doing here. I'm no way good enough to give you any kind of help.'

Matteo got up from his piano stool. He almost ran the five paces it took him to reach me. He came up behind me, put his arms around my neck as I still sat at my keyboard, pressed his head up alongside mine and his chest against my back. In a low voice he said, 'Yes you are. I need your help. Why don't you play me the piece?'

'I haven't looked at it for a year,' I said. But I could hardly refuse his request. I couldn't think of any other way to salvage the moment and justify my being here at his parents' expense. 'I'll have to do it from the music, though,' I said. 'There's no way I could remember it.'

'I'll turn the pages,' Matteo said.

I played the opening. The growling motor-bike ba-rumpb, ba-rumpb in the bass, then the answering clang of bells from high above. Chopin makes the pianist do this twice. Then, having got the listener's undivided attention, he really lets the thing rip.

I didn't get very far however before Matteo stopped me. 'That was brilliant,' he said. 'That thing you did.'

'What thing?' I asked.

'With the pedal just there. Fantastic effect. I never thought of doing that. Can you show me again?' he asked.

I did. He tried it out on the other piano, then we carried on. But he stopped me again after a few more seconds. I'd used a bit of fingering, apparently, that he hadn't considered. 'That makes it so much safer,' he said, and made a note of it.

And so we went on. Gradually my confidence began to come back. Gradually I learned how to teach Matteo. And gradually I began to learn that there is no-one who can't be taught something, provided you've discovered that every individual needs teaching in a different way, and that you allow a bit of give and take between what *you* think they need to be taught and what *they* think they need to be taught.

The morning turned into a journey of exploration, a journey of delight. We took it in turns to play passages from the huge scherzo. We swapped pianos, tried out our ideas on both of them, to see if they would work equally well on both. We had only got a little way through the twelve pages of the scherzo, and it seemed like only ten minutes had passed, when Artemia arrived at our side and interrupted us, asking if we would be having any lunch today, as it was already three o'clock…

However rich you may be a simple lunch has to be a simple lunch, unless you want to be fat as well as rich. So we ate a simple bowl of angel-hair pasta with olive oil, garlic, flakes of chilli pepper and anchovy shreds. It was followed by a large fresh Sicilian peach and washed down with a glass or two of fizzy water. So much for lunch. It was perfect.

'We ought to have a siesta this afternoon,' said Matteo when we'd finished eating, 'and a walk.' He seemed very much in charge for the moment. Why shouldn't he be? He was the son of my employees; I was not. 'The only thing is: which do we do first?'

I checked that Artemia was out of earshot. 'I'm taking it that the siesta might not necessarily involve sleep...?'

'It might involve sleep,' said Matteo carefully. 'But it might not be exclusively a matter of sleep.'

'That's what I thought,' I said. 'What time does Marco get back from school?'

'About five, probably,' said Matteo. 'He may be bringing a few of his – *compagni?* – back with him...'

'His mates,' I said. 'In which case hadn't we better have the siesta first?'

'That's what I'd hoped you'd say,' Matteo said. 'And thank you for the word mates. That's what I was looking for. Just couldn't find it quickly enough.'

'Life's like that,' I said.

We went upstairs, on up past the picture gallery and the parental chambers to our snug top-floor retreat. 'Your place or mine?' I asked.

'Nice expression,' Matteo said. 'I never heard Mama use it. Shall we go to your room? Then if Marco and his ... mates ... come back early we won't have them right next to us.'

Love in Venice

'Good thinking, mate,' I said.

We stood together in my bedroom in full view of anyone who might have been looking out of the top floor windows of the palazzo opposite, on the other side of the Canal Grande while we undressed each other.

Matteo was very fair skinned. But I was new to Italy and I had only my preconceptions of what a naked Italian male should look like to compare him with. For one thing, Venice is at Italy's northernmost edge – it's well to the north of the southern coast of France. For another, Matteo was only half Italian. He'd lived in Venice all his life and had a Venetian father but his mother Annabelle was as English as I was – and had a much posher English accent than I did.

We stood and looked at each other for a minute, fingering each other's dicks a bit uncertainly, the way beginners on the violin finger the necks of their instruments. 'Come to bed,' I said. I was aware that, however much or little sexual experience Matteo might have had, and however good his mother-tongue English was, he had probably never used English while having sex. That might be something I could usefully teach him. I who had never used any language except for English while having sex.

We didn't climb in under the duvet – it was a hot end-of-June afternoon – but lay on top of it, holding each other, feeling each other's nakedness like blind people, getting to know the contours and textures of arms, legs, chests, necks and backs; discovering which bits were hairy and which were not. Actually neither of us was heavily endowed with the furry stuff. My mouth found its way towards one of Matteo's tits. I licked around it then took the nipple very gently between my teeth and nibbled it. He didn't protest at any of this. He even gave an appreciative *Mmmm* when it got to the nibbling bit.

'Lie on top of me?' I prompted. 'Lie on my tummy?'

He did. 'Lie on your belly?' he queried after he'd got there. 'Can I say that?'

'Yes,' I said. 'People do say the word belly when they're having sex, or talking about it. It's only in polite situations, like the dinner table, that you're not supposed to say it.'

'That's more or less what Mamma said,' Matteo confirmed. I guessed the matter had arisen in a different context. And that was the last time that his mother or the nuances of the English language were mentioned during that bedroom hour, our first together and, up to now – in our twenty-two-hour-old relationship – the loveliest.

I wondered if Matteo would try to fuck me. He was well positioned to make a move in that direction but he did not. So I didn't try it either. He might not have experience of fucking or being fucked and I didn't want to frighten him, or turn his first time in bed with me into an alarming experience. After all, we had three months ahead of us.

He did poke his nice cock between my thighs at one point. I gripped it tight and he responded with another

Love in Venice

Mmmm and thrust it up and down a bit. My own dick was getting a lovely massage from his puppy-soft tummy as he did that.

We rolled around and I lay on top. An urge was born in me to say 'I love you' to him. I had to press my lips together to stop the words squeaking out. Why does having sex with certain people make us want to do that? It wasn't possible that I loved him. We'd only just met. I couldn't tell him that I loved him. It wouldn't be truthful. At least, not yet.

Five minutes later we felt our imminent climaxes bubbling up. I knew that mine was, but I could as clearly feel that he too was rapidly building up to it. His body was easy to read: very expressive of what was going on inside it. Some people are like that. I was happy that Matteo was among them.

I rolled off him and we lay side by side on our backs, our hips touching; one of my legs thrown across his. Arms crossed over each other we fiercely pulled each other's urgent cocks until the dams burst inside both of us and our twin jets of semen sprang simultaneously and deliciously out of us.

In terms of visual entertainment I surpassed myself. Under the guidance of Matteo's blurred hand my airborne stream found its way to my collar-bone and across Matteo's chest. Seconds later he exactly returned that compliment. Perhaps he too had surpassed himself.

It took us a few minutes to recover ourselves. When

we had we mopped each other up with a small towel I'd brought from home for this express purpose and had placed with foresight in the drawer of the locker beside my bed. (I'd forgotten it was there when I'd done myself the previous night – hence my resort to my under-pillow handkerchief.) We were still in the middle of the clean-up process when I heard the sounds of doors and stairs and young male Italian voices. Marco and his school-friends had arrived back. Instinctively I froze. Matteo noticed this. 'Don't worry,' he said. Even as he spoke I could hear that his brother and friends had gone into Marco's bedroom, two doors away, and closed the door behind them. 'They won't trouble us. If we go out shortly we can do it quietly. And if Marco does catch us… Well, actually, it won't matter very much.' He paused. 'I'm not sure I ought to tell you this. You might be shocked.'

'I don't think you'll be able to shock me,' I said, looking and smiling into his face. 'Not if it's anything to do with sex.' Then I paused. 'And if it's to do with your brother … perhaps I can guess.'

'We used to do stuff together,' Matteo blurted, an anxious look suddenly clouding his face.

I stroked his cheek. 'That's what I guessed,' I said gently. 'It's OK. Lots of pairs of brothers do when they're very young. I'm OK with that.'

SIX

Matteo took me out to show me the frontage of the house. It involved a trip on the bus.

If you live in a palazzo on the Canal Grande you can easily see the handsome façades of the palazzi opposite but unlike people in most cities you cannot simply step into the street and view the front of your own. This was a feature of Venetian life I had never thought about. I did know what the front of the building looked like – Annabelle had sent me a photo of it by email before I'd come out here, and there was of course Canaletto's painting of it hanging in the collection on the floor below our bedrooms. But I hadn't yet gazed upon the reality with my own eyes. So we walked to the bus stop.

The bus stops here were glassed-in waiting rooms that floated, attached to the quays by hinged walkways, rising and falling comfortably with the tides. Matteo took me to the ticket window and helped me to buy a travel pass at a young person's discount. I simply had to touch it against a reader each time I took a bus.

Most bus drivers use the foot brake to slow down on the approach to a stop, and the hand brake to keep it in position while the passengers get on and off. Here the diesel engine was the only brake. The driver used it and the rudder to keep the bus pressed up against the pontoon jetty of the stop while the conductor moored us temporarily with a stout rope. He threw a loop over an iron rail on the pontoon, pulled on it, then fastened the end with a pair of half-hitches around the two pins of a cleat on the gunwale of the boat. The whole procedure took him about a second and a half. His hands moved so fast that the rope was a blur and the half-hitches appeared as if by magic.

We were chugging past the Dragonettis' palazzo within a minute of setting off. Seeing it as it was meant to be seen I thought it the handsomest of all the palazzi in sight. Though of course I would think that. Its canal-front elevation was approximately square. Its brickwork was invisible, covered by smooth rendering that was painted a dusky pink. The window surrounds, and the arch of the water door were of creamy marble. With their intricate tracery they gave an impression of piped sugar-icing decorating a beautiful iced cake. There were the small lancet windows of the water floor, then above them, centrally placed, the six lancets that together lit the portego with the pianos in it, and six identical lancets that belonged to the picture gallery portego above that. Further pairs of Gothic windows stood a little aside from them, two on each side and on each floor. The lower ones belonged to the dining-room and Domenico's study, while above them the windows lit the master bedrooms. Right at the top of the house was a line of small square windows that the casual bus passenger would hardly bother to glance up at. But I did. There was my bedroom window, behind which I'd had sex with Matteo within the last hour, and Matteo's window next to it, and Marco's next to that. It gave me a wonderful cosy feeling of belonging. To be able to look up at that five-hundred-year-old façade and to know where, behind it, everything was.

But there was something right next to the palazzo that grabbed my attention then. 'Hey, Matteo,' I said, 'there's a garden right there!'

'Right,' he said. 'That's ours. I haven't shown it to you yet. There has been too much else to do.'

'Of course,' I said. My mind flipped back to the hour of intimacy in my bed that had ended just thirty minutes before.

'You get into it from the water floor. I will... I shall show it to you when we get back.'

'It looks lovely from here,' I said. 'Orange trees and stuff... By the way, you don't have to keep worrying about shall and will all the time,' I told him gently. 'Most people just say, *I'll show you.*' I gave his arm a quick squeeze and added apologetically, 'Just trying to help you with your English. Like I said.'

'Thank you,' said Matteo. 'Mamma always says, "I'll do this, I'll do that." But my English teachers at school say that's sloppy.'

'It isn't,' I said. 'Your mum's right. I bet even the Queen says *I'll*, and *I've*, when she's at home. And your mum's English is at least as good as the Queen's.'

'Thank you,' said Matteo again, and he pinched my forearm.

Having seen the palazzo and its garden from the outside we didn't immediately get off the bus at the next stop. We let it take us further up the Canal Grande, heading west. Matteo pointed out other buildings we passed. He didn't know everyone who lived along the Canal Grande of course, but he knew quite a lot, and he told me about them, and the history of their houses.

We didn't go inside the cabin to take a seat but stood on the open deck, the better to enjoy the view and the feel of the place. I'd got used to having everyone tell me that Venice stank in the summer. But it didn't. Not today at any rate. Or if it did, well, I never noticed it. I just stood next to Matteo at the rail, marvelling at everything I saw, but more than anything else, marvelling at Matteo. I wanted to keep touching him, wanted to fondle him, to paw at him, to keep reassuring myself he was real. From time to time he pawed at me, though only for a second at a time. I realised with an exquisite pang of insight that he was feeling the same thing that I was.

We made a circle out of our trip. Our first time together on a boat. All the way up the jaw-dropping Grand Canal as far as the railway station – which might have dropped from Mars, so ill-assorted it was with everything else in the city. There we had to change buses. We doubled back then through a side canal that made its way through the utilitarian end of Venice – past the car parks and the road bridge and then the docks. We even sailed past a rusty old army tank at one point. But then we were back in the Venice that people came to see: on the wide Giudecca Canal, curving its way seaward, roughly in parallel with the Grand Canal but a few blocks south of it. We got off where Matteo knew we needed to, and threaded our way back home through the labyrinthine back streets. It wasn't till we passed beneath the stone head that peered sternly down from the wall above that I knew where we were, knew we were nearly back.

The house was quiet when we got inside. But when we'd climbed the stairs to 'our' floor at the top of the building we could hear occasional sounds coming from Marco's room. He was presumably still entertaining his friends in there. 'Computer games,' Matteo said to me with a momentary upward flick of eyes and eyebrows. 'They're obsessed with them.' Unsure what we were going to do now we went into my bedroom together and closed the door. Only an hour and a half had passed since we'd lain on my bed together in each other's arms and come expansively all over each other. Was it too soon for a replay? Would we get bored with this if we did it too often? Apparently it wasn't too soon to do it again. We were soon back on the bed and undoing each other's flies. And if we were going to get bored with this one day... well, it wasn't showing any sign of happening yet.

*

We didn't get bored that afternoon. But we did eventually get up off the bed and put our clothes back on. 'Show me this garden of yours,' I said.

'Of course,' said Matteo. 'I keep forgetting.

Forgetting this thing the English have about gardens.'

'Don't come all Italian with me,' I said, gently teasing him. 'You also keep forgetting that you're half English yourself.'

Matteo had no answer to that, except to pinch my bottom quite hard as we headed out of my bedroom towards the stairs.

You went out into the garden through a small and unobtrusive door on the water floor. There were no windows onto it from that floor and, except on its Grand Canal side, where it was partially screened by the iron railings I'd first glimpsed it through, it was enclosed by high walls and barely overlooked at all.

There was no lawn in this garden. Its ground was paved with a checkerboard of marble squares. In the bare earthy spaces between the paving stones grew shrubs and medium sized trees. There was a lemon tree, an orange tree and a pomegranate tree. Against the walls grew roses – in full bloom, red, yellow and white, this June afternoon – while white summer jasmine swarmed up the railings between us and the canal. Small hedges of box, just a foot or two high, furnished the ground. The scent of all this, raised from leaves and petals by the warm sun, was a heavenly one.

Four stone benches also furnished the space. They were placed formally, symmetrically, one for each side of the square. We sat down on one and, although potentially partially visible to any determined eyes that might be peering through the fronds of jasmine and the railings from boats on the Grand Canal, put an arm each around the other's neck. 'It's a magic place,' I said.

'I thought you'd like it,' Matteo answered. 'Can't think why I forgot to show it to you before.'

Perhaps because the place was too powerfully magical, I thought, though I didn't say this out loud. Beautiful scenery has been known to make people fall in love with each other too quickly for their own good. I already knew this. This afternoon I was already close to giving my heart unwisely and unconditionally away. I wondered if the same went for Matteo. I wondered if he was alarmed about that prospect. I knew that I was.

*

When dinner time came round we were one extra at the table. One of Marco's friends was staying on to eat with us. His name was Tonio. Like Marco he was bright as a button and extrovert. I couldn't guess from his demeanour whether he too lived in a palazzo. At any rate he seemed unfazed either by his surroundings or by the presence of the Dragonetti parents. He was clearly a regular visitor and comfortable in the company of his friend's elder brother Matteo, whom he bantered with. I was pleased to see that Matteo liked him and I found it very easy, in my turn, to like him too.

After dinner we four lads went out. We took the bus to another part of town. I hadn't yet got used to this; I was anything but blasé about it. We waited a few minutes in the cabin on the bus-stop pontoon, feeling it rise and fall slightly as boats passed. Then our *vaporetto numero uno* pulled in and momentarily tied up while we and other passengers trooped aboard. We untied at lightning speed and accelerated out into the Grand Canal, this time heading eastward to pass beneath the Rialto Bridge and round the big looping bend towards the Salute church and the open water in front of St Mark's Square.

It was dark now, so the water was lit by street lights and the huge windows of the palaces we passed, big as churches. Those lights reflected and made patterns in the black water of the canal. It was a sight such as I had never seen. People said that Venice was like no other place on earth. Without having seen every place on earth (though who has, after all?) I had to agree.

Through the huge high windows of the palazzi I occasionally got tantalising glimpses of their interiors where curtains had not been drawn. Of the painted, coffered ceilings mainly, but occasionally of the tops of tall bookcases and dark works of art in ornate bright golden frames, lit by golden chandelier-light and framed in night.

At last the waterway's big U-curve was behind us and the canal ahead was opening out into the calm open waters of St Mark's Basin and the lagoon that it merged with. The Doge's Palace came into sight on our left, the two great churches – the Salute and San Giorgio Maggiore – off to the right. But we were making for a spot on the left shore beyond San Marco and the Doge's

Palace. It was the area of Castello called Arsenale ... where I had stayed in a hotel, unknown to the Dragonettis, on my first night. Just two evenings ago! That hardly seemed possible now that so much had happened since.

Matteo knew I'd met his brother in a bar that night, and that we'd had sex of some sort. But he might not have known exactly where that had taken place. At any rate, once we had landed from the bus he led us along the waterfront to the very same bar in which his brother and I had met. Neither Marco nor I mentioned this coincidence but walked in with Matteo quite nonchalantly. At least Marco did. I made a point of looking about me in the bar's interior in the interested way of a new arrival who doesn't know the place.

We bought a beer each from the bar and took the brimming glasses outside with us, sitting among a small crowd of other locals at one of the tables in the pedestrian street. It had been a canal once, Matteo told me, but had been filled in during the nineteenth century, to create the Via Garibaldi, one of the wider walkways of the town.

As we sat and chatted I found myself watching Marco's interaction with his friend Tonio, and wondering inevitably whether their friendship, which was clearly a close one, went as far as to involve sex. If I hadn't reached a conclusion by the end of the evening, I could always ask Matteo when we were alone again together, I guessed.

I also guessed at the same time that Marco, having told his elder brother that he'd had sex with me, was unlikely to have stopped short of asking Matteo if he and I had also had sex together. And that Matteo, who had admitted to me that he'd done stuff with Marco at some point in the distant past, would have been unlikely to lie to his younger brother by saying no.

The sexual dynamic between the four of us sitting in shorts around that pavement table, bantering and quaffing beer, was an exciting one, the prospects enticing for all of us. So enticing was it that I began to notice that my dick was hardening inside my shorts. I glanced sideways at Matteo's crotch, just out of curiosity, and hoped I wouldn't be spotted doing it. A similar ridge was appearing in Matteo's shorts. I looked up at him. He caught my eye. And gave me a mischievous smile.

SEVEN

In the morning I did some piano practice. That sounds a prosaic way to begin a chapter. But, remember, I did it in the forty-foot long portego of a Venetian palace, sitting at a nine-foot Fazioli, while the Canal Grande shimmered just outside.

Even nicer – Matteo was sitting near me, listening in. He even took notes at times.

I wouldn't have expected to enjoy this close scrutiny of his – I'd actually asked him not to be there – but in the event it gave me an unanticipated feeling of contentment. It came about like this.

My agreement with Annabelle included her permission to practise for some time each day on one or other of the two pianos. Musicians have to practise or they can't perform. And it wasn't my intention to do nothing but teach piano all my life. I wanted to be a performer too.

At breakfast that morning I was wondering how to raise with Matteo the delicate subject of my need to practise. But he got there first. 'You didn't do any of your own practice yesterday,' he said. 'You were too busy with me.' Had he kept an entirely straight face as he said that I might have understood him to mean only the music, but the smile that quivered at the corners of his mouth and twinkled in his eyes made it clear that he was including the bedroom too. 'If you want to do a couple of hours this morning, that's fine by me.'

'Well, if you say so…'

'Only…' he continued a bit shyly, 'would you be OK if I listened in?'

'You wouldn't want…' I began, but he interrupted me.

'Please. I'd learn so much. Plus … I really like your company.' When he finished that last revealing sentence he covered his chin with the top of his T-shirt, like a kid who's said more than he meant to say.

He'd had my company through the whole of the previous night, waking and asleep, wrapped for much of the time quite uncomfortably – if wonderfully – in my arms. But still he evidently hadn't had too much of me. And I hadn't had too much of him. But it was the bashful way he tucked his chin into his T-shirt that won me now. 'OK,' I said. I grinned at him. 'Flattery will get you everywhere. But I can't promise you'll learn much. And just get up and go when you've had enough.'

But he didn't get up and go. I made a point of practising something I already knew: the Schubert A-minor sonata, whose slow movement I'd already played to him on my first night in the house. I didn't find it a particularly difficult sonata (except for its final twenty seconds – I'll come to that in a moment) but it's a powerfully expressive piece and deeply poignant. Those aspects of it need to be brought out very carefully: the emotions made to speak clearly but without being cheapened by vulgarly over-sentimentalising them. All in all it was an ideal piece of music to work on with an impressionable young man, a fellow musician, with whom I was beginning to fall in love…

Beginning to fall in love! Again I was getting ahead of myself. Last night I had sat out at a pavement table drinking beer with Matteo, Marco and Tonio. The sexual static between the four of us had grown intense, though nobody had said anything. But it had become shyly visible in all our pairs of shorts by the time the evening ended.

There had been no need in the end for Marco and Tonio to tell me that there was a sexual thing going between them, and no need for me to ask them. Their conversation had in fact focused firmly on the fact that their school holidays were due to start in a few days and they would be looking for a holiday job apiece in order to fill their pockets. Tonio knew the head of a gondola outfit, he said, that liked to employ handsome boys in their late teens to sell the tickets. (The gondolas were actually rowed by scrawnier, or else paunchier, but always expert, older men.) With the summer explosion of tourist numbers due any day now, the gondola hire companies would be recruiting armies of presentable youngsters like themselves, Tonio told Marco. Would Marco like him, Tonio, to have a word on behalf of both of them? Marco had said yes. Of course he would.

If I had managed to work out during the course of that evening that Marco and Tonio were not 'just good friends', well, Tonio must have known about Matteo and me. And probably Marco would also have told him about himself and me two nights ago.

So there we had been, the four of us, all connected by interweaving threads of sexual intimacy. I felt, in my excited enjoyment of that moment, sitting round a table in the open air, surrounded by convivial Italian chatter in the warm Venetian night, that I wanted to explore all those threads, renewing and doubling them. To put it another way, more stark and less poetic, I wanted to have sex with everyone I shared that table with. Together as well as separately.

But that was a wish that didn't sit too well with the burgeoning knowledge that I was beginning to fall in love with Matteo. Being in love meant exclusivity. At least, I'd always understood that was supposed to be the case. So I saw a possible conflict here. And I didn't know – perhaps I never would know – whether Matteo's heart was taking its first faltering steps towards falling in love with me.

All these thoughts were at the back of my mind now as I patiently worked my way through Schubert's D 784. Through the stark octave figures of its opening allegro, through the pearly ornaments of its gentle central andante and on into the flying finale whose bubbling triplets made me think of the flight of swallows skimming a river, dangerously near to the water, at breathtaking speed.

Last night had ended with the four of us returning, up the Grand Canal by a very late waterbus, to the

Dragonettis' palazzo. We had all come in together and, because the silence of the place indicated that everyone else was already in bed and asleep, made our way very quietly up the stairs. Nothing was said outside the bedroom doors. Nothing needed to be said. Marco and Tonio went into Marco's room, and Matteo and I went into mine. It was very matter of fact, this tidy way of arranging the day's end. It seemed clear that Tonio was accustomed to sleeping over with Marco. I'd already seen that there were two beds in that room, so there would have been nothing to arouse any anxieties the Dragonetti parents might have had about the propriety of things.

I've written that nothing was said as we parted for the night outside those bedroom doors. But Matteo and I each exchanged a kiss with the other two. Brief and chaste, but on the lips. It was something, I was learning, that Italian men routinely did. But the novelty of it made quite an impact on me. Here I was, not only kissing Marco goodnight, but doing the same with his young friend Tonio. I was still savouring that novelty – as well as the taste of Tonio's lips – when, after entering my own room with Matteo in tow, the two of us started kissing quite earnestly and, after a little time, quite unchastely too.

No doubt, I couldn't help thinking, something similar was happening, in the privacy of Marco's room, between the other two…

I brought my mind back to the Schubert. I had to. The impossible final few bars were approaching. And like a pilot who can see the runway lights coming towards him fast and dangerous, I needed the whole of my concentration to deal with what was coming now.

The difficult bit would last no more than a few seconds. It amounted to just over seven bars of music. But it was the climax of the whole sonata, coming just before the four final forte chords would tell the audience it was time to clap, put their coats on and go. It was loud – meaning difficult, and that mistakes could not be hidden – and it was fast. Schubert had taken his swallow-skimming triplets and added octaves to them – octaves in both hands – so that it was as if each swallow was having to shoot the rapids with a fishing weight hung round its neck.

Schubert required you to play those seven bars legato, that is, with a joined-up sound. Up to a certain speed you can play octaves legato by using fingers three four and five in rapid succession while the thumb bumps along seven inches away. Even that is only possible if you have a big hand.

Even with a big hand – such as I'm lucky enough to have – it was impossible at the speed Schubert wanted you to play it at. Perhaps huge-handed genii like Liszt and Rachmaninoff could have done it. But almost nobody else could. Schubert certainly could not. He was a very small man, with very small hands. He famously failed to manage the rapid octaves in the piano part of his own Erl-King setting.

So what would Franz Schubert, aware of his own

physical shortcomings, have wanted me to do now? If you're an amateur you're allowed to miss out some of the thumb-notes, but as I was a would-be professional that option wasn't open to me. The professionals I'd seen playing the piece had chosen between two unwelcome options. They'd followed Schubert's instruction to play legato, but necessarily slowed the melody down right at the piece's climax, or they'd kept up the pace but played the octaves staccato in defiance of the composer's wishes.

'Franz', I now told the composer in my mind as the terrifying moment loomed, 'you can't have it both ways. I can do it smooth or I can do it fast. Not both. Neither can anyone else. And given that you couldn't follow your own instructions yourself, what should I do now?' Then I added, just to make the situation clear, 'I'm playing this to a young man who is not only my student but someone I'm falling in love with. I know you've been there too…'

I didn't wait to hear Schubert answer me. There wasn't time. But I knew suddenly what I wasn't going to do. I wasn't going to slow down. I hit the octaves running. Staccato and loud. Bang-bang-bang, bang-bang-bang, bang. There are seven repeats of that motif. They take little more than a second each. I managed to blur the hardness a little by carefully fluttering my foot up and down on the sustaining pedal. Then I crashed to a halt with the final four repeated chords.

I was only aware that the piece had come to an end when I felt Matteo's arms around my neck and his cheek against mine. 'How the fucking hell did you manage that?' he asked me. He didn't need to do much more than whisper the question. His lips were practically brushing my ear.

Ordinarily I would have said it was a fluke, or luck, and that I'd never managed to end the sonata as dazzlingly as that before. But I knew at that moment exactly how things stood. I told Matteo the honest truth. 'Because I was playing it for you.'

*

We went out for a coffee. Neither of us needed to voice the thought that the palazzo had become a little claustrophobic at that moment. 'Find the café we had breakfast at yesterday,' Matteo instructed mischievously.

I didn't think I'd have a hope in hell of finding the place, yet somehow, taking my bearings from the stone face that peered down from the alley-way wall, I did just that. Matteo ordered us a double espresso each in rapid Italian and then we sat, exactly where we'd done the previous day, on the narrow walkway between the café's front door and the brink of the slinky side canal.

People who think they may be falling in love with each other rarely mention the fact to each other at the time. They talk of other things. Matteo and I talked about the possibility that his brother Marco might, along with his friend Tonio, be working for a gondola firm in a few days' time.

'It would be a very easy job,' said Matteo. 'Chatting

up the tourists, flashing your teeth and eyes at the ladies, and taking their arms on the stairs. Except that it's... I don't know the English word. You get paid according to how many customers you persuade to go on board.'

'Commission-based?' I suggested.

'Sounds right to me,' said Matteo, stirring his coffee, and I felt that I'd earned another morsel of my own salary – which was not commission-based at all, and I was very glad of that.

'I can just see the two of them in those blue and white striped tops,' I said, 'and those straw boaters with the little ribbon-ends.' I'd seen a few other young men dressed liked that at the tops of water stairs and hadn't failed to notice how nice they looked.

'Mmm,' said Matteo non-committally, and as he said it I wondered for the first time if he, not just Marco, had done the physical stuff with Tonio. I thought I might ask him at some future date when the moment seemed right, but I didn't attempt to do it now. 'How long have they been an item?' I asked instead.

Matteo shrugged and said, 'How long is a piece of string?' His mother must have taught him that, I thought. I couldn't imagine him learning it at school.

I changed the subject slightly. 'You must admit it's slightly confusing. You and your brother having such similar names. Don't other people find that?'

Matteo moved his head from side to side. 'Yes, maybe

some do. I guess that if our parents had gone on to have two more sons they'd have been Lucca and Giovanni. Matthew, Mark, Luke and John: the full set.'

I hadn't thought of that. But I said, 'It was slightly easier when I thought of your brother as Tomassio.'

'I think,' said Matteo seriously, 'that if you have sex with someone you tend to go on thinking of them by the name they gave you when you did it with them. I shall not... I mean I shan't ... mind if you want to call him Tomassio.'

'Well that's helpful,' I said. 'And kind of you. But I'd better check with him first. See how he feels about it.'

Matteo looked at me and lowered his eyelids ever so slightly, giving me a full view of his lashes. I imagined them at that moment as tiny black peacocks' tails. 'That's very diplomatic of you,' he said. 'And very wise.'

I laughed at him and punched his arm.

EIGHT

Everyone who's ever learnt to play a musical instrument or to drive a car knows there are two separate things involved. There are the lessons you have to have, and then there is the practice that has to be done in between. Of course the reality often falls short of this. Most kids don't want to do the practice, or they do the absolute minimum. The kids who are the exception are the ones who have to be torn away from their instruments for meals and at bedtime. They are the kids who are going to be the future's professional musicians. They had included both Matteo and me.

When I began to teach Matteo we were both highly conscious of the difference between lessons and practice: neither of us would have imagined a different routine, a different way of doing things. But on the day that I practised the Schubert sonata while Matteo listened and took notes – and then in the afternoon Matteo practised a big Beethoven sonata while I took notes ... and we discussed it all at length afterwards ... the rigid distinction between lesson and practice began to blur.

The roles of teacher and student began to blur too. In the days that followed Matteo and I became, no longer teacher and pupil, but simply two guys who wanted to play the piano better and better and to learn everything we could from each other. We simply worked together at the two pianos, taking it in turns to practise our pieces while the other listened, took notes, commented and made suggestions for improvement.

I had no idea whether this way of doing things would work for anybody else. I knew, though, that it was working wonderfully well for us. I knew in those idyllic days of June that the harmony of our daytimes, working away at Chopin, Schubert and Bach, was as complete and perfect as the harmony we enjoyed during our nighttimes, in bed sleeping, or awake and having sex.

We used our two bedrooms in turn now, partly in order to give our two sets of sheets an equal amount of use. This was a ridiculous piece of over-caution, we knew. Annabelle did not want us to be mollycoddled by Artemia, and she expected us to change our own sheets at the end of each week. It was our job to put them in the washing-machine on the water floor. And if it was the rule that Artemia later took them out and ironed them herself, that was a concession that the boys' mother made reluctantly, in the knowledge that Artemia would iron the bed linen perfectly in minutes – while we lads would take all afternoon and make a perfect hash of it.

Marco accepted our sleeping arrangements without question and with no sign of jealousy. His friend Tonio obviously couldn't sleep over every night without raising parental eyebrows, but during that first week he did so twice, while on one night Marco stayed over with Tonio at his parents' house. The two of them might have wished for seven nights together, but in the circumstances three out of seven didn't seem too bad.

In the circumstances… Parental eyebrows… All of us

were eighteen or more, so were legally entitled to do as we liked together, and it was no business of the Dragonetti parents. Well, that was the theory. The reality was a bit different. It's still more difficult to come out as a gay teenager in Italy than it is in Britain, and even that, I had found myself as yet unable to do.

The Dragonettis might not have been able to tell their offspring not to have gay sex, but they would have had the right to turn their technically adult boys out of their house. Not that they would remotely have done that. They might, though, have fingered me as their sons' seducer and turned *me* out of their house. So there were good reasons to be careful. And, more reasonably, none of us wanted to upset the apple-cart. Few parents, however enlightened they may be, positively welcome the idea that their two sons – their only progeny – are both gay. It's still an embarrassment they have to carry around with them and decide whether to share it with their friends and other family members or not. Besides, we boys were all still young enough to find later that we'd been 'going through a phase' and not really gay at all. In which case the Dragonetti parents' apple-cart would have been upset for no good reason – and then upset a second time, when they would have to tell everyone their sons weren't gay after all, and that all those daughters of friends who had given up on the idea of making a catch of them could come back and have another try.

*

We were working together one afternoon on Matteo's

Beethoven sonata. It was the very beautiful and virtuosic one that is known as the Waldstein – which was the name of the man to whom it was dedicated – and Matteo was making a very good job of it. Because of the new way in which we were working together I found that I was, relatively painlessly, learning it too.

Annabelle walked into the portego and came towards us. We stopped. Annabelle didn't say *Carry on*, or *Don't mind me*, so we stayed stopped. 'That's going very well,' she said, and smiled. Then she said, 'Have either of you ever heard a quail?'

The question wasn't as mad as it might seem. We were working on the brief slow centre of the sonata, the calm eye amidst the swirls of cloud and wind. Its motif is a phrase of four notes played very slowly. The little phrase is said to imitate the call of a quail.

'Yes,' said Matteo. 'Don't you remember? We heard them on that holiday in the Swiss Alps. Down in the pastures.'

'Yes, I do remember,' said his mother. 'I wasn't sure if you did.'

'I've never heard a quail,' I said. Quite unintentionally this came out sounding very sad, as if I'd missed out on one of the great experiences that life has to offer, and it made us all laugh.

'We'll have to see what we can do,' Annabelle said to me. 'Not that you'll hear quail in Venice. But we'll try and fit in a few trips into the country while you're here.

Venice can be quite claustrophobic after a while.' She paused for a second. Then, 'Actually, it was something like that that I was coming to talk to you about. I think you both need to get out a bit more. You've been working incredibly hard this week. Be careful you don't overdo it. On top of each other the whole time...' I didn't dare catch Matteo's eye at that moment. 'You've got three whole months of working together ahead of you. I think you ought to pace yourselves a bit. You don't want to find you've got tired of each other by the end of the first fortnight. Or tired of music.'

I didn't think I could ever get tired of Matteo. They used to say that you never got tired of the eternal joy that was Heaven. And being with Matteo was the nearest thing to Heaven that I'd experienced in my life. But Annabelle had nearly thirty years more experience of life than we did: it was just possible she knew what she was talking about.

'Why don't you take the afternoon off?' Annabelle went on. 'And Marco's at a loose end too. His friends have all gone somewhere else. He'll just sit plugged into his computer all day in his bedroom. Maybe the three of you ought to get out in the open air...'

Wisely she left it at that. 'There's fresh coffee in the kitchen anyway,' she finished. Then she left us.

*

We did go out. The three of us. We went to the beach, on the bus.

It was typical of this tospy-turvy, looking-glass world, this world of Venice in which we lived, that we drove out of town on water in order to arrive at the beach. The vaporetto number one, which I now thought of as my war-horse, took us down the Grand Canal as usual, into the wider water of St Mark's Basin then, stopping off from time to time along the southern waterfront of Castello and the public gardens, chugged out into the open reach of the lagoon towards the natural harbour wall that protects the lagoon from the Adriatic Sea.

That natural harbour wall, broken by three entrances, was something that I had always imagined, looking on the map, to be about a hundred yards across at most, and with one hotel on it. (The Grand Hotel des Bains, that would have been. Anyone seen Death In Venice?) But as we approached the central section of that protecting spit of land – the Lido, lying about a mile beyond the easternmost tip of Venice proper – I began to see how wrong I was.

The most astonishing thing – I noticed this when we were still a half-mile off the Lido's shore – was that the Lido had cars and trucks, and vans and buses, motoring unconcernedly along it. I hadn't seen a car in almost a week. This sight, coming into focus between the rows of wooden navigation posts, rocked me to the core. Disproportionately. It was a major culture shock.

But you can get used to most things in time. And it took some time to travel that last half mile. So by the time we docked I had come to a broad-minded acceptance of the existence of motorised land transport within a couple of miles of the heart of La Serenessima.

We got off the bus. The Lido turned out to be nearly a mile across as well as seven long, and a sizeable town or suburb in its own right, if no less tourist-dependent than Venice itself. The inward-facing shore gave us a panoramic view of the lagoon and its dozens of islands and islets, of the great city at its centre, and of the pencil line that was mainland Italy beyond that. After a while, though, we turned away from all of that, and trekked down the broad tree-lined, hotel-lined, street towards the seaward side, towards the beach.

Matteo, my guide, gestured widely towards the north. At the top end of the Lido, he said, was Venice's original, often fog-bound airport. It was now principally a military and security base. Beyond it was the biggest entrance into the lagoon from the Adriatic. The Porto di Lido. The big dredged channel used by the tankers and cruise ships.

'Ciao, ragazzi!' – Hi, guys – a voice greeted us loudly, unexpectedly, from across the road. We turned, though the voice was familiar enough. We saw Tonio crossing the road towards us.

'Che bruta visione!' Marco called to him. It meant *what a beastly sight*. Italians use the phrase regularly when greeting close friends. It's meant as a joke.

We all met on the pavement. We all kissed.

'I thought you'd gone to Padova with your parents,' Marco said.

'I thought I had,' said Tonio. 'But plans changed. I called you but...'

'Sorry,' said Marco. 'Forgot to charge it...'

'I called your home. Your mother said you were going to the Lido. I came on over. To lie in wait...'

'An ambush,' said Matteo.

'It worked, though, didn't it?' said Tonio brightly.

The four of us walked on towards the sea, whose light was shining towards us now, reflected in the sky above the trees ahead. Unexpectedly I found myself walking alongside Marco. While Matteo went ahead, chatting with Tonio.

My new companion had no hesitation in coming to the point at once. 'You like my brother a lot.'

'I like you a lot too,' I said in my British, diplomatic way. 'But yes I do. I hope you're OK with that.'

Marco chuckled. 'Of course I'm OK with it. I'm very happy Matteo has a friend at last. Before, it was always me he was into.'

'Oh,' I said. Matteo had told me what he had told me, but I hadn't seen the thing in quite those terms. Then I reminded myself that everyone's take on any relationship was different, especially when it came to the two people most concerned in it.

A thought struck me. 'Has Matteo ever had a

girlfriend?' I asked.

'No,' said Marco. 'Neither have I, before you ask. Though Tonio had one for a while.'

'Hmm,' I said. You go looking for a pattern to things but it never emerges quite as clear-cut as you want it to.

'What about you?' Marco asked.

'Me what?' I queried.

'Ever had a girlfriend?'

'No,' I said. 'I mean, I've got friends who're girls…'

'We've all got those,' said Marco.

'I guess I'm the real McCoy,' I said, mischievously hoping he wouldn't know the expression.

He didn't. 'What's that meant to mean?'

'The real thing. The genuine article. I guess I'm saying I'm a real gay man.'

'Ah,' said Marco. 'I think Matteo may be too. The two of you have so much in common – music and so on, I mean – so you may as well have that too.'

'I see,' I said. 'And you may be right. He seems very comfortable in his skin when he's in bed with me, anyway.'

'That I can believe,' said Marco, nodding knowingly.

'So what about you and Tonio?' I pursued. I couldn't imagine a better moment presenting itself for me to ask this question easily.

'Wait and see,' said Marco, flashing a very twinkly look at me as we walked along. 'We're a year younger than Matteo, remember. Three years younger than you. When it comes to nailing our colours to the mast we're hedging our bets and keeping our powder dry for now.'

'Blimey,' I said, genuinely astonished. 'You're pretty well versed in English metaphors. Even mixed ones.'

'Having an English mother helps,' Marco reminded me. Then he added cheekily, 'I hope Matteo's helping you a bit with your Italian.'

'Hmm,' I said non-committally. Then, 'I'm finding it a bit difficult: you and Matteo having such similar names. I wondered if I could call you Tomassio – to make things easier.'

It was Marco's turn to say *Hmm*. 'But then you might get my name mixed with Tonio's.'

'I see,' I said. 'Yes, there's always that.'

'We could compromise, I suppose,' said Marco. (He could only have got that formula from Annabelle.) 'You go on calling me Marco, and thinking of me as Marco... Except...' He shot me a wicked sideways look that was as sharp as a dart. 'Except when we're having sex together. Then call me Tomassio.'

Love in Venice

'Ah,' I said, trying not to let him sense the earthquake that was happening inside me. 'I'll try and remember that.'

Our road had reached a roundabout, where it joined the road along the Adriatic beach. Beyond it, between two hotel blocks, a narrow pathway led straight towards the blue blink of the open sea. We walked down into the narrow track and our shoes began to skid and slip in sand.

'Race you guys to the water,' Marco suddenly called. I wasn't quite sure exactly who he meant until he grabbed my hand and, pulling me along at first, overtook the other two before we reached the end of the narrow pathway.

It wasn't much of a sprint. In deep dry sand you flounder rather than run. But all four of us were equally handicapped in that respect. Marco and I were still holding hands, and now laughing. We could hear the other two pounding along behind us, laughing too. Whether they were holding hands or not I didn't look round to check.

Marco and I mounted a low slab of rock, accelerated over it, then ran on, on wet sand now, for a few more seconds before we came to a halt, our trainers and socks soaked, in the shallow breaking waves of the Adriatic Sea. Our hands came unclasped and we turned round. Matteo and Tonio were upon us immediately. It looked as though Tonio was going to fall against me while Matteo ran full tilt into his brother. But somehow at the last nanosecond our positions got reversed. Matteo ended up throwing his arms round me, while Tonio embraced Marco. It was a very energetic collision.

We were lucky not to all fall flat in the shallows of the sea. Somehow we remained standing as we, two couples, hugged and kissed. Then, leaning for support on one another's shoulders, we took off our soaked trainers and socks. We tied our shoes together by the laces and hung them round our necks like yokes. While we tucked our socks into the back pockets of our shorts, dryish top ends first, leaving the wet toe ends to stream like pennants down the curves of our butt cheeks. Had only one of us taken this practical step towards drying out our footwear in the sun as we walked it would have looked peculiar. As it was, with all four of us doing it, it looked like we were setting a trend.

We followed the edge of the surf for a mile or so until the line of swish hotels had petered out and we were on a wilder, unscrutinised area of the sandy beach. There we turned and headed up the beach a little way, to where tall reeds and grasses waved in clumps. We threw ourselves down on the ground, invisible as hares among the tall reeds and laughing, began to pull one another's T-shirts undiscriminatingly off. We didn't leave it at T-shirts. A moment later we'd yanked each other's shorts off too. There was nothing left then except underwear. Within seconds we'd removed that.

I was treated to my first sight of Marco and Tonio naked. I thought they looked gorgeous. It goes without saying that all four of us were big and erect. I reached across Marco's bare thigh, simply because his was the nearest, and tweaked his standing dick. But I wasn't sure whether I was supposed to be doing this. Whether we all were. By now Marco's fingers were crawling tentatively down my treasure trail. I wondered – I had never fucked or been fucked by anyone – should we be embarking on a fourway suck or fuck? A daisy-chain, I'd heard that sort of thing called. Would Matteo be wanting this? Would Tonio?

To ask one another verbally would have felt crass, I reckoned. We let our bodies sort things out in the end. I withdrew my hand from Marco's dick and he pulled back from me. Then Tonio staked his claim to Marco gently, dropping lightly on top of him, chest on chest, and snogging him where he lay. At the same time I felt Matteo's arms come round me from behind, in a proprietorial sort of way.

We compromised in the end. Matteo and I stayed wrapped together, devoting our hands and cocks and tongues to each other exclusively, while Marco and Tonio did the same. But we stayed within sight of one another, each pair looking at the other pair from time to time, not hiding the fact that we were doing so … and, boy, what a turn-on that proved to be.

None of us had brought a condom; we hadn't quite envisaged this happening. And as I, at the age of twenty-one, had never fucked a guy before there was a fair probability that the others, all younger than me, hadn't done so either, and wouldn't have wanted to do it for the first time under close public scrutiny. So nobody actually fucked anybody else. Anyway there was a quantity of sand about. But we had a perfectly good time doing pretty well everything else. Two separate couples, enjoying additionally the sight of the other couple's activities. It wasn't long before I felt Matteo come forcefully and hotly up my chest and belly, though I was holding him too close to be able actually to see it happen. Needless to day, this acted as a trigger to my own ejac which came about, equally heavily, just a few seconds later, in the same warm dark space between us.

That all took our minds away from Marco and Tonio. By the time we next focused our attention on them a minute or so later it was obvious that they had both climaxed too. They were sitting up on the sand, wiping each other's fronts down with two of the white socks that had been drying in one of their shorts' pockets. One of them would presumably be going home with sockless feet in his trainers.

There was still nobody about. Still naked we ran down the beach and into the sea. We all swam a few strokes, but that was about enough – in the northern end of the Adriatic in mid-June – then we quickly splashed and washed each other before running out of the water again, to dry off like seals on a low flat slab of rock that lay conveniently halfway between the wave-line and the thickets of reeds in which lay our clothes.

A rattle like machine-gun fire startled us. But it was only a helicopter rising suddenly from behind distant trees over at the air base. It was out of sight and sound before a minute had passed. 'Gone to rescue a cat up a tree,' said Tonio. We laughed.

An hour later, dry and dressed again in our T-shirts and shorts, we meandered back across the narrow landmass of the Lido, stopping for a small beer on the way, to catch the waterbus back to the heart of Venice, whose spires we could already see clearly across the water, sparkling in the evening sun. Tonio and Marco exchanged a bit of ribald banter on the subject of whose socks were whose, and which had been used in their mopping-up operation. In the end they agreed that it didn't really matter. Everything was quite dry now anyway; so nobody went home sockless. We all caught the vaporetto wearing virginally white socks and trainers, and looking as though butter wouldn't melt in our shoes.

NINE

That expedition to the Lido seemed to do everyone good, though its more sensual elements might not have been quite what Annabelle had in mind when she urged us to take the afternoon off. It cemented the bond between Matteo and me. Secure in the enduring quality of our relationship we were now able to leave each other alone for a whole hour at a time occasionally. One of us might head out to a shop on our own, or sit in the garden with a book while the other practised. Although that was about the limit of our separations from each other. An hour apart was about as much as we could manage at any one time without unease setting in. And that went for the daytimes only. We continued to spend the entirety of all our nighttimes snuggled up together in the same bed.

As for Marco and Tonio, on the final Saturday of their school term they got themselves interviewed by the man who ran the gondola company and were hired for the summer on the spot. It may have helped that they were both very cute. And beauty in both of a pair of people is a very potent thing. Somehow it's not a mere ten plus ten but more like ten squared, which is very different.

Their new boss found them uniform navy trousers and navy and white striped shirts that approximately fitted them. Those would be theirs for the duration, and they would be responsible for keeping them clean and washed. They also got a straw boater with fluttering ribbons each. They brought their outfits back to the palazzo and put them on there to show them off. That showed their figures off too. Matteo and I both thought they looked stunning in them. Had the Dragonetti parents plus Albano and Artemia not also been present at this mini-fashion parade I think we two would have wanted to yank the uniforms off and do with their ex-wearers what we had only just restrained ourselves from doing on the beach.

Marco headed off to work early that next Monday, leaving the palazzo while Matteo and I were still in bed. We spent the later part of that morning working at the pianos – on the big Chopin scherzo – resisting the temptation to wander across the city to see how Marco and Tonio were getting along on their first morning. But that evening the two younger boys reassured us when they came back for dinner that their first day had been a success. The boss had been pleased with them and they had notched up an acceptable amount of commission, which they would receive in cash at the end of the week.

So, confident that things were going well for them, on the afternoon of the boys' second day as gondola touts Matteo and I took a walk through the town streets to see them at work. I was learning that it was possible to walk through much of Venice without travelling by water – provided that you were prepared to zigzag a bit. As for getting lost among the labyrinth of alleyways and multiple dead-ends, well, that was all part of the Venice experience, Matteo assured me. Despite having been born and brought up there he sometimes got lost himself, he admitted. But it didn't matter, he explained. You never got lost for long. The city was small and bounded by water on all sides. You would always eventually find yourself beside the Grand Canal or the lagoon shore and could easily re-orient yourself. This afternoon, at any rate, we would be sticking to the well-trodden routes of the city centre; I would have Matteo with me; we would not get lost.

We headed away from the palazzo, zigzagging beneath the glowering head in the alleyway wall and past the café that had become our regular local hang-out. We were soon in the tourist-thronged area that was the Rialto. Hundreds of years ago it had been the world's equivalent of Wall Street and the Square Mile rolled into one; now it was a picturesque huddle of tourist shops.

Oh, and the fish market. In this great historic shed we saw display after display of pouting crabs and twitching pink prawns. One large and clever species of langoustine had large deceiving eye-patterns on their fanning tails. There were massive fishes like giant perches such as I'd only ever seen in old master canvasses of apocalyptic biblical scenes; I'd never imagined they also existed in the real world. Though perhaps, after all, Venice was not the real world.

Cod, tuna, hake and skate. Flounder and other flat fish whose names I didn't know in English, and neither did Matteo... He yanked me away from the clean, water-sluicing fish sheds and towards the Rialto Bridge.

The Rialto Bridge was a bridge of steps, a bridge of shops, but not a bridge of views, I realised. We shouldered our way up its steep stairway, against the heaving tide of tourists pouring down. Alongside us came barrow-men, bumping their specially designed carts expertly up the stepped incline. Expertise certainly played a part in their ability to pull off this mini-feat, but they must have tremendous muscles too, I thought.

At the very top of the steps, before they descended again the other side, the lines of shops on both sides of the bridge were at last pierced by archways. And from this high point there was a view. If we could muscle our way through the crowds taking selfies with their cameras out on stalks we could peer along the lovely curve of the Grand Canal towards the north and south…

I must have had muscles on my mind because, once Matteo had shepherded me towards the short parapet-rail of carved stone, my eyes focused not on the famous curve of the canal but on the equally spectacular double curve of the jeans-clad buttocks of a young man: he was leaning over and taking a photo of the famous view of the canal that opened out below.

He seemed big and handsome, with well-shaped legs. At least that was how he appeared from the rear. Many people display those attributes, however, yet prove a disappointment when they turn round. In a way I hoped that he wouldn't turn round: I didn't want to have that disappointment. Yet I also hoped he would.

And of course he had to, unless he planned to spend the whole day leaning over the narrow parapet (or jump from it), and after a few seconds he did.

He was not a disappointment from the front. He stood tall. His face had a blue-eyed, almost Nordic, look. His hair was blond and his lips were full. I guessed he was about three years older than I was. He was hemmed in by the press of tourists now, with Matteo and me at the front of the press. *'Scusi,'* he said to us. His accent wasn't very Italian. It might have been British, I thought.

Matteo and I parted like the Red Sea to let him pass. *'Va bene,'* Matteo said, in polite response to his *Scusi*, while I said, 'No worries,' in English. He glanced at each of us in turn for a split second, and I could see that in that moment he'd clocked us as a couple. He looked at us a second time, again for a bare half second, but this time with a half-smile that was somehow both tender and complicit. He said, 'Have a good day,' then disappeared into the crowd behind us. I turned, and Matteo turned, to watch him as he was swallowed by the crowd, his handsome butt disappearing last.

The whole encounter had lasted no more than three seconds. 'Well, that was nice,' I said to Matteo, but half regretting that I'd spoken as a soon as the words were out. I was new to the experience of being a couple. When it came to acknowledging the attractions of third parties I wasn't sure what the rules were yet.

But Matteo was smiling at me. He nodded his head. 'Handsome guy,' he said, then dropped the subject as we in our turn now leant over the bridge. So evidently everything was all right.

We made our way down from the summit of the

bridge, once again against a surge of tourists, this time coming up. We continued along the tourist trail, winding our way through the skein of streets between the Rialto Bridge and the Square of St Mark. Winding though the way was, this was one area of Venice where you could not get lost. At each street corner an arrow painted on the wall indicated 'Per Rialto' or 'Per San Marco', and if you were unable to make sense of those, you simply followed the other tourists.

Midway between those two key points we came to a junction of two side canals where, beneath the crumbling but still imposing façade of an ancient palazzo, a little basin served as a gondola rank. At the top of a flight of queasy wooden steps two smiling young men in striped T-shirts were accosting the passing tourists, handing out photocopied itineraries and price lists. One of them was Tonio. Halfway down the rickety staircase two more young men, similarly shirted and boatered, were helping unsteady elderly and not so elderly passengers into the rocking sleek black boats. One of those two young men was Marco.

Both boys greeted us happily but went on with their work. We stayed and watched awhile, unconsciously hoping perhaps that one of the tottering tourists would slip into the water, and that from our comfortable dry vantage point we could observe our comrades' efforts to haul them out.

When they had a second to spare, rare though that was, Tonio or Marco would come and chat to us. After fifteen minutes or so, though, Matteo and I felt we'd seen enough and made noises about heading back.

As we were turning to go, Marco came rushing up to his brother and said, though in Italian of course, 'Hey, wait. Could you do me an enormous favour? On the way back could you slip into the school? I left my sports bag behind at the end of term. There'll still be people there today but it's closed from tomorrow…'

Matteo nodded. 'And it'll be closed tonight by the time you finish work. Yeah, I know.' I noticed that he hadn't said whether he would do Marco the favour or not.

'Please,' the younger brother added.

'Lick my boots?' said Matteo, laughing. This was obviously a traditional bit of banter between them; probably it went back years.'

'Fuck your arse!' Marco laughed back.

'Of course I'll do it,' said Matteo. 'Arse or no arse. See you back home. Don't be late for dinner, though. It's roast pygmy. Artemia's been working on it day and night.'

With that the two brothers gave each other a hug and then Matteo and I turned back along the narrow quayside towards the Rialto Bridge.

'There's a little bar I wanted to show you,' Matteo told me as we re-crossed the bridge. 'But I need to make a five-minute detour to the school. You can head for the bar and I'll meet you in there – with Marco's stinking sports clothes – in ten minutes.' With his hands Matteo indicated the way I was to go. To the Bar All'Arco. I was to turn left into the Ruga Vecchia San Giovanni, then take the second alley on the right. It was a sort of tunnel – a *sotoportego*, Matteo called it. I would spot the bar at the far end of the tunnel. 'Set me up a glass of something red,' he said before diving down a side street and leaving me on my own to remember the names of the streets.

Not that I was in danger of getting lost. I had my phone, with access to Google Maps. And even without Google I didn't get lost. The ancient little bar showed up in the light at the end of the tunnel that ran beneath the nearby houses. I opened its heavy glass door and went in.

The space inside was tiny. The walls were stacked with wine bottles as high as anyone could possibly reach. Most of the small counter was occupied by bottles too. The rest of it by attractive displays behind glass sneeze-guards of the kind of tasty morsels the Spanish call tapas and the Italians *cicchetti*. There was no seating. The three or four customers who were in there this early evening stood with their glasses in their hands in the small space between the counter and the door. One of them I recognised, although he had his back to me. But his buttocks were memorable. He was the guy we'd seen at the crowded top of the Rialto Bridge and who had told Matteo and me to have a nice day.

Hearing the door knock shut behind me he turned to

see who had come in. He smiled when he saw me, and I smiled when I saw him smile at me. Neither of us could help that. 'Well, well,' he said. 'The boy from the bridge. Or one of them.' He might still have looked Nordic but he sounded pretty Scottish to me. I could see his eyes stray towards the plate-glass door behind me, expecting now that Matteo would follow me in. But he didn't, of course, so the guy went on straightforwardly, 'Where's your mate?'

'He's gone to pick up his brother's sports bag from his school,' I said. There are contexts in which the most banal of truths will sound extraordinary, barely believable. 'He's on his way.'

'Then let me get you a drink before he arrives. My name's Sol.'

Sol, I thought. God of the sun. I wished I had a name that could eclipse that. Like Zeus or Posseidon. But I didn't have. Anticlimactically I said, 'I'm Ben.'

'Short for...?'

'Benjamin,' I said. I heard myself sounding a bit apologetic about it. 'As in the Bible.'

'Tell me about it,' said Sol and flicked his eyes upwards self-deprecatingly. 'Mine's short for Solomon.' I laughed. Sol reached out with his free hand and shook mine. 'My parents are a bit...'

'I know,' I said. I corrected myself quickly. 'I mean, I understand.'

Love in Venice

'Red wine, I take it?' Sol asked, becoming businesslike again. 'Seems that's what everybody drinks round here.' I said that would do fine, and Sol named a wine at random, reading from the label of one of the bottles on the bar, I guessed. He knew as little as I did about Italian wine, I realised, and my heart did something funny. We had a bond.

'So what brings you to Venice?' Sol asked me as soon as he was facing me again and I had a glass in my hand. 'You're English, I'm guessing, but your friend's not.'

'He's Italian,' I said. 'I'm working with him. Coaching him as a pianist... Piano student, rather, I should say... Actually he plays better than I do...'

'Hey, hey,' said Sol very gently. 'I've hardly met you and already you're putting yourself down. I'm sure you're both brilliant musicians. Classical...? Or...?'

'Very classical,' I said. 'Loud and proud,' I added, determined not to put myself down again.

'That's way out of my league,' said Sol. 'I never even mastered Chopsticks.'

'Chopsticks is harder than you think,' I said. 'Don't put yourself down.'

I gave him a searching look. He gave me one. Then his face melted into a smile. I guess that so did mine. 'Cheers,' he said.

'Are you a tourist here?' I asked him next.

'Well, yes,' he said. 'Because how can you not be when you come here for the first time? But, like you, I'm here on business.'

Now it was my turn to ask him what that business was. And I would do. But the question I really wanted to ask him was, *Are you gay?* Though that would have to wait a few moments, for politeness's sake. But I was pretty sure of what, when I did eventually put the question to him, the answer would be.

TEN

'So what are you doing here?'

Sol gave me a smile that I'd have to spend time trying to decipher later. 'I'm learning how to build yachts. I'm on a six-month placement with a boat builder in Venice. Over on Giudecca.'

'Oh,' I said. 'I haven't been over there yet.' I only just stopped myself from adding that now I wanted to go to the place.

'I only started last week,' Sol said.

'Me too.' I was eager to seize on things we had in common.

'Where do you come from?' Sol asked. 'I mean, England obviously, but…'

'Redhill,' I said. 'Just south of London…'

'I know,' he said quickly. 'On the way to Gatwick.'

I nodded promptly. 'And you…?'

'Leith. Just outside…'

'I know,' I cut in much too keenly. 'Edinburgh.'

This time Sol's smile was a less complex one. 'Well done,' he said. Then his expression changed again, grew careful, almost diffident. 'The guy you were with, your

Italian – er – protégé... Is he...? Are you and he...?'

'He'll be here in a minute,' I blurted quickly, anxious to deal with my own immediate concern before coping with Sol's. Then suddenly, 'Yes.'

There was a second's silence during which we looked at each other in minute shock. Then the tension snapped and we both laughed.

'I'm gay too,' Sol said. 'In case you were wondering.'

'I was and I wasn't,' I said. 'Wondering, I mean. I mean, you don't look gay or anything. I guess a boat builder wouldn't. You look more like a boat builder...' I didn't usually get into tangles like this.

'And you look too nicely muscled to be a pianist.' Dear God! Sol was paying me a compliment. 'Your friend likewise.' Even if it was a compliment that would have to be shared fifty-fifty it was still a compliment.

Well, you talked of the devil and... Matteo walked in at that moment. Saw me being chatted up by a handsome stranger. He looked suddenly vulnerable and shy. Almost afraid. Because he was the local boy, a better pianist than I was, and usually in charge when we were together, I tended to forget that he was two years my junior. Now the look on his face reminded me that he was.

'Matteo,' I introduced him. 'This is Sol from Scotland. We met him on the bridge.'

'I know,' said Matteo. 'I recognised him.'

'He's nice,' I said. 'And one of us.' I thought I might have gone too far there – outing Matteo to a stranger when he was far from fully out among his own circle – but Matteo didn't seem to mind. I thought of telling him there and then that Sol had praised his muscles but decided just in time that that should wait. There's going too far and there's going too far.

Matteo turned to Sol, smiled – which I was relieved to see – then said, 'Hi,' and the two of them shook hands. A minute later Matteo also had a glass in his hands, purchased by Sol, and the three of us were chatting happily. A feeling of elation seized me suddenly. There was something so perfect, so right about this moment. Like juggling with three balls – that brief moment when you feel it will go on for ever and that nothing can go wrong with it.

We had a couple of titbits each to mop up the wine. Pickled anchovies on slices of crusty bread, salt cod whipped with garlic mayonnaise, tentacles of baby octopus... You must come and see where we live, we said. Come and see my place, said Sol. Though his would be hard to find. So would ours, said Matteo. We were on our second glass of wine by now. Why didn't Sol come round to the palazzo with us when we went back shortly? A coffee or something...? That was Matteo's invitation. It wasn't one that I was in a position to make myself. But Matteo hadn't used the word palazzo. I did that.

'His family have a palace on the Grand Canal,' I said boastfully, and I was careful to use the English words, just in case Sol's Italian didn't extend to palazzo, or Canal Grande. Few gay men in their early twenties would have said no to an invitation like that from two gay guys a couple of years younger than themselves. Sol was not among that few. He said yes at once.

Sol walked between us. We chatted all the way. I thought Sol might at some point throw an exuberant arm around each of our necks but he didn't. Perhaps he wanted to and had to make an effort to restrain himself. I know that I kept wanting to touch Sol and was making an effort to restrain *my*self. I wondered if the same went for Matteo too. I would probably find out in time anyway. For the moment though, the atmosphere between the three of us, a feeling of things simmering powerfully beneath a lid, made me think that the answer was probably a yes.

'Oh hey,' said Sol suddenly. He came to a stop. He pointed upwards at the surly stone face that peered from the alleyway wall.

'No-one knows who he is or where he came from,' volunteered Matteo. 'Some relic of a long demolished Gothic building, I suppose. Someone with a sense of humour cemented him up there. He was there before my grandfather was born: that's all I know.'

'His main purpose in life,' I added, wanting to contribute something and to show off to Sol, 'is to tell us that we're nearly home.'

'Home.' Sol picked up on the word. He turned and grinned at me. 'Looks like you've really arrived.'

A moment later we had all arrived. I watched Sol's reactions with keen interest. Perhaps he'd been born in a Scottish baronial castle like Balmoral, I mused, but much more probably he hadn't, in which case he would be as impressed as I had been. And he was.

Neither Matteo nor I gave the game away too soon. We took him in through the grubby and unassuming door at the end of the alley. We let him see the junk-filled water floor without offering much in the way of comment. Then we took him up the stairs. Matteo opened the door at the top and we took him into the huge portego, now filled with the light of the late afternoon. Sol wasn't exactly speechless. 'Wow,' he said. Then after a pause he said it again. 'Wow.' Then he was speechless.

'I'll make us some coffee,' said Matteo. 'Kitchen's this way.'

*

Half an hour later and Sol had had the full guided tour. Well, not the bedrooms, obviously, but he'd seen all the paintings on the upper grand floor, and he'd successfully cajoled Matteo and me into playing him a duet on the Fazioli piano... We did the four-hand arrangement of The Arrival of the Queen of Sheba that we'd crashed through on our first evening together. Now we crashed it again, laughing exuberantly at the end, and

Sol joined in. Joined in the laughter, I mean. Not joined in with the duet... Then I felt Matteo's body tense suddenly on the piano stool beside me. 'Oh fuck,' he said is his most finely-tuned English. 'I've left Marco's sports kit in the bar.'

'We can get it later,' I said.

'We can't,' said Matteo, looking at his watch. 'It's a daytime bar. Opens early morning. Closes early evening like a shop.'

'We can pick it up tomorrow,' I said. I was enjoying the presence of Sol in the palazzo with us. I didn't want this little upset to turn into his cue to leave. 'Marco can't need his sportswear tonight, can he?'

'I'd just rather get it now,' said Matteo with a firmness I hadn't often heard before.

Sol did take that as his cue to go. He got up from his elegant armchair. 'Time I went home.'

I wanted to say something that would keep him longer, but wasn't sure what I could. This wasn't my house we were in; it wasn't my place to ask him to stay on here while Matteo went out and brought the sports bag back. But before I could think of anything else that would prolong the contact Matteo did. In a softer tone he said, 'Maybe we could all head back to the Arco and have a before-dinner drink?' He looked a bit diffidently at Sol. 'Though maybe it's not on your way home...?'

Sol nodded vigorously. 'Yep. Nice one.' I thought that

Love in Venice

he would have said the Bar All'Arco was on his way home even if it wasn't and he'd have to go a mile out of his way to get there.

'I'm up for that,' I said. As if there was the smallest chance I wouldn't be.

Then we were down the stairs and heading out again, going back the way we'd come.

'So, where are you staying in Venice?' I asked Sol as we walked.

'Over in Giudecca. On Giudecca. Whatever one's supposed to say. I've got a room in the house the family own. The family that also own the boat-building yard.' He made a wry face. 'Of course it's nothing like...'

'Of course,' I said, then, realising I'd sounded like a prick, added, 'That didn't come out the way I meant.'

'No offence taken,' said Sol. 'You must come over and see the yard. Do a few of the Giudecca bars... Both of you.'

That prompted Matteo to ask him, a bit carefully, 'Have you met many people since you came here?'

'To be honest, no,' said Sol, looking slightly pained. 'Though I've only been here a few days. The couple I work for are very nice. Very hospitable. They've got young kids... I've been eating with them in the evenings. Then I've headed out to a bar or two. But on my own... And not speaking Italian.'

'Then we ought to take you about a bit,' Matteo offered. 'Let you meet a few more people...' His confidence failed him then. He was talking to someone nearly half a dozen years older than himself. 'Actually I don't go out very much in the evenings. Venice is a very quiet place. For nightlife you'd need to go to Mestre or further away to Padova...'

'That's Padua to you and me,' I put in.

Matteo ignored that. He went on, 'And I don't know any gay people really. Well, hardly any...' He tailed off.

'It isn't easy to be "out" in Venice,' I said, trying to help Matteo.

'But now Ben's here...' Matteo added in a voice that tried to be up-beat about the situation.

'I'm very pleased just to have met you two,' said Sol. There seemed to be real warmth in his voice. Though maybe he was just acting it.

We reached the bar and went in. There, among the tiny crowd that was sardined into the small space, were Marco and Tonio, standing next to the counter and drinking a Venetiano spritz. Between their feet, and heavily guarded by the pressure of their two pairs of trainers, Marco's sports bag lay like an obedient dog. The two boys turned towards us. Marco gave us a look in which pleasure mingled with puzzlement. He said, 'What the hell's been going on?'

*

That night as we were undressing for bed Matteo said, 'Sol's nice. Hmm?'

'Yes,' I said. I'd wondered which of us would be brave enough to be the first to say so. Turned out it was Matteo. 'Very nice.'

We'd had a convivial pre-prandial beer, the five of us, and then Sol had left us – a bit reluctantly, I couldn't help thinking – to make his own way home. Though not before Matteo had invited him to come for a meal at the palazzo in a couple of days, and not before we'd arranged that Matteo and I would go over to Giudecca the following morning and have a look around the yacht-building yard. Tomorrow morning was something we were looking forward to.

But first we were looking forward to tonight. Matteo and I stood, confronting each other naked, admiring the sight of each other, two lean strong bodies with lean strong erections, just prior to catapulting ourselves into each other's arms.

'Do you want to fuck me?' Matteo said suddenly. His voice was all husky, thicketed with a tangle of desire and fear.

'I've never fucked before.' My voice came out exactly the same way.

'Nor me,' said Matteo. We hadn't told each other this before. But somehow we already knew.

'We haven't got a...' I began to say. Although, if

neither of us had had penetrative sex before…

'Yes, we have,' said Matteo quietly. 'I got some from a machine.' He dropped his eyes towards the floor the way he did when he was feeling awkward about something. Those twin peacocks' tails his eyelashes made… 'On my way back from getting Marco's sports bag. While you were in the bar with Solomon.'

I chuckled to put him at his ease. Or was it to put myself at ease? 'Then hand me one, please?' He bent down. The packet was actually in a pocket of the shorts he'd just dropped to the floor. He handed it to me. I took one of the rubbers out of its foil. 'I've never put one on before,' I admitted.

Matteo shrugged. I'd never seen a naked man shrug before. A shrug involves every muscle in the body above the knees, I now realised. Including that one. Matteo said, 'Neither have I. We can learn together.'

I knew enough at least not to end up with a bubble of air, and had soon rolled the thing onto me. Before I could find a way to frame the question – which way round do you want to go? Matteo had answered it wordlessly by kneeling beside the bed and laying his upper half across it. His buttocks faced me cheekily. His voice came a bit muffled now. 'I've seen it done like this in videos.'

'Me too,' I said. I'd also seen the next bit, fortunately. I knew enough to moisten a finger with my own saliva, and gently enter him with that before trying to batter the door down with my dick. The tactic worked. I could feel Matteo relax as I fingered my way softly into him.

Then... There's a difference between seeing how a thing is done and doing it yourself. Watching another kid play Für Elise is hardly a full preparation for actually doing the same thing. Yet somehow I managed to get my cock into my friend. Somehow I managed not to hurt him as I was doing so, though I heard him gasp, and felt the tremor of him, as I got fully engaged.

I was fiercely excited. I knew, as I began to heave my hips and piston deep into him, that this would not take long. 'I'm going to come,' I said with a catch in my voice.

'Me too,' said Matteo, rather to my surprise, as he wasn't touching his cock and neither was I. It must have been the friction of the bed-sheet, I thought, caused by my thrusting into him. Now he too was thinking of the bed-sheet, it appeared. He said, 'Put your hand under me. Catch me as I come.'

And so I did, worming my hand between his hot belly and the bed. I found his cock and allowed my hand to become his drip-tray. I was only just in time. He spurted as soon as I got there, and the hot wetness triggered my own eruption instantly in his inside.

We lay half-kneeling where we were for a minute or two, while neither of us spoke. Then, 'Wow,' I said, and Matteo repeated, 'Wow,' and I remembered the dumbstruck reaction of Sol on finding himself in the portego earlier today.

And then I wondered whether this whole episode – our sudden desire to cross the Rubicon of anal penetration on this particular night – might have just a little bit to do with our encounter with Solomon.

ELEVEN

I had seen Giudecca from the waterbus the first time Matteo had whizzed me around the water city, and I'd seen it several times since. It's separated from the central part of Venice by the half-kilometre-wide Giudecca Canal. And if that explanation doesn't help, and if you don't have Google Earth or a good old atlas open in front of you, I'll try and help you picture where it lies.

Venice, viewed from above, looks like a fat fish wedged rather tightly across its safe triangle of water, the lagoon. The lagoon itself is dotted with dozens of much smaller islands, but the centre of Venice is the biggest island by far. The head end of it, where the docks are and the car-parks and the railway station are, is tied to the shore – as if by a fisherman's line – by the long bridge that carries rail and road and all the other services like electricity and gas. The Grand Canal winds through the body of the city just like the alimentary canal winds through the body of a real fish. The hundreds of other, smaller canals are like the fish's arteries and veins and from any great height above the ground are too small to be seen.

But the fish's underbelly, Venice's southern shore, does not give directly onto the lagoon. The long narrow island of Giudecca hugs it, following its curves, for a kilometre or two. The place looked pretty from across the water of the Giudecca Canal, I thought. And it was across this canal that we took the waterbus number 82 that next morning to keep our appointment with Sol.

When we got off the lightly rocking bus we were not in a different world – as we had found ourselves when we travelled to the Lido. There were no cars here, and it was still unmistakeably a part of the city of Venice. On the Lido few buildings were more than a hundred years old and most were much younger than that. But here on Giudecca we were still in a world of crumbling ancient palazzi, grand Renaissance churches, and thread-like canals that hump-backed bridges crossed with flights of steps.

But this was Venice without the tourist throngs; it was the Venice that belonged to the locals as it had done for hundreds of years. And it was less claustrophobic than much of the more central part of the city. Down each canal you glimpsed the dazzle of the sun on the lagoon, just four hundred metres away. For – so Matteo informed me – Giudecca was at no point more than four hundred metres wide. If it was difficult to get lost in central Venice then it was impossible here.

Matteo and I went looking for the boatyard where Sol worked, following the directions we'd been given. Matteo wore the slightly anxious expression of someone who, in an unfamiliar part of his own town, doesn't want to let his foreign visitor see that he doesn't already know the way.

But it was easy. You kept count of the bridges you crossed (it only came to two) then turned left, walked the four hundred metres, and you were there. The yard consisted of a fair-sized stretch of muddy foreshore and a large boathouse like a miniature aircraft hangar. Its doors were being slid open as we arrived and the person doing the sliding was Sol.

He saw us before he'd finished opening the doors and gave us a wave. We walked towards him, arriving at his side just as he got the shed fully open. He turned to us and enfolded first Matteo and then me in a very warm hug. You could do that here. It was good to be in Italy, I thought.

Four sailing boats sat inside the shed on wheeled trailers. They were all at different stages of build or repair and three or four muscular young men in shorts were at work on them, drilling, cleaning, sanding, varnishing...

'We have to get a boat into the water this morning,' Sol told us. He grinned. 'You've arrived just in time. You didn't know you were going to have to put some work in when you got here.'

It didn't feel at all like work, actually. But doing other people's jobs for a short time seldom feels like work. Real work is what you have to do every day, have to get up early in the morning for, and come home tired from at night.

Few things could have been more fun that sunny June day, I thought. Helping to wheel a medium-sized yacht out of its hangar alongside a couple of other hunky bare-chested men. Using our strength to nudge it this way and that, positioning it exactly beneath the chains that dangled from two cranes.

We attached the chains to cradles, attaching those fore and aft from below. Then... well, we weren't invited actually to drive the cranes. We stood back and watched as two other guys climbed into the cabs, then, with all the precision of synchronised swimmers, lifted the boat evenly, swung it slowly out across the water and lowered it gently into the dock beside a jetty that stuck out into the lagoon.

It took longer to lower the boat than to describe the process. Ropes had to be attached, and then adjusted, at different stages. The chains had to be unfastened and the carrying cradles gently eased out from beneath the floating hull. By the time all this was done... Sol turned to Matteo and me and said, 'Time for a wee bite and a beer?'

Confidently Sol led Matteo and me up one lane, across a tiny bridge, then down another lane to a café-bar that, like the boatyard, looked out across the sun-sparkling lagoon. We ordered a beer each and some bruschette, then sat in the sun and enjoyed them beside the water. 'Do you know the names of all the islands?' Sol asked Matteo, jerking his head towards the sea view. The southern lagoon was studded with islands of varying sizes, some with buildings clearly visible on them, others not.

'Hmm,' said Matteo. 'Some of them. But it isn't easy. They change position according to where you're looking from, I mean they seem to.' He pointed to one of the nearer ones. 'That's San Clemente, I think. There's a luxury hotel on it. And that one over there…' He twisted round in his chair to point to it, 'is called Sacca Sessola. There's one called Santo Spirito…' He gave up at that point. 'Some of them are so small. They may not have names at all.'

'Well, thanks for trying,' said Sol. 'I'll try to remember those.'

'It's a pity we couldn't bring my brother and Tonio with us,' Matteo said next. He seemed at that moment suddenly very innocent and very young.

'When they get a day off I'll ask them over,' said Sol in an even tone. But – or did I just imagine this? – I saw on his handsome face a look I'd seen on the faces of diners who are reminded to leave room for pudding when they're only just about to start the first course.

After our light lunch we all walked back to the boatyard. Matteo wanted to take some photos, he said, and walked away from us towards the water's edge. Sol told him to come and find us inside the shed when he was done. Then he led me indoors and showed off one particular boat that he was working on. This involved walking round the boat into a gloomy corner, where no-one else was working, at the back of the shed. In the middle of pointing out some rather fancy methods of gluing fibreglass Sol suddenly said, 'Is it just the two of you or can anybody play?'

I said the first thing that popped into my head. 'Well, not just anybody.' Then I paused. Matteo and I had never discussed the question of whether our sexual relationship was going to be an exclusive one or not. The matter hadn't arisen yet... Or had it? My mind went back to the afternoon on the Lido with Marco and Tonio. To what had nearly happened, and to what actually had. There was the complication that I had had sex with Marco the day before I met Matteo... The whole area seemed a bit complex and unclear.

Sol plunged into the silence I'd left after my brief reply. 'So not just anybody. What about me?' He gave me the loveliest smile at that point, and I guess I must have returned it in kind, since something encouraged him to take me in his arms and kiss me on the lips. The sensations of this were wonderful. A second later I felt Sol's hand dive confidently down behind the waistband of my shorts and grab my cock. Which was standing to attention like a soldier, I discovered with a shock.

I pulled sharply away, vigorously escaping Sol's embrace. 'It doesn't belong to you,' I heard myself say. I meant my cock. Then I said, 'Matteo will come in,' in an urgent tone. But my actions belied my words. I found myself reaching out – as if my hand had a will of its own – and touching Sol's cock through the fabric of his denim cut-offs. My hand found its target unerringly. It was fully erect. I grasped it firmly for an instant – might as well be hung for a sheep as a lamb – and it was the biggest one I'd ever held in my hand.

Sol didn't speak. But I heard his breath involuntarily

sucked in. As quickly as I'd reached out to grab him I released him and withdrew my hand.

Only just in time. Matteo's silhouette appeared against the bright light of the shed's doorway. 'Over here,' Sol called to him. His voice was fully under control and he had a confident and relaxed air. Practice made perfect, I guessed, in this as in everything else.

A few minutes later Matteo and I left Sol to get on with his work. We had to get back and make a start on ours. We retraced our steps to the bus stop. As the vaporetto chugged across the Giudecca Canal the island that was Giudecca grew small and distant behind us. I tried to make the moment that had occurred there, that hug and kiss with Sol, that quick mutual grab, grow small and distant too. But I couldn't do that. I couldn't shrink the moment down. Instead it grew huge in my mind. And apart from anything else, I realised as I stood next to my lover Matteo at the rail, sniffing the salty air, my now flaccid dick was laying a trail of wetness inside my shorts.

*

Matteo had been delighted to meet the Schubert sonata I had played to him – or rather practised in front of him. I had been surprised to find, in talking with him about it later, that he had never learnt anything by Schubert. 'He's reckoned to be one of the big four where I come from,' I told Matteo, pulling rank for once – the older and more experienced musician, the graduate of Trinity College, London. 'You know, after Bach, Mozart and Beethoven…'

'Where I come from,' Matteo had answered, a mischievous smile playing about his lips, 'we tend to think of the fourth one as Rossini…'

Well, Matteo was Italian, I was British. We didn't turn the matter into an argument. I was pleased enough that Matteo wanted to make up for lost time and start getting to know the piano works of Schubert now. I did ask him if he had ever accompanied singer friends in the songs of Schubert, but he said he hadn't even done that. 'You're in for a treat when you do,' I told him. Then I wondered… Who might that unknown future partner in music be? Whoever it might be, I would be bound to be jealous. I wished for a moment that it might be me, but I put the thought aside. My homely baritone, tuneful but untaught, was nowhere near good enough for Schubert songs. My piano-playing, though…

We decided to learn a Schubert work together. Following our new and unorthodox procedure of working on music in harness together, learning from each other as we went along. We weren't quite sure what to choose. Schubert had written not only five hundred songs, ten symphonies and loads of chamber music but also well over a dozen big sonatas for solo piano, eight pieces he called Impromptus and…

Surprisingly it was Marco who decided this for us. 'Do the Three Piano Pieces,' he said. 'Our music teacher at school played a recording of them. They're fantastic.'

Love in Venice

I knew the pieces slightly. Other students had played them at college. The name Schubert had given them – Drei Klavierstücke in the original German – was off-puttingly dull but I had to admit, remembering them, that they had wonderful inventiveness and flair. I actually had them with me. They were in a volume of Schubert's music that contained some other things that I did play. I hauled the book out of my case. The case I'd brought here with me, and had packed with my summer clothes and a weighty assembly of piano music scores. It now lived, tidied away but not forgotten, at the bottom of my bedroom wardrobe.

Once we started work on the Three Piano Pieces it was impossible not to fall in love with them. That was quite easily explained. We were still in the process of falling in love with each other. Falling in love with every piece of music we worked on together was part of that. It was like the music was a lightning rod for the powerful and potentially destructive forces that were building between the two of us like massive summer storm clouds that tower into the sky and can bring down the giantest of planes.

The Three Piano Pieces were put together almost like a sonata of their period. That is: the first and third pieces were quite fast and spritely and they bookended the second piece, which was slower and more thoughtful. It was more than just thoughtful, though and, while it was less challenging to the fingers than its companions it quickly became our favourite.

'There's nothing to it really,' Matteo observed when

we were talking about it once. 'It's just a little magic trick done with key changes.'

'Yes,' I said, 'but what key changes! Essence of Schubert.'

'It's like he builds you a comfort zone in the first minute or so, then takes you right out of it. It gets uncomfortable and scary…'

'Then just when you're about to say, Mamma, take me home, Schubert does just that.'

'Exactly,' said Matteo nodding. 'But he was only… How old when he wrote it?'

'He died at thirty-one,' I said. 'He wrote this shortly before that.'

'He would have done,' said Matteo, still nodding, and with a poker face. Then the poker face collapsed and we laughed, finding the weak joke a good enough excuse to throw our arms around each other's necks.

'It's like being taken for a walk in the woods when you're a very small kid,' I said, after we'd disentangled ourselves and were running on with our thoughts about the piece. 'It's all full of wonders but frightening at the same time, and your feelings about it change second by second.'

'Then when you're really scared,' said Matteo, 'at that *Mamma take me home* moment, you see your house through the trees. You're so relieved…' He stopped and

Love in Venice

I could see that the vision and the feelings he'd conjured had brought him close to tears.

A thought struck me. 'Were you ever taken for a walk in the woods when you were very small? Venice being what it is…'

'No,' Matteo said. 'But I can imagine.'

'I'll take you for wonderful walks in the country, and the woods, when we're in England together…' I stopped and we looked at each other. It was the first time either of us had dared to think into the future. To the idea of us spending time together in England…

'I'd like that,' said Matteo. The words were understated, but I heard his voice and saw his face and both were once again stoked with emotion.

TWELVE

I couldn't decide whether to tell Matteo that Sol had kissed me in the boat shed or not. To tell him that I'd kissed Sol back? That Sol had put his hand inside my shorts and grasped the shaft of my excited cock? That I'd grabbed Sol's through his shorts immediately after that? I thought about telling Matteo some of this but not all of it. I could simply mention the kiss – Sol's kiss rather than mine – and leave the rest of it out.

Days went by while I wrestled with this. I was very inexperienced in the ways of love. I knew from hearsay, though, that there were two opposing views on this. One was that you should get it all out in the open, be totally up-front. Start the relationship as you meant it to go on, in total mutual honesty. The other view could be summed up quite easily in two words. The words were: never confess.

I knew one thing for certain. That the longer I left it the worse it would get. The worse it would be when I did eventually tell Matteo. Or – heaven forbid – if Matteo found out from someone else. But who could he find out from? Sol would have to want to tell Matteo himself for that to happen, and I couldn't easily envisage any scenario in which that would come about.

Of course there had been other men working in that half lit, half dark boat shed. But I was pretty sure we'd been out of their sight. Sol wouldn't have embraced me unless he'd been sure no-one could see us. But how could he be sure we hadn't been seen? How can anyone ever be sure that at any given moment they are unwatched?

I reassured myself with the logical thought that there was no reason on earth why workmates of Sol's would tell Matteo – someone with whom they'd only exchanged a hallo and a handshake – that Sol had been kissing someone else. For all they knew that was a normal part of our relationship. It might rate a mention among themselves if one of them had seen us and the others hadn't. But I knew just enough about the male sex to be pretty sure that none of them would take the trouble to track Matteo down and, for no reason at all, share the information with him.

Time passed. A week passed. I hadn't told Matteo. By now it seemed probably that I wasn't going to. We hadn't seen Sol during that week. But we were going to see him tonight. We had already arranged that Sol would come to dinner at the palazzo. In the last few days we had firmed up day and time by text.

We arranged to meet initially at the Bar All'Arco. Partly because this would give us all (including Marco and Tonio who were joining us on their way back from work) a chance to have a casual drink without the slightly constraining presence of the Dragonetti parents. Partly so that Sol wouldn't have to find the palazzo on his own, running the risk of getting lost.

Matteo and I arrived at the Arco first. A minute later

Marco and Tonio turned up. Working together had done nothing to cool their friendship. If anything it had done the reverse. This evening they were puppyish in each other's company, like two young people who are just falling in love.

Then Sol came through the door. He looked splendid. I couldn't help thinking of the sun. He'd been out of doors in it for the past week and his face was acquiring a golden tan. For all his blond hair. It seemed he was one of those (few) lucky blond Scots and Scandis who go the right colour in summer. I rather envied him. I could only guess how far the tan extended. He wasn't wearing shorts – out of courtesy to his dinner hosts – but rather badly pressed chinos. It was the badly pressed aspect that suddenly endeared him to me even more.

I looked at his face carefully as he came in. There was a trace of nervousness, of sheepishness, on it for just a nanosecond. It read, Does Matteo know about the kiss and grope? Do the others? But in the same nanosecond he read in everybody else's face, including mine, the information that I hadn't kissed and told, and his features resumed their usual confident, comfortable expression.

'Listen,' Sol said when he'd got a drink in his hand, 'I've got to do a bit of sailing in a day or two. That yacht we put in the water last week...' He looked at Matteo and me. 'She needs a bit of a test sail round the lagoon before we return her to her owners. Just wondered if any of you would like to join me?'

I would, for one, but I didn't want to be the first to say

so. Marco spoke first. 'Actually, Tonio and I already have a date to go for a sail on our next free day.'

'Oh?' said his brother. 'With anyone we know?'

'No,' said Marco. 'Two gay tourists. They are ... I would say ... middle-aged. Very rich and very nice. We met them when they went for a gondola ride.'

'Did they invite everyone who works on the gondola quay to join them?' asked Matteo, pretend casually.

'No,' said Tonio. 'Just us two.' He sounded quite proud of that.

'You've been hit on, picked up,' said Sol with a laugh in his voice. 'You be careful now. Wouldn't want you both to be sold into slavery.'

'We can take care of ourselves,' said Marco, and I saw his biceps twitch, perhaps involuntarily, below his T-shirt sleeves.

'Sure we'd like to come with you,' I heard Matteo say. 'Wouldn't we, Ben?' It took me half a second to realise that he was talking to Sol.

'Of course,' I said, happy to agree.

Sol proved a delightful dinner guest. He quickly charmed Annabelle and Domenico and was friendly without being over-familiar with Artemia and Albano. We had a pasta dish with fresh sardines, then roast chicken with salad. Lastly a mousse made of summer fruits. I tried to be careful not to look at Sol too often across the dinner table, but to parcel out my attentions to everyone fairly.

But I couldn't help thinking about Sol even when I wasn't looking at him. He seemed lonely. I didn't know if he had a boyfriend back in Scotland (with his looks it was unlikely that he didn't) but he certainly didn't have one in Venice – and if his kissing of me was anything to go by, it looked like he could do with one.

Might that turn out to be me? We both spoke the same first language after all, different national accents notwithstanding. The mutual attraction was evident: we'd both acknowledged it in the boat shed. And Sol would be quite a catch for me, I thought. A handsome, very fit guy, slightly older, slightly bigger, considerably more muscular than me. He was masculine and outgoing; good with his hands – made yachts and sailed them too…

But what was I thinking here? I already had a boyfriend. I had Matteo. Not as extrovert as Sol, not quite as muscular or tall … yet almost so. Younger than me and brilliant in his field in music. He was just as handsome as Sol was. And his family was richer by far… I banished that last thought at once, as being unworthy of me. That didn't come into it at all. Yes, Matteo was my boyfriend and I was his. We just hadn't used the word. We still hadn't used the other word either. The one that began with L. We were afraid of that word. Well, I knew that I was. But I knew I was falling in love with Matteo. I thought – all right, I hoped – that he was also falling in love with me. Perhaps it was time for me to take the risk – go out on a limb and tell him I loved him. To brace myself against the possibility that he'd say I'd misread the signs and that he didn't feel the same about me. In which case – I clung to the silver lining – I could fall back on Sol.

After we'd eaten we took Sol down the Grand Canal on the waterbus, to the bar in Castello where I'd first met Marco. That meeting didn't come up in the conversation – let alone the details of the encounter: we talked about other things instead. We planned an evening in Mestre across the bridge to the mainland sometime soon. There were gay bars there, unlike in Venice where most places were shut by midnight, when the footsore, sight-sated tourists were in bed in their hotels. There was a lively night-life in Padua too, Matteo said, since there was a big university there. But when Sol questioned him about it he admitted he'd never spent a late night out there. Neither had Marco, it seemed. Or if he had done he wasn't going to say so.

Before we parted for the night – Sol heading off on the late bus back to Giudecca, Marco going in another direction to sleep over at Tonio's, and Matteo and I returning up the Canal Grande to the palazzo – we firmed up the arrangement for the sailing trip. As Marco and Tonio wouldn't be coming it could be any day of the week. Matteo and I managed our own schedule; we weren't bound by the duty roster of a gondola hire company. We settled on Friday, just two days away.

As we said our goodnights we all kissed each other, as Italian men do. Sol's goodnight kiss with me was a very simple, chaste affair. But it was on the lips. So was the kiss that Sol gave Matteo.

As we briefly turned our backs on the Grand Canal, threading our way back from the bus stop through the narrow lamp-lit alleys I thought about saying to Matteo, 'I love you.' But somehow the moment didn't seem right. Not so soon after that goodnight kiss from Sol. If the moment didn't feel right to me then it probably wouldn't feel right to Matteo. He, after all, had also had a kiss from Sol. There must be a right moment for this, I thought, but when would it be? And how would I know when it arrived? I had no experience of this. I'd had no practice, no rehearsal. I'd never said *I love you* to anyone. I didn't know whether the same went for Matteo.

Instead I found something else to say. It wasn't as important as the matter of love but it wasn't totally unimportant. It was the matter of how I would earn my bread for the rest of my life.

'I've no idea what I'm going to do after I leave Venice,' I said.

Matteo didn't say anything. He didn't move a muscle except the ones he was using to walk with. Nor did he look at me. But I felt his reaction keenly. He somehow made the temperature in the air around us drop by ten degrees.

'I mean in terms of work,' I clarified hurriedly. 'How to earn my living for the rest of my life.'

'I see,' said Matteo. The temperature went up, though not yet by the full ten degrees. There was a pause. Then Matteo asked, 'What would you have done – about work, I mean – if you hadn't met my mother and me?'

'Done what I need to start doing now. Writing round to all the music colleges in London to ask about teaching opportunities. And when they've all said no, writing round to the schools.'

'Yes,' said Matteo a bit flatly. We both knew the realities of the pianist's life. Only one person could win the Leeds Piano Competition, or the Moscow. There was only one Daniel Barenboim, only one Lang-Lang. Only about ten concert pianists in the world made an ample living from giving concerts alone. The hundred or two hundred others made most of their income from teaching in music colleges. And there were only about two hundred in the world. The rest of us ended up teaching music in schools. I expected Matteo to say some of this now. But he didn't. He said, 'Schools in London, I hope.'

'I guess so,' I said, a bit surprised. Yes, I'd probably assumed I'd be looking for work in London or around.

'Well that's OK then,' Matteo went on. 'I don't mind if you end up cleaning the toilets in a London school. So long as it is London. London for the next three years. Because that's where I'll be.'

It felt like the sun had come out and was blazing in the midnight sky, shining down into our lamp-lit alleyway. I turned towards Matteo, embraced him fiercely, kissed him urgently. He did the same to me.

We did the last bit of that walk home arm in arm, then hand in hand. We met no-one on our way upstairs. Domenico and Annabelle, Albano and Artemia, all had gone to bed.

And so did we. I said it – so that Matteo wouldn't have to. 'Tonight I want *you* to fuck *me*.'

Matteo's face registered an expression of wonder that was only halfway to being a smile. He seemed awed by what he was about to do. But, without speaking, he took charge of the situation from that moment on. He undressed me before undressing himself and gently guided my willing body into the position he wanted it to be in. That turned out to be lying on my back on the bed. Once he was naked he surprised me by fishing his packet of condoms out from the pocket of his shucked jeans: they'd been in his shorts pocket the first time we'd used one, a week ago.

Then he did what I'd done to him that first time: he relaxed my entrance with a moistened finger or two. He hoisted my legs up over his shoulders. (He must have seen this, as I had done, on video: we hadn't done this together before.) Then he very gently pushed his cock into me.

I was suddenly anxious about how it would feel. I was still a rectal virgin – Matteo had lost that status a week before me. This was my first time … and he was gentle with me. As he went in I had the feeling I got when walking into a cold sea or jumping into a swimming pool: the shock of entering a new world. Next I felt a burning inside me, and then a new sensation as I realised this was a feeling I could enjoy.

Once he'd reached inside me as far as he could go – and that was quite a way; his penis was long, like mine – he paused a second, leaned his face towards mine and smiled. Then he spoke for the first time. 'I wanted to see the light in your blue eyes.'

'Like a mirror,' I answered, surprising myself as much as him by those words. 'They're just reflecting the blue light in yours.' As the blue waters of the Venetian lagoon are reflectors of the blue light of the sky.

Then he started to pump with his hips and I felt his piston gently moving to and fro inside me. Like a steam engine gathering power and speed he got into his stride. I was concentrating on the feelings inside me – the physical sensations in my bowels, and the emotional ones ... which centred, to my surprise, in a feeling of pride, of feeling proud of and for Matteo. I wasn't thinking about my own cock, half lying, half standing between our two bellies. But it turned out that it was doing some thinking of its own. It suddenly brought itself to my attention in the most spectacular way.

'I'm coming!' I said in astonishment to Matteo. Urgently I grabbed it and helped it to release its contents – for maximum pleasure and effect.

Both were startling. It was the most powerful orgasm of my life to date. It showered my shoulder and the monogrammed sheet. Watching it, equally startled, Matteo clearly found himself triggered to let go himself. He cried out something in Italian. I didn't know the word but its meaning was as clear as the meaning of any word could be. He thrust hard into me with urgent strokes as he shot his load. Then as his unseen spasms died away his thrusts diminished to little pushes, then mere nudges. Then they stopped.

Matteo's whole body relaxed. He let himself fall forward onto me. He didn't pull his cock out, nor did it slip out of its own accord. For some minutes we just lay there, still connected most intimately. We kissed from time to time but didn't speak.

At last Matteo did speak. 'Together in London.'

'Yes,' I said. I paused. 'I want that.'

'I want it too,' Matteo said. I was acutely conscious that he was still plugged into me.

At last it slipped out. Not his cock, though, but something else. From Matteo's mouth. A whisper that brushed my cheek like a shy kiss. 'I love you, Ben.'

'I love you, Matteo,' I whispered back. I felt my eyes well up with tears.

THIRTEEN

What a difference a word makes. That next morning I felt like I was embarking on the first day of my life. I could tell that it was the same for Matteo. We went out for breakfast: to our usual café by the side canal. As we sipped our coffees and tore our croissants meditatively into pieces that we could dip into the jam, we kept looking at each other with expressions of wonder and astonishment: expressions that said, 'Wow.'

We worked together on our music after that. On Schubert, Beethoven and Chopin. As I heard us playing to each other – or practising or working I should say – I realised I was listening to two new people playing the music. Two people I hadn't known or even met before today.

Annabelle also noticed it. She commented when, at one point in the morning, she happened to walk through the portego. 'That sounds really splendid. Both of you. Better even than yesterday. It seems you're making great strides together.' She turned to me and gave me a gorgeous smile. 'Well done, Benjamin,' she said. 'I'm so pleased I found you.'

'Thank you,' I said. It was a very mealy-mouthed reply, she must have thought. But what else could I say? That we were playing better because we were two men who had just acknowledged their love for each other in words for the first time? She would discover that for herself at some future date, assuming things didn't suddenly go wrong. But it seemed a bit soon to spring the news on her right now.

Marco came home briefly after he'd finished work. He didn't stay long, though. He was going to the gym with Tonio, he said, then staying over with him at his parents' place. He'd just come to get his sports clothes, and had found his brother and me relaxing in two of the armchairs in the portego. We weren't snogging or cuddling or anything. Domenico could have returned from work at any time, while Albano and Artemia were going to and fro.

But Marco stopped beside our chairs and gave us each a very searching look. 'You two look very happy today. I mean, even happier together than you look usually. I wonder if I can work out why...'

'Get away,' I interrupted him. I changed the subject. 'Which day is it you're going sailing with your sugar daddies, you and Tonio?'

'Day after tomorrow,' he answered. 'Saturday.'

'And we're going tomorrow,' I said. 'Pity. We won't be able to ram you in mid-lagoon.'

'Well, enjoy – both of you – if I don't see you before,' Marco said. A mischievous smile appeared on his face. 'Don't let Sol kidnap you.'

Matteo came in. 'I think we can handle Sol between us. It's *your* virtue I'm worried about. Yours and

Love in Venice

Tonio's...'

'*My* virtue?!' Marco batted back. 'I think that got lost somewhere some time ago.' Another mischievous grin. 'As both of you should know,' he finished archly. He turned to go. 'Don't get up,' he said finally when he reached the door to the stairs. 'I'll see myself out.' The three of us laughed, then Marco was gone.

*

That evening I got an email, rather to my surprise, from the violinist who had been my chamber-music coach at Trinity. Martin. He had a proposal, he wrote, in which I might be interested.

He had a recital date at London's Purcell Room in November. He didn't need to tell me the Purcell Room was part of the Royal Festival Hall complex on the South Bank and a very prestigious venue for a concert. His usual recital partner had had to bow out from the engagement. Martin didn't demean the man by using the term accompanist: he was a piano soloist with an international reputation. Martin wondered if I might be available as a substitute...

I called excitedly to Matteo at that point and we read the rest of the email together. Martin listed the repertoire he would be playing. The concert would begin with the Mozart sonata I'd made such a spectacular success of with Jake at the college a year earlier. It was because of that success that Martin was contacting me now. Second item would be the big Beethoven C minor sonata

(Martin reminded me he'd also heard me play this, with a different violinist, in my second year at college.) In the second half he would play an unaccompanied sonata by Ysaye, then finish with some popular fireworks by Sarasate and Kreisler. Those pieces, I knew, were spectacularly difficult and showy for the violinist but quite undemanding for the pianist.

'Wow,' Matteo said. 'What news could be better than that? You will say yes, presumably?'

'I will say yes,' I said. I could feel myself shaking with the surprise. 'I'm kind of gob-smacked. It's like hearing I've won the lottery. But it's only the second-best bit of news I've had in the past twenty-four hours.'

Matteo looked puzzled for a half second but then he was on it. 'The best being...?'

'What you said last night.'

'What did I say last night?' Matteo teased me.

'You said, "I love you." Then I said it too. I'll say it again. I love you, Matteo.'

'I love you too,' said Matteo. Then he twisted me round on the computer chair and wrapped his strong arms round me.

Later, when we were in bed and once again entwined around each other, Matteo asked me who Jake was.

'Oh, just a guy at college. A very good violinist actually... Actually, I had a bit of a thing with him.'

Love in Venice

'Oh?' murmured Matteo.

'He wasn't really gay,' I said. 'It didn't have a future.'

'Lucky for me, then,' said Matteo. He gave me a squeeze.

*

We took the 82 across to Giudecca and walked round to the boatyard, meeting a boisterous see breeze on each street corner. Matteo had been saying that it was a bit surprising that Sol should be able to sail a state-of-the-art yacht belonging to someone else around the Venetian lagoon after only three weeks here.

He explained. 'It looks like it ought to be easy – sheltered water, plenty of wind and so on – but it absolutely isn't.' (That was another of those expressions he'd obviously got from his mother.) 'It's full of shallows and sandbanks just beneath the water. After all, what are we walking on? Just another shoal or sandbank that happens to be just above the water.'

'There's all the dredged channels, though,' I countered, trying to sound knowledgeable. The lagoon was crisscrossed with double rows of wooden marker posts. The waterbuses and taxis ran between these, as if on roads. And there were a couple of very wide, deeply dredged channels that were used by cruise ships coming into the lagoon and tying up at the docks, and by container ships and tankers going in and out of Mestre.

'The channels are not easy to use under sail,' Matteo

said. 'If you need to tack to and fro, for instance. And there's some parts of the channels where you have to take your sails down and use the engine. All sorts of rules and regulations...'

But Matteo's doubts about Sol's competence to navigate the lagoon's waters evaporated once we got to the boatyard. For Sol would not be navigating; his role today would be that of technical trouble-shooter. There would be four of us on the yacht; it would be skippered by a fit and wiry thirty-year-old called Alex. He was a Venetian born and bred and had sailed the lagoon since childhood. His surname was Canal. Of course he got ribbed about this endlessly but he took the tediously repeated joke with patient good humour. As well he might. He was a distant descendant of one Giovanni Antonio Canal – better known to the world as Canaletto.

The other noteworthy thing about Alex Canal was that he was extremely handsome.

We all got involved with untying the mooring ropes, jumping onto the deck like cats the second we got them undone. I was the only man aboard who had never been sailing before. I hadn't admitted that even to Matteo who, Venetian born, was at home on most kinds of small craft ... even up to the size of biggish yachts, it now appeared. But I had been watching the waterbus men and other boatmen on the canals doing their stuff during the past weeks and now I found that even a bit of careful observation helped at least a little bit when you were learning something new.

Love in Venice

We inched cautiously backwards under engine power from our berth into the lagoon. Sol was in charge of the throttle and the wheel for the moment. No local knowledge was required at this stage. It was simply a question of not banging into the quay or the other boats tied alongside. When we were clear of those obstacles Sol changed into forward gear and pointed the boat eastward. A moment later he handed the controls to Alex. Very correctly but, I couldn't help imagining, a bit reluctantly.

A new view of the lagoon and the city now appeared around us. Wherever you moved in Venice or in its surrounding waters you got a different view. That was one of the great joys of the place. To our left the raggedy southern shore of Giudecca now expanded across our eye-line, the island and great pinnacled church of St Giorgio Maggiore coming into sight just beyond, tacked on to Giudecca's end. On our right, looming suddenly close, the Island of San Clemente rose up, lapped by the cross-threads of small-boat stern-waves. Ahead of us lay the two islands of San Servolo and San Lazarro while between them the long low line of the Lido, two miles beyond, formed the far horizon for now.

It was the Lido we were aiming for, Sol told us as we half sat, half stood in the cockpit, around Alex at the wheel. Still under engine power the yacht dipped and rose a little as we accelerated and negotiated the resistance of the mass of water below us and in front of our bow. The movement, the thrust and the encountered resistance reminded me inevitably of something I'd done quite recently, and also for the first time, with Matteo.

White and grey gulls swung through the air around us, their clear cries cleaving the breeze, and the salt spray licked our cheeks while the pungent sting of iodine got into our nostrils and lingered there.

'You know how it all works, I suppose?' said Sol to me and Matteo. He was talking about sailing boats. Matteo said that of course he did, but that he didn't know the names of the parts of the rigging in English. His Italian father, not his English mother, had taught him to sail. At this point I came clean. I didn't know the names of the bits and pieces in any language. Nor how they worked together to make a boat sail.

'Then now's your chance to learn,' said Sol. At the same moment a gruff few words from Alex told us that we could now set the sails. We were in open water by this time and far from the channels used by the buses and cabs.

Then I found myself out on the forward deck, leaning over the side and adjusting the trim of the foresail, under careful supervision from Sol and Matteo. I learned which lines were stays, which were shrouds and which were halliards. I was told to thank my luck for modern science. The halliards worked by electric buttons these days. The sails appeared to run up the mast by themselves. Not long ago, the guys told me, we'd have been pulling the halliards strenuously arm over arm, hoisting the heavy canvas into the bumptious wind with only our own muscle power.

Love in Venice

With all this moving around on the small area of the tilting deck and in the cockpit a certain amount of physical contact between the three of us was inevitable. Sol was very easy and generous with his shoulder claps and semi-accidental hugs, and I saw that these were dispensed, shared out, more or less evenly between Matteo and me. And we were both quite ready to return them in equal measure, I noticed. Nothing wrong with this, I reckoned. In fact I thought it was nice. My only momentary regret was that Alex took no part in this touchy-feely laddish behaviour. He had one hand at least, and often both of them, firmly on the wheel.

But out on the water, beneath the open sky, where blue above was reflected in blue below, I felt myself as happy as I could ever be. Safe in the comforting love of Matteo and in the friendly, sexy company of Sol, I found myself enjoying one of those rare moments when life seems as perfect as it can be and nothing can ever go wrong in it again.

Away from the city the water was claimed by birds less familiar than sea-gulls. There were flocks of black ducks that rode the swell a while then took off together and flew, skimming the wave tops till they were out of sight. Tufted, rufted grebes sat on the waves and stared at us affrontedly as we breezed along. Cormorants plunged, re-surfaced, then re-plunged.

We passed between San Servolo and San Lazarro. San Lazarro homely with cypress groves and campaniles – home to a community of Armenian monks, Matteo told Sol and me. San Servolo a creepier, more forbidding place: once the site of Venice's insane asylum – a building Shelley had described, so Matteo said, reciting the lines in English, as: *a windowless, deformed and dreary pile, such a one as age to age might add, for uses vile*. The island was peaceful this afternoon. None of the *yells and howlings and lamentings keen* that had curdled Shelley's blood when he heard them came from it now. All the same it was with a feeling of relief that we let it slide astern.

Alex carved a route for us that went around the shoals. The landmarks on the Lido ahead of us moved sometimes right and sometimes left. But gradually, cutting across a staked-out bus lane or two, we came closer to its shore and then headed south, parallel to it, in search of a particular place to moor for an hour or two. Alex said he knew a good place for lunch…

We trooped ashore and Alex led the way. We had spaghetti with vongole, the little local clams, washed down with a small glass of white wine each, then after a short walk around, returned to our yacht and continued on our way. The plan was to head right down to the southern end of the lagoon, pay a visit to the town of Chioggia there, then return north to Venice, to Giudecca, before evening.

Sailing down the inside shore of the Lido, in the calm waters of the lagoon began to seem tame after a while. The boat was working perfectly. Alex and Sol decided, and Matteo and I agreed, that we would head out through the next opening in the lagoon's protecting wall and continue our journey to Chioggia on the seaward side, enjoying the more bracing adventure of the Adriatic waves.

So we left the safety of the lagoon by way of the Porto di Malamocco, bowing to Neptune a couple of times as we hit the first breakers, and headed down the seaward side of the next spit of land, little wider than a harbour wall, that is the Pellestrina Littoral. Like the Lido, its northern counterpart, the Littorale di Pellestrina is about seven miles long. At the end of it is the Porto di Chioggia, with the town of Chioggia tucked snugly into the bottom corner of the lagoon just inside it.

The Adriatic wasn't really rough that afternoon, but there was enough of a swell to make the change of scene exciting. We hadn't travelled halfway down the Pellestrina shore, though, before the wind fell light and our speed slowed almost to nothing. This was fine for a bit, but as the same landmarks on the shore stayed with us while we travelled at less than a walking pace it at last became boring. Alex decided that if we were to get to Chioggia at a reasonable hour we had better start the engine.

Alex tried the electric starter and nothing happened. A few goes later Sol had recourse to the back-up pull-cord. Still nothing. Sol and Alex hauled out a tool box that was stowed beneath the cockpit seating, and set to on the engine's weather cowling with screwdrivers. It was I, the non-sailor (who nevertheless drove cars and knew roughly how they worked) that took the trouble to check the fuel gauge. 'Do you want to look at this?' I called to Sol and Alex. 'I think we may be out of Diesel.'

FOURTEEN

There were no fuel stations on the Adriatic side of the Pellestrina strand. We had no alternative but to sail on down towards Chioggia at one mile an hour and hope the wind picked up before we turned into the lagoon again at the Chioggia entry point.

The wind didn't pick up. We crawled down the coast, made our way through the Porto di Chioggia, saw the town with its belfries just inside the lagoon to the left of us and headed towards it like an invalid on a walking frame. Alex told us he had a friend in Chioggia who would let him tie up alongside his own boat. That was a piece of luck. Boats lay three abreast in the crowded basin, and it would otherwise have been difficult to find a space. We were less lucky in that by the time we got there it was seven o'clock in the evening and all the fuel stations were shut.

Even though we were in early July – not long after the week of longest days and shortest nights – there remained only two hours before sunset. It was a good dozen miles home to Venice from Chioggia and without wind, without engines… We didn't want to find ourselves limping painfully home in the middle of the night. We decided to stay in Chioggia for the night, finding something to eat in the town and sleeping rough on the boat.

Love in Venice

Alex phoned the boss of the boatyard to explain the situation and then Sol spoke to him too – since Sol was living in his house – to add the obvious footnote that he wouldn't be in for supper that night.

Matteo called his parents and delivered the same information. He didn't expect there to be any problems there; his father sailed and knew the way of sailing trips. But Matteo's expectations were happily exceeded. If we wanted to stay in a hotel for the night, he'd pay for that. Just put him on the phone when the time came and he'd settle with a credit card. The same went for dinner out. There were four of us, Matteo pointed out a bit sheepishly. That was OK, his father said. So long as we didn't all make a habit of it…

I did notice that Alex made no other phone call. Maybe there was no-one in his life who needed to know he wouldn't be home that night. Or maybe he'd sent a text and I hadn't seen him do it.

We made the most of it. Chioggia turned out to be a miniature version of Venice itself, complete with canals, bridges and church towers, though more workaday and less magnificent. Matteo pointed out the very un-ferocious stone lion atop its stumpy column in the Piazzetta. 'We call it the Cat of San Marco,' he said with a laugh. 'We Venetians.'

'We patronising bastards,' I paraphrased, and mock-punched him in the ribs.

Beyond the Piazzetta the town's main street, the

Corso del Popolo, led our eyes past a sea of café and restaurant awnings and pavement tables towards the cathedral and its campanile at its far end. We didn't walk as far as the cathedral. Before we got there we succumbed to the temptations of the café tables. If we were having our board and lodging paid for, then we reckoned we could afford to treat one another to a few drinks.

After a couple of beers our eyes focused on the fascia board of a small hotel directly across the Corso. As it was now eight o'clock we reckoned it wasn't too soon to try and bag rooms for the night. As we crossed the road I was aware that none of us seemed to want to bring up the subject of how many rooms we wanted. Perhaps that would become clear when we got to the reception desk.

It did. 'We only have one room left,' they told us. 'It's the weekend. Did you not think to book earlier?'

We explained our situation patiently. The receptionist nodded her *heard-it-all-before* understanding. Then she spelt it out. The room was a double, furnished with two single beds. We could take it or leave it; there was nothing else.

We all looked at one another, feeling very awkward. Alex, our skipper, had been very much in charge for most of the day. Now he seemed tongue-tied. Suddenly Sol took command of the situation and of us. After a very brief look at each of us in turn he took a breath and announced to the receptionist that the arrangement would be OK. There was a moment during which Matteo

Love in Venice

and I held our breaths, expecting to hear Alex say that it would not be OK at all. But instead he nodded, then looked at Sol for half a second with an expression I couldn't read. Relieved, Matteo and I muttered to Sol that, yes, this would do fine, and the deal was done.

Matteo explained the arrangement his father had made to pay the bill, a phone call was made, and then we were outside again on the Corso, where we picked another bar at random and had another beer. As we sat and chatted, in a mixture of Italian and English, about this and that, no mention was made by any of us about the unusually intimate accommodation we'd booked for the night. Though I noticed that Alex was becoming visibly more relaxed than he'd seemed all day, and quite endearingly tactile with Sol. He was sitting very close beside him at the pavement table we were sitting out at, and wasn't shrinking from rumpling Sol's hair if Sol said something teasing or funny, or patting his thigh. Perhaps he was just being Italian. Though Sol was giving as good as he got in this respect. Perhaps it was simply the beer.

We walked one block away to a restaurant that Alex knew. It looked onto the picturesque throng of fishing boats that nearly blocked the Vena Canal. Fish was the mainstay of Chioggia's economy, Alex and Matteo explained. They hardly needed to. The streets were full of fish-heads dropped by gorged sea-gulls, and being pulled to pieces in tugs-of-war among the hungrier birds.

Our restaurant's menu was a fish cornucopia. We toyed with the idea of bucking the trend and ordering steak instead, but it seemed a pity now that we were here. We had sea-urchins, bright gold and iodine-tasting in their spiky shells, then prawns and a dish of salted cod. A bottle of local wine. Coffee and amoretto biscuits...

Retracing our steps towards our hotel we stopped off at one last bar. The midsummer night had fallen at last, and we drank our final nightcaps of Amoretto under a dome of brilliant stars. And then it was time for bed. Whatever that would entail...

The last few yards were a bit of a lurch, I have to admit. But we were sober enough to claim our key politely enough from the reception desk and to unlock our door successfully. Once we were all inside the bedroom which, with the four of us in it, now seemed curiously cramped and small, there was a moment's hiatus as we each individually confronted the question of who would sleep with whom. I wanted to sleep with Matteo, of course. And yet... Well, I have to admit, I also wanted to get my hands on Sol. While Alex was a new and very attractive unknown in the equation. He looked to be about ten years older than me – twelve years older than Matteo. To my surprise that didn't diminish his attraction in my eyes.

Alex suddenly pulled off his shirt.

Nobody else spoke. Then one by one we copied him. We were all standing close, facing each other, in the space between the two single beds and the door. Like a performer gauging his audience Alex looked at all of us, then smiled hesitantly. Judging us and the moment he smiled more confidently, dropped his trousers and underwear. His dick sprang out and up, fully erect.

He was the smallest of us all in stature, though older and with the tautest musculature. His dick wasn't the longest, either (I had some knowledge of Sol's as well as Matteo's.) But it was a beautiful tapering shape, thick at the base, and with a fine point to it, which was being revealed to us millimetre by millimetre as his foreskin slid back automatically, the way the sails of our yacht slid down the mast when the halliards were operated by the electric switch. As we other three obediently followed his example in dropping our trousers and underwear to half mast (Captain, oh my captain) I was astonished to hear Alex say – in Italian, though even I couldn't fail to understand – 'Who wants to suck it, then?'

I had never heard anyone say anything like this. On a porn video site maybe, but never in real life. I was young and I was shocked. Especially to hear the words on the lips of a macho Italian yacht captain who was descended from one of the best-known painters of all time. And I could see that Matteo, two years younger than me and having had an even more sheltered life, was vastly more shocked. But ... to cut a short story even shorter ... we all – all three of us – wanted to suck Alex Canal's beautiful penis and, getting down on our knees, we all did.

*

Nobody fucked anybody that night. I would have

known if they had. I shared one of the two small beds with Matteo. I think we both came twice. Two feet away Sol and Alex were snuggled up together in the other bed and, from the sound of things, something similar happened over there too. Drunk though we were, we didn't actually compare notes, calling the score across the room in the dark.

Breakfast, which we ate in the midsummer morning sunshine outside a café on the Corso, was as socially uncomfortable as any of us had a right to expect. Casting about for something to say I reminded Matteo that this was the day that his brother was going sailing with Tonio. 'Ha,' said Matteo. 'Perhaps we'll cross their path in the lagoon.' An amused smirk appeared on his face momentarily. 'Assuming their sugar-daddies know how to sail.'

Then we took refuge in the practical necessities of the morning. We found a supplier of Diesel who was prepared to chug round and refuel our yacht where she lay berthed, boat to boat. Then, with a rather tight-lipped Alex at the wheel, we powered our way out of Chioggia's northern basin and headed towards Venice.

La Serenissima hid herself at first. To begin with she lay behind outcrops of the Pellestrina Littoral and the Lido on our right. And then as those bulwark landmasses curved away she remained eclipsed by the small islands that lay in between: Poveglia, Santo Spirito, Sacca Sessola. Even after we had nosed our way past those after an hour or so our view was still partly obscured by the bulk of San Clemente, La Grazia and San Servolo.

Love in Venice

But now we had tantalising glimpses of the sea city in between those rocky obstacles. The southern shore of Giudecca appeared in dismembered segments.

We tried to spot our destination – the boatyard where Alex and Sol worked – but it was difficult. Sol was little more experienced in sailing home to it than we were and Alex was giving little away. Since casting off from Chioggia he had more or less regressed to grim and silent mode. My heart went out to him. If he was a straight guy who had behaved out of character one drunken night in a shared hotel room, he might well be feeling bad today. He would in any case be dealing with a hangover. We all were.

At last Giudecca, with the spires of Venice behind it, came into full view as we passed alongside the uninhabited island of La Grazia. We hugged the walled shore of this island – an abandoned leper colony – because a mud shallow lay a little way to the side. Alex mentioned this, though he probably didn't need to. Another sailing boat was sitting nearby; her sails were set but she didn't appear to move. As we drew closer we could see why. She had strayed too far from the island wall and was now stuck in the treacherous mud that lay, invisible, just below the surface of the lagoon.

We could see two men on board. From a distance they were mere stick figures. After a while they hauled the sails down. 'They'll have to wait now, to be floated by the tide,' Alex explained. It was one of the first things he'd said in the past hour.

'Unless we throw them a line,' said Sol. 'Give them a tow.'

'Can do,' said Alex.

'Of course we should,' said Matteo.

Alex turned to him and, for the first time this morning, grinned. 'Then of course we will.' He told us where the towing line was stowed, though Sol already knew.

Sounds travel easily over water, human voices particularly. I became aware that the two men on the other boat were having a conversation. I didn't pay attention to that; they were talking Italian anyway and I probably wouldn't have understood even if I'd tried. They would be talking about their situation, of course. Perhaps they were about to hail us, to ask us for help, just as we were about to hail them and offer it.

Alex didn't hear them at all. He was talking to Sol about the towing line, which Sol was pulling from beneath a seat, uncoiling a length of it. But Matteo did hear the men talking on the other boat. He must have picked out some of the words. I saw him go rigid with shock. 'Don't stop for them,' he hissed to Alex. 'Sail on round the corner. We need to talk ... but not here.'

I didn't know the Italian for *What the hell are you on about?* But I knew that was what Alex said to Matteo; I could tell from his tone of voice.

Matteo stopped being a teenager then. A very adult

expression formed on his face as he stood tall and said to the considerably older Alex, 'Just do as I say. I'll explain in a minute.' Alex grunted, a hint of displeasure mixed in with his surprise, but he obeyed. We didn't stop. We continued to sail. I tried not to look towards the other boat and the men who were on board. I expected them to call out to us, to ask for a tow, perhaps to be indignant that we'd sailed so close and not volunteered our line. But they did not, and that surprised me too. In a few seconds we'd left them astern.

Some of the islands had walls around them, I'd noticed yesterday and today. They were the ones that had had religious communities on them – or still did – and were hospitals, monasteries or cemeteries. So when Matteo ordered Alex to sail on round the corner he was describing the layout of La Grazia in quite an exact way. We sailed on for a minute, close in under the long straight stone wall, then when the wall turned at a right angle Alex turned sharply too. As soon as we were out of sight of the other boat, and presumably out of ear-shot too, Matteo spoke. Urgently he said, to all of us, 'It's a kidnap. Those men on the boat. They've kidnapped Marco.'

FIFTEEN

'You're joking,' said Sol.

'I'm not. There've been kidnap attempts before. When we were small…' That was news to me. I knew the family was very rich, but still…

Matteo went on, 'I heard them speaking. I didn't catch many words. I heard my name – Marco's name. I heard *the Dragonetti boy*. That made me listen hard. I heard *Che … fare con l'altro.* What to do with the other one. Something like that. They meant Tonio. They must have meant my brother and Tonio. The thing is…'

Sol interrupted Matteo. 'What time was their sailing trip supposed to start?' Not waiting for an answer he started rapidly to explain to Alex about the trip the two boys were supposed to be making today with two middle-aged gay men.

'I've no idea,' Matteo said. He turned to Alex and took over from Sol, explaining to Alex in Italian about the younger boys' planned boat trip in case Alex hadn't understood Sol's rapid English. Or hadn't believed him… Alex was turning the wheel. Intending to return to the other boat? Or to go round in a circle while we tried to make sense of Matteo's excited outpourings? Till we decided what to do? At any rate he was clearly taking the situation seriously.

Alex spoke. 'The thing is… It's whether they have the

boys already or if they're still on the way to pick them up.' He said that in Italian but I got the meaning easily.

'Try his phone,' I said to Matteo, but Matteo was already doing it.

'It's off,' Matteo said. 'Gone to voicemail.'

'Tonio?' I tried. 'D'you have his number?' I knew I didn't.

For the next few seconds we all made rapid suggestions about who should be phoned. Matteo's parents? The gondola-hire company where Marco and Tonio worked? The police?

'I don't want to call Mamma or Dad for the moment,' said Matteo. 'Mamma would have a kitten.' I had to smile, in spite of the desperate seriousness of the moment. It was also touching, the way Matteo and Marco called their English mother Mamma and their Italian father Dad.

I said, 'If you could get Tonio, you might find out what time the rendez-vous was set for. Whether it's happened already or...'

'I don't have Tonio's mobile number,' Matteo said curtly. 'I know the number of his parents' home ... if I can remember it. But they'll both be out at work...'

'You can ring it anyway,' I said. 'You never know. But would you tell them their son's been kidnapped, or about to be?'

'Of course not,' said Matteo, sounding a bit impatient with me. 'It would only be to ask if they knew what time he was supposed to…'

His composure began to collapse at that moment: I could see it in his eyes. I wrapped him in my arms, held him tightly. As we laid our heads on each other's neck for a second or two I felt like kicking myself for not having done this a minute and a half before.

Then it was back to business immediately. I let Matteo detach himself. He tapped out what he hoped was Tonio's parents' number on his phone. And to his great surprise he got an answer right away. Tonio's mother happened to be at home this day. We'd all forgotten, returning home to Venice a day later than we'd intended to, that it was Saturday.

There was no sign of terror or anxiety in Matteo's voice as he smoothly asked Tonio's mother if she happened to know what time her son was going sailing. 'I've tried to contact Marco,' he went on, acting casual, 'but…'

A moment later Matteo ended the call. 'Twelve o'clock,' he told us. 'By the Fondamente Nove.' He was sharing the only two pieces of knowledge we craved. On a reflex we all looked at our watches. It was a little after eleven.

I had no idea what or where the Fondamente Nove might be. But Alex knew it, clearly, as he nodded his head and said, 'They'll be late for their appointment, then. Stuck on a mud bank...' He permitted himself the ghost of a smile.

At least we knew now that Marco and Tonio weren't already on board the stranded yacht. But what were we going to do now? Go back to the boat and confront the kidnappers face to face?

I said, with a bit of a swagger, 'There's four of us. Only two of them...'

'We only *saw* two of them,' said Sol sensibly. 'It's a biggish boat. There might be more below deck. Anyway, what would we do? They haven't committed any crime yet, as far as we know. We heave them overboard? Murder them?' He shrugged in an achingly beautiful way. 'I don't see what else we could do.'

'You're right,' I climbed down. 'I hadn't thought it through.'

There was a moment's pause as we all tried to think the thing through. Then Sol reached out to Matteo and gave him a hug. 'It'll all be OK, kid,' he said. I saw Matteo hug him back gratefully and found, to my surprise, that I didn't mind that that had happened. I found I was grateful to Sol.

Then it seemed it was Alex's turn. He too gave my lover a very brief though bracing hug. He rumpled Matteo's hair and said something unintelligible in what I presumed was Venetian dialect. Just a couple of words. Whatever they were they somehow made Matteo smile, and I was grateful to Alex for that. But I was glad that I had been the first to give Matteo a little physical show of support. If I hadn't done that, then I might have been less happy about the others' gestures of comfort towards my man.

'I think the next thing is call the police,' said Alex. 'All agree?' We all nodded. Alex spoke to Matteo. 'Want me to do it?' He was older than any of us. He was now firmly in charge.

'No,' said Matteo crisply. 'I'll do it.' He tapped out 113 on his phone.

He spoke for a long time to the police once he'd been put through. And, to judge from the long periods of time when he wasn't speaking, they talked a lot to him. Early on, I noticed, he gave the Dragonetti name. But before he had finished his call we heard the sound of a boat engine. A yacht came round the corner of the walled island. Its wasn't under sail; it was powering along as fast as it could go under engine power alone. It was the boat we'd seen stranded, with the two men on board. The tide had been coming in fast. It had evidently risen sufficiently to allow them to float clear. The yacht was heading towards the main island of Venice, making for its eastern end.

Alex didn't consult Sol or me. Nor even Matteo, who was still on the phone. He hauled the canvas down – at least he pressed the button that did this electrically – then started the engine and turned to follow the boat that had by now sped past.

Love in Venice

A minute later Matteo ended his call. Looking around he took in the new situation. 'The carabinieri said not to follow them,' he said.

'Too late for that now,' said Alex, looking very determined as he adjusted the wheel. 'Because that's exactly what we're going to do.'

*

The Fondamente Nove was quite simply a bus stop, Matteo explained to me and Sol. It was on the north shore of the main island of Venice. It was the departure point for transport to the main islands of the northern lagoon: Torcello, Murano and Burano. I hadn't been to any of these places yet. They were popular with tourists, especially Murano where the Venetian glassmakers had their furnaces. Burano, Matteo had told me, was prettier and they made lace there. He also told me that because of the similarity of their two names tourists often embarked for the wrong one by mistake.

So the Fondamente Nove was a busy place, I supposed, and I wondered for a moment at the kidnappers' choice of such a place for an abduction. But then I remembered a character in a TV series saying, "Where better to hide a book than in a library?" So, I guessed, where better to get people onto a boat without anyone noticing than a place where hundreds of other people were getting on and off boats? And if the Fondamente Nove was where the yacht ahead of us was going, then so, it seemed, were we.

Adam Wye

By now we were only about a mile from the boatyard on Giudecca. We could make it out clearly now, just off to our left. But to reach the Fondamente Nove we would have to turn right and go round the city in a big loop of its eastern end. It was a distance of about seven miles, Alex said. Though from the place where Marco and Tonio worked at the gondola steps it was just a ten-minute walk. You couldn't however, take a sailing boat on a short cut through the city-centre canals.

We didn't attempt to catch the other boat up, or to follow it too closely. We kept it just in sight, allowing it to grow vague in the light haze that lay low on the water in the growing morning warmth, but never letting it completely disappear.

Che fare con l'altro? What to do with the other one? The words kept ringing in my head like a terrible bell, a knell of doom. What would they do with Marco too? All too vividly I saw a finger arriving in the post: a finger now cold and bloody and blue, yet that had twice touched the most private piece of my anatomy and in the most intimate way. A finger – or an ear... Almost automatically I reached out and put my arm around Matteo as he stood inside the cockpit next to me. But it wasn't so much because I wanted to comfort him, I realised with shame, but because I wanted his proximity, strength and warmth ... to comfort me.

At such a moment it seemed almost equally shameful to find myself admiring the views. Yet admire them I did. I couldn't not do. Giudecca curved away out of sight as we came round the back of San Giorgio Maggiore,

Love in Venice

proud and aloof on its own special island; then St Mark's Basin opened out in front of us, the Doge's Palace shining towards us from the water's edge a blue mile away, and the great Campanile behind. Two miles further on we were approaching the eastern tip of Venice, the point of Sant'Elena. Along the shore that led there great trees stood proud and green behind the railings of the public gardens and the locals strolled, untroubled by the tourist hordes, in the sun.

The yacht we were following turned sharp left when it reached the point of Sant'Elena, and of course it disappeared from sight. A few minutes later we too rounded the little cape, where the shoreline abandoned its high-falutin palace façades and tree-lined walks and gave way to tin sheds and scruffy boatyards. The northern half of the lagoon lay spread out in front of us, its mushroom crop of islands appearing to move against each other as we powered through the water. Beyond them lay the Italian mainland, where the airport was. I hadn't been out on this half of the lagoon since I'd crossed it in a speeding water taxi after landing at the airport on my first day, three weeks or more ago. Now just as then the water around and in front of us was full of boats criss-crossing the lagoon. Full of boats... But of the particular one that we were following there was no sign.

'Well, we know where they're heading,' said Sol. 'We can carry on following them there.' Nobody disagreed, and we continued to furrow our way through the lagoon, a little way off Venice's northern, shaded, shore.

Alex spoke suddenly, unexpectedly. 'Last night,' he said. 'I'd had a bit to drink. I don't usually…'

'It's fine,' I said, feeling sure I spoke for everyone. 'It doesn't matter.' It had been nice, though, to suck on his beautiful cock, albeit briefly. But probably this wasn't a good moment to say so.

'I'd prefer if you didn't…' Alex began, in a very bashful way that was at odds with everything we'd seen and heard of him up till now.

This time Matteo cut him off. 'None of us are going to talk about it. Solemn promise. Only us three here will ever know.'

Well, Alex would be unlikely to forget it in a hurry, so that made four of us. But I didn't point this out either.

*

Perhaps it was a good thing in the end, my enjoyment of the panoramas around us. I turned round and looked behind us when we were still about a mile away from the Fondamente Nove. I thought I might find myself looking directly out to sea through the Porto di Lido but two long flat islands blocked my view. A yacht was putting out from the Venice shore behind us, though, beginning to run up its sails. I focused on it for several seconds, not thinking anything in particular, before I realised. This was the boat we were supposed to be following. It had dived into the city's edge well before the Fondamente Nove and was now on its way out again. With the boys on board?

'They're over there,' I said excitedly, touching the others' shoulders, pointing across the water behind. The boat was under full sail by now, and turning east, away from us, heading back the way it had come.

Alex didn't bother to tell us what he was going to do; we knew anyway. We were soon turned right round and once again pursuing the other boat. Matteo took out his phone.

The carabinieri had given him a special number to ring. He used it now. The police had planned to thwart the kidnap attempt by intercepting the yacht at the Fondamente Nove. Now it seemed – perhaps because of the delay caused by the yacht's running aground off La Grazia – that the rendez-vous point had been changed. I saw Matteo's eyes move and his body tense as he told the person he was speaking to that we had been following the boat, had observed its change of route-plan, and that we had it in sight now.

There was silence from Matteo as he listened for some time to what was being said at the other end. I guessed he was getting a thunderous dressing-down for disobeying police instructions and my heart went out to him. At last he put the phone down.

'Change of plan,' Matteo announced smoothly. 'We're to keep the boat in sight, though without being seen ourselves if possible.'

'That's not a change of plan,' Alex said laconically. 'That was always what we were going to do.'

Ignoring this, Matteo went on. 'We report its position back to the carabinieri, and note any change of course. They'll intercept it somewhere – with a *motoscafo*.'

Venice and its lagoon were home to a vast number of different types of boats. Matteo had told me about them and I was learning to know which were which. I knew about the vaporetto, the water bus, the gondola, of course, the *sandolo* and the *topo*, the *cavallina*, the *bissona*, the alarming-sounding *vipera*, the *barcobestia* and the ceremonial barge, the *bucintero*. The *motoscafo* was a speed-launch. The fastest ones were, unsurprisingly, used by the carabinieri – the military police.

SIXTEEN

We followed the other boat at a distance, back the way we'd both come. We kept the yacht just in sight, though allowed its outline to be blurred by the heat haze that shimmered above the water's surface. If they looked back and spotted us they would see us similarly hazed, with any luck, and in any case we would be just one among a myriad of other small craft on that boat-starred sea.

We passed the headlands of Venice's northern shore, heading back towards the island's eastern tip, St Elena. On the other side of us two rural-looking islands floated past. Certosa and Le Vignole, Matteo introduced them when I asked him. 'Venice's vegetable plots,' he said. I hadn't thought about this. Yet obviously the sea city had to get its five a day from somewhere.

We approached the point at St Elena. Would the boat ahead of us turn right, retracing its steps back into the southern lagoon where we had first encountered it? Would it carry straight on towards the Lido, which we could now see a mile or two ahead of us? Or would it turn left…? After a minute or two that seemed like an hour or two the boat turned left into the main shipping lane. 'Fuck,' said Sol. 'They're heading for the open sea.'

'Where will they be making for?' I asked Matteo. My knowledge of the Adriatic's geography was patchy to say the least.

'Could be anywhere,' he answered reasonably, though his voice was scared. 'Turn left and the next big place is Trieste. Maybe … I don't know … a hundred miles away… Turn right, if they didn't go in to Chioggia they'd come to Ravenna. I don't think that's quite so far. But they could go straight across, I suppose. To the Croatian coast…' He tailed off. I don't think either of us wanted to contemplate how far that might be.

I thought about my stomach then. We'd eaten breakfast. We'd planned to be back in Venice before lunch. We had bottles of water on board; that I knew. But did we have an emergency ration of food? How long would it take to sail across the Adriatic, from one side to the other, anyway? Was our boat prepared for such a journey? What about fuel…? Alex and Sol would know the answers to those questions. There was little point my asking them aside from idle curiosity. We were going to get Marco and Tonio back at whatever cost. Alex's grim determination as he turned the wheel to take us into the big shipping channel told me that. And I was as steady in my resolve as he was. As was Matteo. As was Sol.

Matteo called the carabinieri again. He told them about the yacht's new heading and roughly where both boats were. A minute later they called Matteo back. 'You can stand off,' he was told. 'We've got you both on radar now.' Predictably the advice to stand off was ignored by Alex at the wheel.

Ahead we could see the open Adriatic, framed in the

Love in Venice

Porto di Lido between its two entrance piers. And now we had joined the big boys in the shipping lane. Tankers, container ships and cruise liners all used this narrow gateway, travelling at three times our speed. Our skipper gave me an order for the first time. 'Ben, keep a watch astern. Anything big, gaining on us, tell me immediately.'

'Will do,' I said. Then thought I should be a bit more serious about this. 'Si, capitano,' I amended. And hoped that hadn't been over the top

'Of course,' I heard Matteo say to the others (I had my back to them all), 'they may not go far at all. They could put in at any little beach or cove...'

But then what? I thought grimly. Where would they go from there? And what would we do?

Every ten seconds or so I turned round quickly, just for a second, to glance at the way ahead. I felt quite guilty about disobeying orders in this way, but I reckoned that anything coming up fast behind us would not materialise in the space of two seconds. We were concerned about container ships, not fighter planes.

My once-per-ten-seconds snapshots showed me the Porto di Lido coming quickly closer. Its two piers, running out to sea, protecting the lagoon alike from silt and storms, came towards us like the two ends of a pair of pincers or tongs. Between them the waves of the Adriatic rolled green and laced with white. The boat ahead of us was making its way between the piers. It would be difficult to see the moment at which it entered the sea. Except I knew we'd be able to tell from the rocking-horse rise and fall it would display when it hit the first wave. Bowing to Neptune.

I remembered to return my gaze to the traffic astern. Nothing big was coming up behind. I thought again of fighter planes and on a reflex peered up into the sky. There were no fighter planes up there. But suddenly a clatter arose from behind trees on the Lido shore, where Venice's air base was, just half a mile away. I turned quickly and saw a helicopter come into sight, climbing fast above the trees. At that moment I heard Sol shout, 'Look!'

'Helicopter,' I said.

'Not the 'copter,' said Sol. 'Ahead.'

Disregarding orders yet once more I spun towards the bow. The boat ahead of us appeared to be exactly between the two pincer tips of the piers. But from each of those pier-heads a small boat was powering towards it, their speed lifting their sharp-pointed bows high above the water; their departures from the twin piers were immaculately timed. From the water near the yacht rose sudden plumes of spray.

The helicopter was overhead the yacht now – arriving so suddenly that it took us by surprise – and then the two speedboats were alongside the yacht, one on each side, their interceptions perfectly synchronised, and men were swarming aboard. The sounds of the shots that had been fired across the yacht's bows some seconds earlier now reached us, meshed up with the helicopter noise. The yacht bobbed up then down, quite violently. So did the two police launches that were grappled on either side. Bowing to Neptune. They had met the first wave of the open sea.

I took hold of Matteo then and held him tightly. I said, 'I love you.' Those were the only things I could usefully do. He said,

'Ben, I need you.'

A vertical row of green lights ahead of us on one of the piers – which we'd taken no notice of up to now – attracted our attention suddenly by changing to red. Alex had slowed the engine to a crawl. There was nothing to be gained by charging onward now. We heard the ring of another shot or two. Then, quicker than we'd have guessed possible something or someone dropped from the helicopter on the end of a line we couldn't see. Like a spider whizzing down its thread of silk. Then something or someone was winched up again. A minute later the process was repeated, though more slowly this time. Then the helicopter turned and clattered back towards where it had come from. Within a minute it had sunk out of sight behind the trees on the Lido shore.

I had to keep reminding myself I was supposed to be keeping a lookout behind.

There was more activity on the boats ahead of us – now bobbing in the waves just beyond the piers. Figures came off the yacht on both sides and went – some seemed almost to tumble – aboard the police boats. Those two boats then detached themselves and pulled away. They turned quickly about and began to head our way. Behind them the yacht began a more stately, leisurely turn among the waves.

We didn't have time to move to the side of the channel to let the carabinieri speedboats pass. They came past us rapidly, blue lights flashing, one on either side. They didn't acknowledge us, and we bounced up and down quite heavily as their two stern waves crisscrossed beneath our bow. Seconds later they had disappeared astern in twin mists of spray.

Matteo – I still had one arm round him – got a call on his phone. It was the police again. The message was short. Matteo acknowledged it with a curt yes and thank you, then ended the call. He turned to us, his face curiously devoid of expression. 'They said go home. That the boys would be back home before we get there.'

I thought that he would break down and cry just then. But he didn't. Then I thought that I would. But I didn't, and the moment passed. I looked at Sol. A smile of relief was just beginning to appear on his face. It was Alex, the oldest among us, our brave decisive captain and the bold sexual exhibitionist of the previous night, whose handsome face crumpled into tension-dissolving tears.

Sol put his arms around his shoulders from behind as he turned the wheel and began the turn that would take us back home through the lagoon. Sol rubbed his head and chest against Alex's neck and back the way I did sometimes to Matteo when he sat at the piano... The way Matteo sometimes did to me.

Standing behind our two sailor friends Matteo and I held each other now.

*

The boss of the boatyard heard the bare bones of our story but no more. 'Tell me more another time,' he said. 'You need to be home now.' He was already calling up a water taxi.

Matteo said to Sol and Alex, 'I want you both to come back with us too.'

'I don't think so,' said Sol. 'It would look like we expected gratitude.'

'Quite right,' said Alex. 'Another time, perhaps, but we won't come back with you now.'

'OK,' said Matteo, 'but if you're there in person you can tell my parents to their faces that you don't expect anything.' He said that quite firmly, but then his tone changed. 'Please come back with us. Both of you. I want you to.'

All four of us climbed down the water steps into the taxi when it came.

We cut right through Giudecca on a narrow waterway, whizzed across the broad expanse of the Giudecca Canal, then plunged into the heart of Venice on the other side. Twisted through tiny capillary canals whose existence I hardly knew ... until we emerged onto the Canal Grande just a stone's throw from the front of the Dragonettis' palazzo.

We pulled up at the landing stage beneath the grand façade. I'd never arrived at the palazzo in this way. Nor had I ever seen the great water door opened, as it was opened now for us by Albano. He had cash in his hand for the taxi driver and came down the steps to pay him before shepherding us inside and bolting the door behind us as Matteo led the way upstairs.

In the portego, beyond the pianos, Annabelle and Domenico sat with Marco and Tonio. Annabelle, on the sofa, had an arm around her younger son. She seemed to be holding back tears. A policewoman was sitting on another chair nearby. Domenico stood up and came to greet us. With offers of prosecco. Alex began to say that he and Sol wouldn't stay for the drink; they had just come to see we got home safely, but Domenico waved his words aside. We all went after chairs and pulled them up to where the others sat. It was handy, I thought, to have a living-room in which you could easily find nine chairs and still leave a decorous row of them against the walls.

*

We told our story and Marco and Tonio told theirs. 'They weren't very professional at all,' said Tonio. 'Just two stupid chancers who thought they'd have a go. They could barely sail a boat. Let alone put up a struggle against armed police. They just crumbled and gave in. Fired one shot each then let themselves be overpowered.'

'Fired a shot each?' I said, feeling my stomach churn with dismay. 'Was anybody…?'

'They both missed,' said Marco. 'More or less. One policeman had his epaulette grazed.'

I let the boys have their moment of elation. They would learn in time how easily it could have gone the other way. That the bully who is defeated – by luck or by cleverness – will always look inept and a weakling once he's down. It's a different story when the bullet that might have grazed the epaulette instead strikes home. When the police don't arrive in time. When there's no handy pair of breakwaters from which to spring a pincer trap…

'I don't know how to thank you,' Domenico at last said to Alex. Alex hadn't said much while he sipped his prosecco. Sol and Matteo had taken it upon themselves to make it clear that Alex had been the hero of the day. Without his decisiveness, his clear thinking, his astutely weighed decision to ignore the police's instructions not to interfere…

I can't bear to think through to the end of that sentence even now.

'You've thanked me already,' Alex said. He looked around. 'You've sat me down in your beautiful room, despite my scruffy sailing clothes, without knowing anything about who I am, and shared your wine with me. Shared your celebration of your son's return with me. I would never ask for anything more.'

The Italians certainly knew how to express themselves grandly and nobly when the moment came, I thought. And to act grandly and nobly too. It was something I was just learning today.

'Come upstairs,' Matteo said suddenly to Alex. 'We've got a picture by your ancestor hanging on the next floor. It's a painting of this house. I'll show it to you.' The two of them disappeared through the door.'

A hastily prepared dish of pasta was announced by Artemia, Matteo and Alex returned from their brief tour of the gallery upstairs, and the policewoman took her leave. Six of us hadn't eaten since breakfast and it was now five o'clock in the afternoon. Pasta... That was another thing about living here in Italy. You came home starving, at an unexpected hour, and a substantial rib-sticking dish could be concocted within ten minutes. Ours was penne with chilli flakes and garlic, tomato paste, anchovies and olives ... with capers and Parmesan cheese. We crowded round the table in the kitchen and wolfed it down. No meal could have been simpler, or more quickly prepared. But, eaten in the circumstances that we found ourselves in, ravenous and high on relief and adrenalin, it tasted like angels' fare.

Matteo and Marco wanted the six of us all to go out to a bar, before dinner time arrived, before we said goodbye to Alex and Sol. Annabelle protested. Tonio's mother had arrived by now and she protested too. Neither of them wanted to let go of their precious sons – the more precious for having been nearly lost. Their prodigal sons, who were lost, then found...

Domenico came to Matteo's aid. Yes, we youngsters should indeed go out if we wanted to. We were all adults, after all. 'But come back in time for dinner.' He spoke to Marco and Tonio. 'Your mothers have special needs today, not just you. Respect that, please.' Then he looked at Sol and Alex. 'You guys are older. You'll understand. So please bring them back safely a second time. And do us the honour of sharing our evening meal with us too.'

That would make two big meals in the space of three hours. I was up for that, though. More than up for it. As Sol and Alex accepted their dinner invitations graciously I felt that I was flying six miles high.

It was late that evening when Sol and Alex took their leave. Later still when Tonio's parents took him home. Then Annabelle and Domenico went to bed. It was like the Farewell Symphony. Just Matteo, Marco and I were left sitting together in the portego. A little tipsy by now. Matteo and I sat together on a sofa. Only after the departure of the Dragonetti parents were we able to sit with arms around each other's shoulders, lover-like and intertwined. Marco sat on another sofa now, alone.

I felt for Marco. Tonio's parents deeply needed his presence tonight, with them at home. But Marco needed Tonio too. His need went unacknowledged, though.

Because...because that's how things were.

'Come here,' I said to Marco and, 'Budge up,' to Matteo. I motioned to Marco to come and sit between us. And between us we cuddled Marco, and tried to make things right for him.

We slept the night together. All three of us together in Matteo's big bed. None of us attempted any kind of sex at all. We just held one another. And though Matteo's bed was big for two, it was a tight squeeze for three. It was dreadfully hot and dead uncomfortable really. But sometimes... Sometimes it's the thought that counts. And the fulfilment of a tactile need.

In the morning we woke up early. It was midsummer and the sun rose at half past five. Marco departed for his own bed for the remaining hours before breakfast time. He'd probably had enough cuddling for the moment, just as a cat has, when it knows it's time to get down from your lap. But before he left us Marco said something that shook Matteo and me to the core. 'I've been thinking. I'll need to talk to Tonio of course. But I think it's time he and I told our parents that we're gay.'

SEVENTEEN

There are moments in life when the whole thing – life, I mean – seems suddenly just too big for you. That morning, which was Sunday, we went to church. Together, as a family. Domenico, Annabelle, Matteo, Marco and me. Albano and Artemia too. None of us were believers as far as I knew. Yet we went there.

Went where? There were a hundred and more churches in central Venice. One stood on every canal intersection. Each block was a parish, a *paroquia,* of its own. We walked to the nearest one. It was called San Stae. A classical building of the early eighteenth century, its 'west' front, actually facing north, was painted obsessively by Turner during his visit here.

That didn't matter. Actually nothing mattered this morning except that Marco was alive. I looked at the great glass windows and at the vault above us as we listened inattentively to the Mass that was being said. That Marco was alive, and so were we. Nothing in the world could ever matter more. I thought I'd read that a famous politician, standing in church the Sunday after escaping death in an assassination attempt, had looked at the sunshine streaming through the windows and thought to herself, *This is the day I wasn't meant to see.* It was the same for us, the Dragonetti family – plus servants, plus me. This was the day we were meant to grieve and be shattered by. *The day that Marco wasn't meant to see.* I felt my chest begin to heave, and then I felt Matteo's fingers steal in amongst mine.

*

Neither of us could bring ourselves to touch the piano for days. Marco and Tonio were given leave from work. And so was I. 'Would you prefer it if I went away?' I asked Annabelle. 'If I went home?' My heart was in my mouth as I asked the question. I needed so much to be with Matteo, and he needed me. But I had to put the question. I had to know.

'Where is home?' Annabelle looked into my eyes very seriously. 'What is it? If home is where you're needed most at any given time, then maybe – for the moment at any rate – your home is here.'

I didn't have words to respond to what she had just said. I could only give her hand a momentary squeeze and quickly turn away.

*

We were four. The famous four, the fantastic, fabulous four. Matteo, Marco, Tonio and me. We four against the world. We kept in touch with Alex and with Sol constantly during those next few days but we didn't meet up. They went back to work on Monday. They were grown up and so nothing less was expected of them. But I felt for them too. They too had been touched by the events of Saturday; they would never forget that day. But I remembered the embrace that Sol had locked Alex in when he'd lost his composure at the moment when we'd learned the kids were safe. I wondered if that might herald the beginning of something for them... In my silly romantic heart I did hope so.

We four. We happy four. We band of brothers...Well, two of us actually were brothers... Anyway. We roamed Venice together. The invincible four. Death should have no dominion... People turned in the street and looked at us. We wore such an aura of command and power. We had survived Marco's brush with death. Nothing, not even the lightning that clove the heavens, could touch us now.

We explored the mysterious reaches of Cannaregio, where the long straight canals repeat themselves like reflections in a series of mirrors, and you find yourselves as remote from the centre of Venice, just a mile away, as if you'd gone to Mars. The others were showing me the way, yet it was a way they barely knew themselves. Matteo, Marco and Tonio were being intrepid explorers on their own doorstep. They took me, by labyrinthine paths, into the Ghetto – the Jewish quarter of medieval Venice that gave its name, and a whole queasy concept, to the world.

As we walked into the grey central square of the Ghetto Vecchio I felt something happen to the hairs on the back of my neck. Then I felt as though the air was thick with ghosts from centuries long, and not so long, ago. It was as though I felt them brush my skin. I told Matteo. 'Do you feel it too?' I asked him.

'No,' he said. 'But I do know. I felt it the first time I came here.'

Adam Wye

Henry James wrote that you could stand in the Venetian Doge's Palace for the first time only once. It seemed that the same went for Venice's Ghetto.

We walked the length of the Cannaregio Canal. We stood on the pavement at the seaward end of it, where the low, long waves of the lagoon reached out to touch our toes. Until the railway bridge was built a hundred and fifty years ago this was the city's front door to the mainland. You could enter or leave the city only by boat. Right here. It was hard to imagine, standing at this quiet spot where land met water, now.

We stayed out late some of those evenings but in the end we always went home. Home together. We four. We lucky four.

Coming home to a palace... I couldn't help thinking of the little Schubert piece that Matteo and I were learning, and growing to love. The one where Schubert takes you frighteningly far from home. through a galaxy of ever remoter keys, then brings you back – heart-meltingly – to the place he built for you at the beginning. That little tune was no Venetian palace, for sure. It was no Emperor concerto, no Jupiter symphony. It was humble, modest, unassuming... Like my own parents' house on the fringe of London from where I used to see the planes... Be it ever so humble, home is home.

One night when we were late returning Marco startled us by asking if one of us – Matteo or I – would play that Schubert piece for him and Tonio. Of course it had been at his suggestion that we'd learnt it in the first place.

'It's one o'clock in the morning,' Matteo objected. 'Mamma and Dad...'

'They're asleep one floor above, at the other end of the building,' Marco said. 'Anyway, I don't care.' He'd become rather more self-willed since his ordeal. I supposed that was understandable, but I hoped it would only be a temporary phase.

Matteo shrugged. 'OK, then. But I'd better be the one to play it. If there's going to be a complaint in the morning, it had better be directed at me rather than Ben.' I thought that was sweetly selfless of him, but I didn't demur.

For some reason we other three stood rather than sat while Matteo played it. Which, despite the fact that we'd had a good few drinks during the evening, he did beautifully. We listened to the menacing key shifts of the central episodes, and then the tantalisingly slow return to home. Then there we were. And to my surprise – or maybe not; maybe I was half expecting it – Marco turned to me, grabbed hold of me and buried his face against my neck. I felt the sobs run through him as he cried, painfully, achingly. I was pretty sure this was the first time he'd cried since the kidnap and rescue nearly a week ago.

Tonio moved towards him immediately and I handed Marco to him. While Matteo played Schubert's final comforting bars the two younger lads held each other tight. Home is home is home, be it never so grand.

Adam Wye

*

That impromptu midnight performance by Matteo broke the spell. Neither of us had felt able to touch the piano since the kidnap. Now suddenly it came unlocked for us again. For days music had held no beauty for us. Against the stark realities of death and life all art had seemed trite and contrived. But now it lived for us again. Thanks to the second of Schubert's Drei Klavierstücke. Thank you, Franz Schubert, for writing that modest little piece ... for us four.

*

The night that Marco had spent in bed with Matteo and me remained a one-off; the event was not repeated. On the nights that followed Marco had Tonio staying over with him in his room, or else he stayed over at Tonio's house. Neither of them had yet had the conversation with their parents that Marco had told us they were planning to – the conversation during which they would tell them they were gay – but they still brought up the matter from time to time with us. That difficult conversation was now a part of both their plans; Tonio had turned out to be as much in favour of the idea as Marco was.

The devil was in the detail, though. Timing. When to do it? Method. How? Should they tackle their separate sets of parents? Deal with them as a couple, standing shoulder to shoulder before each pair of parents? Call everyone together and announce it like at a press conference? These were not easy things to decide, and

Love in Venice

the two boys spent much time discussing them.

Matteo and I were involved in this too. If the younger boys were going to come out to the Dragonetti parents then probably we ought to also. Perhaps we should set the example, leading the way, coming out first. After all we were the senior pair.

On the other hand, where Matteo and Marco were concerned, it was the second announcement that was going to be the more difficult one for the parents to hear. I said to Matteo, 'Do you know what Oscar Wilde says in The Importance of Being Earnest?'

'No,' said Matteo.

I laughed at him. 'You don't know what I'm going to say.'

'It's still no,' said Matteo reasonably, and with a shrug. 'I've never read or seen the play.'

'You might recognise the odd quote, though,' I argued back. 'Anyway, one character, told that another character has "lost" both his parents, answers that: "To lose one parent may be considered a misfortune; to lose both looks like carelessness."'

Matteo laughed at that but he took the point too. It's one thing as a parent to discover that one of your offspring is gay; it must be a very different matter to learn that they all are. For whereas Tonio had an elder sister who had a boyfriend, the Dragonettis only had Matteo and Marco. Who seemed both to have made the initial step of admitting their orientation to themselves at some point during the last week or two. During the few weeks I'd been living with them. I couldn't help wondering if this sudden leap along their journeys of self-knowledge had anything to do with me. If it had ... then I wasn't quite sure how I felt about that.

As for me, I was also the sum total of my parents' offspring, being an only child. I wondered how my own parents would feel, how they would react, when at some point in the future I came out to them.

But that was for the future. My parents weren't here. The Dragonettis all were. We had to deal with them – and Tonio's parents – first.

*

But life is what happens while you're planning other things. Marco and Tonio appeared at the palazzo one morning after they'd slept over at Tonio's looking oddly tense about their faces but also, somehow, excited. 'You'll never guess what's happened!' Tonio said as soon as they came into the portego. He looked around to check that nobody else was listening.

'We'll go somewhere more private,' Marco intervened at once. 'Garden?'

Matteo and I nodded our heads and we all trooped downstairs and out through the water floor's garden door into the open air.

'My mother sort of cornered us at breakfast,' Tonio

began even before we'd found a bench to sit on. 'She asked me if there was anything I – we – wanted to tell her. I said, "Such as?" and she gave a sort of smile. She said she couldn't help noticing that we spent all our time together. That we were always inseparable, even at night. That we seemed to have "grown even closer" – those were her exact words – since the kidnap attempt. She said, "So was here anything you wanted to say, connected with that?" It was becoming a difficult moment...'

'You're telling me,' put in Marco. Matteo and I were sitting now on one of the benches. Marco and Tonio stood facing us. Behind them the garden was a background of roses, white, pink and gold. It was like being in a foreign, distant time. Perhaps in a medieval bower.

'She said,' Tonio continued, 'that nothing we might say would shock or surprise her. Nothing we might say would hurt her or my father. So...'

'He came straight out with it,' said Marco. He evidently didn't want to be left out of the news-giving process. 'He said he was gay and I was his boyfriend. She smiled and said, yes, she'd thought that was the case...'

Tonio cut back in. 'I said that now I ought to tell Dad as well, but she said it wouldn't be necessary. That she'd tell him we'd had the conversation...'

Matteo jumped in, sounding a bit uncomfortable. 'Did

she say she'd also tell our parents?'

'No, of course not,' said Tonio. 'That was the end of the discussion. She wished us a nice day and we came straight on over here.'

I felt myself heave out a long deep breath. 'Wow,' I said. I couldn't really think of anything else.

*

Well, that was one third of it done. One quarter if you included my own future coming out to my parents, all alone. But for now there was the urgent question of the Dragonetti parents. Would Matteo and Marco talk to them separately? If so, who would go first? Or would all four of us collar them together? That might be easier for us four (safety in numbers) but it might be a bit heavy on Domenico and Annabelle. They might feel rather bludgeoned. And that in turn might affect their reactions. 'Remember,' I warned at this point in the discussion, 'it's not just that one moment they've got to deal with. They're going to have to live with the knowledge that both their sons are gay for the rest of their lives.' I had to admit to myself privately that of course I was also thinking about my own parents.

We spent some of that day on the water. We took the ferry from Fondamante Nove across the northern lagoon to the island of Torcello.

Torcello was a sleepy little rural place. There were few buildings on it, though quite a number of grass-grown ruins. Canals crisscrossed it just as they crisscrossed Venice, but for the most part the blocks of land they enclosed were pastures, scrubby woods or market gardens.

It hadn't always been that way. Torcello, founded a millennium and a half ago was actually the ancestor of Venice. Its squares were full of palaces and houses. But it was less safe from attack than the bigger islands in the lagoon's centre, so the population moved lock, stock and barrel to the biggest group of those ... and there created the settlement that became Venice.

They left behind their buildings, most of which fell down eventually, or were plundered for the stones that went to build the new city. But there was a still a cathedral standing. Much of the building dated back to the ninth century, so the guide book told us. Inside, behind the high altar rose one of the most beautiful mosaics I'd ever seen. Only a couple of centuries younger than the church it decorated, it depicted the Virgin Mary holding Jesus. We didn't need the guide book to tell us how much that image, the plainest mosaic in a church that was all mosaics, would move us.

We returned outside to the sunshine. There was a high-end restaurant here on Torcello but it was famously expensive. We didn't go into it. We'd brought a picnic. We ate that sitting on a grass bank between a canal and a little orchard. Then one thing led to another and we had sex there. Well, there was no anal penetration, and we didn't turn it into a four-way. We did what we had done once before on the Lido, behaving like two couples, though we were all in sight of one another. And just like on the Lido we found that last detail an amazing turn-on. Well, it hadn't done our relationships any harm that first time, we reckoned. It worked fine for us. Perhaps it would be one of our regular things for the future…

The future. A cloud crossed my thoughts as I considered that. Outdoor sex – the four of us – in London – in the winter… Somehow I couldn't see it. But what would be would be. I made sure to enjoy the moment. This moment of June, on a canal bank, in the sunshine, on Torcello.

EIGHTEEN

It happened quite suddenly. That evening, after our return from Torcello. We were having dinner. We, the Dragonetti family – and I include in that idea of family myself and Tonio.

Annabelle said suddenly, during a lull in the conversation over the veal and artichoke stew, 'Have you heard anything of your sailing friends. Alex and … what was his name? … Sol?'

As it happened, we had. Sol had texted just an hour earlier and we'd arranged to meet for a drink – the six of us – the following day. For the weekend had come round again, and tomorrow was Saturday. Matteo relayed that innocent little piece of information to Annabelle and Domenico.

'They're nice,' said Annabelle. 'I mean Alex and Sol.'

'Nice?' objected Domenico. 'They're bloody heroes, the pair of them. Between them they saved the life of our son.'

Annabelle was not fazed. 'The word nice in English has a wide range of meaning,' she told her husband sweetly. 'It's often an understatement to a quite extreme degree. Something the Italian consciousness can not easily perceive.' She clasped Domenico's hand across the table and laughed lightly at him. This was presumably a long-standing joke between them. A joke that in a way was not a joke – the kind of intimate banter that all long-married couples share.

Then Annabelle turned away from her husband and looked towards us younger four. 'Sol and Alex… Are they … are they a pair? I mean a couple. An item. What's the word young people use these days?'

There was a general sense of discomfiture among us four young guys. Nobody could find the most appropriate, careful, thing to say. I managed to organise my thoughts first for once, and to find suitable words to carry them. 'We don't know,' I said. 'That might be the case.' I shrugged. 'Or it might not be. They've only known each other a fortnight. They might not yet know, themselves.' Sometimes you know that you've said all that you need to on a given subject but all the same you find yourself carried away and imprudently blurt out more. Well, maybe you don't, but it certainly happens to me occasionally. I added, very unnecessarily, 'Alex at any rate would have some baggage to deal with if it were true. Cultural background and so on…' I heard my words come tumbling out and was horrified. I shut up. And wished the floor would swallow me.

Domenico looked at me sharply. He said, 'You sound like quite an expert on the subject, Ben.' His tone of voice was neither hostile nor encouraging. It was neutral in the extreme. I looked back at him in deep discomfiture. I had no idea what to say.

Then I heard Matteo's voice. Calm and measured. 'Dad,' he said, 'I think there's something we need to tell

Love in Venice

you.'

'We?' asked his father. 'Who's we?'

My heart was in my mouth for Matteo. I felt I was watching someone step out blindfold onto a plank that led who knew where.

'I'll speak for myself, then,' said Matteo with infinite dignity. 'Dad, Mamma, I'm gay.'

The atmosphere was changed no less than it would have been had a rock fallen through the ceiling and landed on the table in the midst of us. There was a silence that probably lasted only a second. It felt more like an hour. Then I heard Marco's voice pipe up. Unlike his brother's voice, which had risen to the momentous occasion with an adult gravity, Matteo's sounded small and childlike. Fragile and close to tears. All the same, he said it. 'Dad. Mamma. So am I.'

In all my life I'd never heard anyone say a braver thing. I realised I now had to say something myself. I couldn't just sit and watch as the two brothers I loved – for yes, I did love Marco too – hurled themselves against the barbed wire. I heard my voice – it came out reasonably strong, thank goodness – say. 'I need to say something here too. I love your son Matteo.' I stopped, and waited for the ceiling to fall.

Then Tonio spoke. In a voice that was little more than a husk or a whisper, he pitched in. 'And I love Marco.'

Annabelle stood up. Quite slowly. Very gracefully.

She touched her husband's hand across the tablecloth and said, not directing the remark at anyone in particular, 'I think perhaps I always knew. Maybe mothers always do know. Deep down. It's all right, all of you. But you'll have to excuse me for a minute or two.' She walked towards the dining-room door and exited through it into the portego. That left the four of us with Domenico.

It was Domenico who found his voice first. 'Well, that was a bit of a bombshell, boys.'

'Sorry,' whispered Tonio. I didn't try to look at him. I could tell from his voice that he was already in tears.

'It's OK,' said Domenico, sounding more as if he wished it was OK than as if it really was. 'I'm not angry with any of you. It's just that it's been … a bit of a shock, that's all.' He got to his feet. 'If you don't mind… I think I need to go and see to Annabelle.' He left the dining-room.

'Well, said Marco, to my surprise recovering more quickly than the rest of us and sounding quite upbeat, or at least pretending to. 'That went well.'

*

We met up with Sol and Alex early the next evening in the Bar All'Arco. We four briefly became us six. Customers already overflowed the small interior space and so we took our drinks outside into the paved alleyway. Although surrounded by people at very close quarters we naturally had to tell the story of the previous night. It was the biggest thing that had happened to us since the kidnap attempt.

'It ended reasonably happily,' Matteo said. 'When the parents had got their breaths back they told us they were OK with it, though it might take them a while to get used to it.'

'They asked us not to tell Albano and Artemia for the moment,' Marco added. 'Because they're a bit conventional and traditional. That they would handle that themselves in due course.'

They didn't want an affronted, scandalised pair of servants walking out on them, I thought. I didn't go public with the thought.

'They said our sleeping arrangements up on the top floor were our own business,' Matteo went on. And if Marco wanted to exchange the two single beds in his room for one of doubles that were in both of ours...' He looked towards me when he said that last bit.

Tonio said, 'We're going to do that tomorrow – move the beds, I mean. When Artemia and Albano are out at church.'

'It all seems to have gone about as well as could possibly be expected,' Sol said. 'I mean, with all four of you nailing your colours to the mast at the same moment.'

I wondered if Sol, aged twenty-three, had come out to his parents yet. As for Alex – who had remained thoughtful and silent as he listened to all of this – I couldn't even imagine what his status was in this regard, and found I didn't want to think too much about that. But I felt I owed it to Sol to add something, just in case he hadn't yet come out to his folks and didn't know what to expect. 'It was a bit of a rough ride for everyone, though,' I said. 'Emotionally, I mean. A few tears were shed.' I left it at that. Sol (and Alex?) didn't need to know precisely who had cried and who had not.

We moved on from the bar to a restaurant just around the corner. Matteo had taken the precaution of booking a table earlier. Otherwise we'd never have got in. It was the height of summer now and day by day Venice was filling up even more uncomfortably with tourists.

After we'd eaten there was a feeling among five of us certainly that it would be fun to take a train over to the mainland and go to one of the gay clubs in Mestre. But the feeling went unspoken because of the presence among us of Alex. We were unsure about his sexual orientation and probably so was he. Had we made the proposal we wanted to he might well have said no, he'd rather go home instead, and that would have put the damper on an evening that was meant to be a celebration that included all of us.

But then something unexpected happened. Alex, who had been quietish for most of the evening, suddenly said, 'Do you guys want to come back to my place for a nightcap? I have wine, I have whisky…' He shrugged hopefully. 'Beer too.'

We tumbled boisterously through the streets. At some

Love in Venice

point Alex must have told us where he lived, but the name of a street in this labyrinth of tiny streets would have meant nothing to me. It turned out to be a mere fifteen minutes' walk from the restaurant and the Arco, in the general direction of the prison and the docks.

You needed to be fit to live where Alex did. It was on the fifth floor of an apartment block in which there was no lift. I wondered, as we made our way up the grey concrete, iron-railed, staircase, what to expect when we got to the top. A room in a palazzo on the Canal Grande was a bit of an unusual experience when it came to living abroad for the first time, and I had little idea of how ordinary Italians, ordinary Venetians, lived. Did Alex live like a student, in a bed-sit, and we'd all sit in a row on the single bed as we quaffed our drinks? Did he live with his parents still? Or share the place with other boatyard folk? At last we reached the top of the stairway. Alex unlocked his front door. And his living arrangements turned out to be none of the above.

He was the sole occupier of a comfortably if simply furnished two-bedroom apartment. There was a reasonably-sized living-dining-room and a separate kitchen. 'It was my parents' place,' Alex told us. He shrugged. 'They're both dead.' Sorry, we all said.

I asked, 'Do you have brothers and sister?' It's the question that an only child, such as myself, will always ask.

'One older sister,' said Alex. 'She lives in Verona with her husband and their kids.'

We drank what Alex offered us. Some had wine, some whisky, some beer. I don't remember what, or how much, I drank. We talked about this and that, and made plans for future sailing trips. The six of us. No kidnap attempts, of course. Laughing tipsily we promised one another that. Earlier in the evening we'd already gone over the events of a week ago, recounting again and again, like old soldiers, the details of an event we'd never forget. A day we'd lived through together and that had bonded us – the six of us – for life.

We knew eventually when the evening was about to break up. It was the moment when Alex's store of drink – which had been considerable – finally gave out. We all went bouncing down the five flights of stairs together, and said our goodnights when we were out on the pavement. The goodnight embrace and drunken chat between Sol and Alexa seemed to last a bit longer than Alex's farewells to the rest of us. There was mention of the last boat across the Giudecca Canal and whether Sol might already have missed it. There were always water taxis, of course... Eventually Sol broke away from Alex and came to say a final goodnight to the rest of us. He gave us a grin that was part sheepish, part elated, and part simply drunk. 'Well, catch up soon, guys,' he said to the four of us. 'It looks like I'm … um… It looks like I'm invited here for the night.'

We responded with whoops and shouts that were part mocking and part congratulatory. But though our drunken exclamation might have woken Alex's neighbours there was no surprise in them for us. We'd already guessed where Sol would be spending the night.

*

On Monday we went back to work. Marco and Tonio went back to their gondola landing stage in the heart of the tourist quarter, and Matteo and I resumed our explorations of Schubert, Beethoven, Chopin and Bach. It didn't feel like work, of course, for Matteo and myself.

In any case we took care to spend some time away from the portego and the instruments that inhabited it. There were still plenty of things to see in Venice. Matteo took me inside the Doge's Palace... It was like walking inside a Renaissance painting that had been turned inside out like a glove. And then we walked directly from its gilded chambers through the claustrophobic Bridge of Sighs into the prison on the other side of it. It was hard to imagine a starker contrast.

We experienced another contrast in the square outside the palace. I'd been there in the daytime, when tourists and pigeons competed to see who could be the most numerous. But then Matteo took me there one clear night around midnight, when a full moon rode high and bathed the empty square in bone-white light.

We didn't get to see inside the Basilica of St Mark that summer midnight: we had to make do with the outside of it – spooky, spiky domes and finials in the moonlight. But when we did go inside the ancient building it seemed to be existing in a state of perpetual midnight, its high vaults like the heavens, from which the eyes of saints picked out in mosaic glittered, star-like, down at us.

One Saturday Domenico and Annabelle took us to Florian's for coffee. The famous coffee shop seemed to be vying, when it came to décor, with the gilded Doge's Palace that stood just around the corner of the square. But, as Matteo had told me more than a month ago, the coffee was just the same as everywhere else in Venice. When something is as good as the coffee in most places in this city, it can be hard to better it.

But over that coffee at Florian's, Annabelle made an announcement. 'We'll be taking our usual holiday in August. Dad and I, that is. In the Alps.' She looked now at her two sons. 'This year, well, you're grown up now. You might not want to join us…'

Matteo came in quickly. 'Is Ben invited?'

'Yes,' said his mother.

No prizes for guessing what Marco said.

'And yes, of course,' said his mother. She smiled, and tried not to appear triumphant. She looked at me. 'You might get to hear a quail at last.'

NINETEEN

We left Venice by train. Just Matteo and I. Crossing that long bridge to the mainland I'd seen so often but not travelled over before now. Leaving Venice and its waters after two months there was an oddly wrenching experience, even though we were going to an equally lovely place and would in any case be back on the lagoon in just over a fortnight.

The Dragonettis owned a villa in the hills above Lake Como. From its front windows it looked down on the lake and, behind, had a view up to the still snow-capped Alps. We let the train take us as far is it could, then got a taxi for the last bit. Annabelle and Domenico would be joining us in four days' time, bringing Marco and Tonio. They had let us go on ahead 'to get the place ready'. But there was very little to be got ready. The house was clean and sun-filled. In real countryside, it was not overlooked. Its garden not only had those views of lake and mountain but also contained a swimming pool. Matteo and I hadn't been there half an hour before we had taken all each other's clothes off.

'Actually,' I confessed, 'I can't swim.'

Matteo gave me one of his special looks. 'Can't swim? And you're going to be an honorary Venetian? You know they keep saying it's sinking. You'll need to swim when it finally does. Looks like I'd better teach you.'

So Matteo did teach me. What could be more idyllic than being taught to swim, naked in a swimming pool, by your equally naked lover, under blue Alpine skies, with the sparkle of Lake Como a little way below you, and the calls of quail floating up from the pasture of a side valley?

Just one thing, possibly. Matteo's words: you're going to be an honorary Venetian. Would he and I one day live together in Venice? Neither of us could know the answer; life never takes us to the places we expect it to. The wonderful thing was that he was thinking the thought, that he was actually imagining it as a possibility. What would actually happen was less important.

We spent most of that four-day period before the others arrived in a state of total nudity. When life presents you with such an opportunity it seems a shame not to take advantage of it. I thought that Matteo looked lovely without his clothes on. He thought that I did. We weren't unalike physically, though his light fuzzes of leg and body hair were dark while mine were golden. He was an inch taller than me, and his cock was half an inch longer. We were in love with our similarities, in love with our little differences. In love, quite simply.

I liked the way Matteo looked when he was naked. He liked the way I looked naked. How do I know that? Because he said so, and he'd never lied to me yet. Because the way he looked at me told the same story. And the way he looked at me... Well, that had never lied to me. It never would, it never could. And if one day it told me a different story to the one his words were telling me – then I would know about it and have to deal with whatever lay behind that.

But that was if, not when. I knew we liked the way we looked now. But would that still be the case in five years' time? In ten years' time? In twenty … when we'd both be around forty? I couldn't know; I didn't have the experience. But I knew the way that Domenico and Annabelle still looked at each other sometimes and I thought … well, yes, maybe. Then I realised the implication of what I was thinking. That I wanted Matteo and me to be together in five, ten, twenty years from now… The thought was a difficult one. Like when you sit and think for a few minutes about the size of the Milky Way and then the constellations beyond it.

We rarely left the house and its garden, except to go to the village shop for beer and other essentials occasionally. (OK, we did put on shorts and T-shirts when we went there.) And to go for night-time strolls along the lake shore, on the edge of the range of the shore road's lamp-lights. For most of the day we lounged by the pool, reading, or simply playing with each other. Fucking each other on the short grass or impudently wanking each other by the pool-side and coming on each other's bellies.

There was a piano in the villa. Of course there was. A baby grand Steinway. We spent a little time each day at it, but not too long. We were on holiday, not really working. But my music had come: the scores for the pieces I was to play with my former teacher Martin in

November. Martin had got hold of the piano parts for all the pieces we were doing and had posted them over to me. There was nothing too stressful about this. At least, not for now, on holiday in August. The two difficult works were ones I knew already, while the accompaniments to the showy violin solos by Sarasate and Kreisler were easy. I played them through to Matteo just for his information.

Then, punctually, the senior Dragonettis, with Marco and Tonio, arrived in the car that Domenico kept garaged for most of the time at the Piazza di Roma in Venice. Matteo and I heard its engine coming up the track-way. We had just time to get into our speedos before going to the door to welcome them.

*

And so began our fortnight's family holiday. Sometimes we all went to places together. Sometimes we younger people went around in fab four mode, and sometimes we divided up into couples. Then we were just two: me and Matteo. Doing our thing together. Our thing? What would that thing have been? Being in love. That was what it amounted to.

There were barbecues, occasional dinner and drinks parties with neighbours, visits to lakeside restaurants. It was like any family holiday. I said that – I used those words – one night to Matteo. We were sitting by the pool, under the garden lights, out of the others' earshot. 'Except that it isn't my family,' I added.

Love in Venice

Matteo looked at me very seriously. 'It is,' he said. 'It is now. As much as it's my family. It is and it always will be.'

Sometimes I found I had no words to express things with. I just said, 'Thank you.'

*

One day Annabelle and Domenico were invited to lunch with neighbours down in the village who were old friends of theirs. We younger four found we had no particular plans for the day. The weather was hot and the sky clear. We told the Dragonetti parents that we'd decided to spend the day lounging around in the garden, beside the pool...

...We were like children when their parents have gone out. No sooner had the sound of the car faded down the track-way than we boisterously ripped one another's shorts off, laughing as we got naked all together, for the first time (for the first time as a group of four, that is) since that day on the Lido, weeks ago.

We rough and tumbled each other on the grass beside the pool. I reacquainted myself with Marco's cock, and Tonio's. And, of course, so did Matteo. They hadn't changed in shape or size. Matteo's was still indisputably the largest of the four. Mine was second biggest, followed by Marco's. Tonio's was the smallest by some way. But it was also the prettiest of the four: life has a way of balancing one thing with another...

The other thing that hadn't changed about our four

penises since we'd had them all out and on show together on the Lido… They were all long, straight and hard.

I found myself lying on my back with Marco lying on top of me, rubbing his cock up and down against mine. Shoulder to shoulder, elbow to elbow with us, Matteo lay sprawld on top of Tonio, getting Tonio and himself excited in the exact same way that Marco was doing with me.

After a while I could feel the wet warmth of Marco's pre-come drizzling on my belly. Then I heard him say, 'Oh fuck, I'm going to come!'

I had an instinct, somehow, that he shouldn't come with me. I said urgently, 'Do it with Tonio.'

We must have all had the same idea. For we all put it into practice within the space of about a second – as was evidently vital if we weren't all going to end up coming in a place we weren't supposed to be. Marco rolled off me, and Matteo slid himself across from Tonio into the space Marco had vacated on top of me. Marco quickly hoisted himself over his brother's back, sliding over him, brushing him with his wet dick (obviously I couldn't see that … but it was more than easy to imagine) and quickly sliding onto Tonio.

'You're all wet,' said Matteo, as he continued from where Marco had left off on top of me.

'Blame your brother for that,' I said. A second later it was clear that Marco had climaxed – he did it quite noisily and energetically – and Tonio, lying underneath him, followed his example a second after that. Then I shot my own load almost simultaneously with Matteo and we felt each other's hot wetness spurt forcefully, unseen, between our two tummies.

For the rest of that day I called Marco Tomassio.

Later, when we were in bed together, Matteo and I talked in the darkness about what had happened by the swimming pool. Somehow we'd managed to get things 'sort of right', we agreed. And I thought that 'sort of right' was about as good as things ever got in this imperfect world.

'You know…' Matteo said suddenly, then stopped. His voice sounded as if it was going into confessional mode.

'Yes?' I prompted, and scratched the back of his head as he lay in my arms.

'You know that night in Chioggia when we were drunk with Alex and Sol… And we all took turns to take Alex's cock in our mouths for a minute or so.'

'Yes,' I said. 'I won't be forgetting that easily.'

'We also stroked Sol's cock a bit, didn't we…?'

'It would have been hard to resist,' I said robustly. 'He was wagging it in our faces. And it is spectacularly big. Even compared to yours.'

'Yes,' said Matteo. 'But that wasn't the only time I

touched Alex's…'

'Ah,' I said. I felt my heart begin to sink. 'Then I suppose I ought to tell you that wasn't the only time I touched Sol's.'

'I see,' said Matteo. 'Do you think we ought to tell each other?'

'I suppose so,' I said. 'Now we seem to have started.' But I wasn't looking forward to this at all. 'You first?' I offered generously. I wondered with dismay what I was going to hear.

'It wasn't a big deal,' Matteo said. But I felt him tremble in my arms.

'It's OK,' I said. 'It's OK.'

'That first time Alex came home with us… I took him upstairs to see the paintings. To see his ancestor's picture of our palazzo…'

'You were only gone a minute…'

'We didn't come or anything,' Matteo said nervously.

'Neither did Sol and me…' I found I needed to get this in right away.

'We just put our hands down each other's jeans and had a bit of a feel…'

'It was the same with Sol and me…'

Matteo asked, 'When...? Where...?'

'In the boathouse that day. When you were taking photos...'

'I was only gone a minute...'

'That was all it took. Like with you.'

'Umm,' said Matteo thoughtfully. Now he stroked my hair. 'Did you kiss Sol?'

'Well, Sol kissed me... Oh, all right. It was a two-way thing. Yes, I did kiss Sol.'

Matteo said softly, 'It was the same with Alex and me.'

We held each other in silence for a minute, but our hands and arms and legs and lips and noses gave each other all the reassurance that at that moment we craved.

Then I asserted my seniority for a moment: my pathetic little seniority of two young years. 'Listen,' I said. 'If we really are in for the long haul – and I so hope we are – and if nothing worse than those things come between us ... then we'll be one of the luckiest couples in the world.'

After a short pause for thought Matteo agreed. 'You're right,' he said. 'And your call this afternoon was right. Getting Marco off your belly and back to Tonio for his ejac. Replacing him with me...'

'Thank you,' I said. 'It suddenly seemed the right

thing to do.'

'Then could you do just one more thing for me?' Matteo ran his hand down my spine.

'What's that?' I asked a bit suspiciously.

Matteo giggled in my ear. 'Just stop calling my brother Tomassio.'

TWENTY

While we holidayed beside Lake Como two subjects seemed to be off-limits where discussions between Matteo and me were concerned. One was the question of where Matteo was to live during term time while he was studying in London. The other was the matter of what I would do, once I'd finished coaching him in Venice, with the rest of my life.

We hadn't been back in Venice before the first of those questions was broached ... as it happened, by Annabelle. She said to Matteo, over dinner on our second night back and a-propos of nothing we'd been talking about till then, 'I spoke to Sarah today.' The name meant nothing to me, though since Matteo nodded in response it evidently did to him. His mother went on. 'You've said nothing about making plans for accommodation while you're in London. Well, Sarah has a big spare room and she'll very happily let you have it, plus breakfast and evening meals, for a very modest charge.'

Matteo continued to look at Annabelle like a rabbit caught in headlights, while Marco turned to me with a look on his face that plainly said that the next move was up to me.

I made the move immediately, before Matteo could open his mouth. 'That won't be necessary, Annabelle. Matteo will be living with me.'

A rare frown crossed Annabelle's features as she turned to face me across the table. 'I thought you just had one small room in a house-share.'

'That's true,' I said. I didn't mention the fact that it had only one very narrow single bed in it. Annabelle had enough information to be going on with. 'But it'll do for us till we find something bigger and better.' I noticed that Matteo had remained mute. Domenico hadn't spoken either.

'Sweetheart…' Annabelle was addressing me. She'd never called me sweetheart before. It alarmed me. I kind of knew what was coming next. 'How will you get something bigger and better? Matteo has only a small allowance from us to live on. And you… Well, I haven't heard you say anything about a next job yet.'

This was what happened when you became a son-in-law, I suddenly realised. 'I'm working on it,' I said. 'You know about my concert in November…'

'Yes, and I think that's wonderful – and you know I think that. But it won't pay the rent and bills for October, will it?'

'I'll get a job,' I said. 'Doing anything.' I remembered something Matteo had once said to me. 'I'll get a job cleaning school toilets. Whatever it takes.'

Annabelle looked at me. I tried to make out the expression on her face. She seemed a bit affronted, I thought, but was also trying not to laugh. I realised then that if I had managed to capture Matteo as a partner for life then part of the prize was having a mother-in-law for my remaining years. Ah well, if I had to have a mother-in-law and it turned out to be Annabelle ... I could do much worse.

Domenico spoke. Quietly, reasonably. 'I think we need to hear what Matteo thinks. It's his future, his life we're talking about.'

Matteo took a breath. Then, 'I'll stay with Ben,' he said. 'Wherever he lives. Whatever he finds himself doing for a living. If he ends up cleaning toilets ... I'll lend a hand in my spare time.'

Those pianist's hands of his...

There was a second's silence. Marco broke it. 'Well, that's sorted, then,' he said. 'Good.'

*

My last month and a half in Venice went by in a flash. Matteo and I resumed our happy way of working at the two pianos, Marco and Tonio put in a couple more weeks working at the gondola company (the boys accepted no more lifts in sailing boats from strange men) and then returned to school. While returning to work meant nothing particularly new or different for Matteo and me, going back to school was a very different thing for the younger pair. At the end of the previous term they had been two boys who had sex together. Now they had openly proclaimed themselves a couple who loved each other; at least they had admitted the fact to themselves and then come out to their parents. But would they do the same at school? Matteo and I wondered about this between ourselves, but didn't stick our noses in.

After a few days back at school, though, Marco and Tonio brought the subject up with us. 'We don't go trumpeting it around that we're a couple,' Marco said. 'But people can see that we're closer than we used to be. We don't pretend we're not. And if anyone wants to ask us if we're a couple of *culos* we'll tell them the score. But so far no-one has.' It seemed like a reasonable way to be going on.

During that tail-end of August and through September we all went sailing with Alex and Sol a few times. It was Alex who brought up the subject of the gay bars and clubs on the mainland, in Mestre and Padova. We went to both places, all six of us, a couple of times. From Mestre we got taxis back to Venice, a tight squeeze for six, but we were all quite intimate after all. From Padova we simply returned by the first morning train.

Alex in gay clubs? Gay bars? It might have surprised us a month earlier but it didn't now. For one of the first things Sol had told us when we returned to Venice from Lake Como was that he was moving out from the room he had in his boss's house on Giudecca and moving in with Alex in his apartment near the prison and the docks. 'That's great,' I said. 'You'll just be fifteen minutes walk away.'

'Handy for drinks at the palazzo,' Sol had said. Then his face went sort of shy and he said, 'It makes good

Love in Venice

sense, after all. Alex has plenty of space at the apartment.' Sol had blushed faintly as he said it. ...And plenty of room for Sol in his double bed too, I thought. And in his heart also.

*

The move back to England frightened me. Not because I had no job to go to. Not because I knew I would miss the beauty of Venice and life in a palazzo and on the lagoon. My worry was that Matteo wouldn't settle there. That he wouldn't be happy, sharing a tiny room in a terraced house in Woolwich. That, seeing me in such a setting would take the gilt off our gingerbread relationship for him and that, in time, he would want to move on and away from me. It was one thing to boast to your mother, under the coffered ceiling of a Venetian dining-room that you loved your partner so much that you would clean school toilets with him. It would be a different matter altogether if it actually came to that.

Happily I didn't have to go cleaning school toilets. I got a temporary job in the box office at the Royal Festival Hall. It wasn't far from Woolwich on the train. The work was fairly demanding – you needed a clear head and an iron refusal to panic as you dealt with the conflicting requirements of your customers and your computer screen – but at least it kept my hands quite clean. And there were concessionary classical concert tickets to be had for Matteo and me.

There was a small irony attached to this particular employment though. The Royal Festival Hall is part of a complex that comprises three concert halls. The Festival Hall is the biggest, the next one down is the Queen Elizabeth Hall, while the smallest of the three, used mainly for solo recitals and chamber concerts, is the Purcell Room. The Purcell Room was the venue for the recital I was going to give with my former chamber-music coach Martin in a few weeks' time. The box office system was shared between the three auditoria. Some evenings I found myself selling tickets at the box-office desk in the Purcell Room's foyer. And sometimes I found myself selling advance tickets for the concert I would myself be playing at. I wondered how many box-office clerks had had that experience … and then thought that that perhaps the number was greater than most people would suppose.

Saying, *'Buona giornata* – have a good day,' to Matteo on the morning of his first day at college, when he got off the train at Greenwich while I stayed on for the last few miles to Waterloo, made me feel like a parent sending a child off to his first day at school. Matteo looked nervous but as though he was trying to hide it. I didn't ask him if he was nervous; that would have made it worse. But I worried about him all day. Not until he came home, radiant with relief at the way the day had gone, did I relax and share his relief with him. That took the form of a fuck on our single bed before we went out for an Indian meal. The latter experience was a new one for Matteo. But he took to it like a duck to water – no less so than he'd taken to having sex with me three months ago.

Love in Venice

The following day I travelled to the college with Matteo. Not because he needed his hand held – far from it – but because I needed to talk to Martin about the concert at which I was to be his accompanist – or as he kindly put it, his recital partner – in just over a month's time.

I had known Martin for three years. But only as a teacher. He was a tall spare man in his early forties, with glasses and receding hair. Nothing spectacular to look at. Though he had plenty of personality and was a wonderfully encouraging coach. This was my first encounter with him in his role as concert soloist.

We talked about the music, we arranged to run through the programme in a fortnight's time, and then to do some proper rehearsing in the days immediately before the concert date. In the meantime – I had to explain to Martin – I would need to practise, and I didn't have a piano at home.

'One day,' said Martin, 'you will need a home with a piano in it.'

'Yes,' I said. 'And so will my partner.' Martin gave me a slightly puzzled look. 'Partner as in boyfriend,' I clarified.

Martin nodded his understanding. 'Right. Got you now.'

'He's a student here.' I suddenly felt I had to explain everything all at once. 'You won't have come across him yet. It was him I was teaching in Venice all this summer.'

'Would that be Matteo Dragonetti?' Martin asked.

'Yes,' I said. 'How did you know?'

'His piano professor was talking about him yesterday. He's pretty good, to put it simply. You must have coached him well.'

'I'm not really sure…'

'Listen,' Martin interrupted in a businesslike way, perhaps afraid I was going to go into more detail about my life in Venice with Matteo than he wanted to know. 'Until you've got a piano of your own, you must use the practice rooms here. Just carry on like you did when you were a student here. Book any room that's available as and when you want. Book it under your name and add mine underneath. If anybody queries it they'll have to come to me.'

So that was what happened. Matteo did his practice at the college, of course: in the evenings if I had an evening shift at the Festival Hall, or sometimes at other times of day. And I practised there when I was free. Sometimes I coincided with Matteo and we'd travel home together, sometimes we'd be setting out together on a morning train.

Matteo accepted our domestic arrangement. He adapted to living in a poky little room with me – it must have been a major culture shock after a Venetian palazzo – and showed no signs of going off me or getting tired of me. Life seemed to be going through a period in which everything was perfect. Except there's never a time in life when everything is perfect. One major minefield still lay ahead of me. I hadn't yet told my parents that I lived with Matteo. Not in the sense that we were a couple at any rate. I hadn't told my parents I was gay.

Adam Wye

TWENTY-ONE

During our first month or so in London I took Matteo down to Redhill twice to have Sunday lunch with my parents. I hoped that they might see the situation for themselves and I wouldn't have to spell it out. Yes, that was cowardly of me, I know. But who hasn't found himself a coward at times like these?

It was soon obvious that Mum and Dad didn't want to see the situation for themselves. What could be more natural, they must have thought, than that Matteo and I should have become good friends during our three months working together in Venice? What more natural than that he would lodge with me, as I shared a house just a couple of miles from the college where Matteo was now a student? What more natural than that I would want to bring him home and introduce him to my parents? I was on pretty close terms with Matteo's parents, after all.

My parents had invitation tickets to the Purcell Room concert. They would be joining me and Martin and his wife plus a small group of other selected friends for a restaurant supper afterwards. Would Matteo be able to join us too? I would have to ask Martin nearer the time.

I didn't have to ask Martin. Matteo answered the question from the other end. One night when we were in our cramped bed together he said to me, 'You'll need a page-turner, of course.' Violin soloists traditionally play without the score in front of them, but their piano accompanist usually plays from the music. Not least because, should one of the partners take a wrong turning in the music, somebody has to be able to find the way back to the correct road. But it helps if there's someone there to turn the pages of the pianist's score.

'It's OK,' I said with an insider's knowledge. 'The Festival Hall has a small fleet of page-turners. They'll provide one.' OK, I had an insider's knowledge. But for the moment I'd lost touch with my lover's instinct. I was reminded of it pretty quickly though, as I felt Matteo stiffen in my arms.

'I just thought you might prefer to have someone who knew you, that's all,' he said a bit coolly.

'Oh God,' I said. 'I'm sorry. I thought you wouldn't want to demean yourself by turning pages for me. I thought you'd want a seat in the front row…'

'Then you didn't know me well enough.' He sounded huffy. Also very close to tears.

I pulled his head close against mine, rubbing it with my hands to comfort him. I heard the brittle crackle of his hair beneath my finger ends. I said, 'I'd love nothing better than for you to be on the platform with me. Turning the pages. Sitting by my side. I'm sorry for being stupid. Sorry for getting it wrong.' Then it wasn't Matteo but I that cried, and it became Matteo's job to comfort me.

The upshot of that was that I told Martin the

arrangement: Matteo would be my page-turner for the evening. And I didn't need to ask Martin if Matteo could join us for supper afterwards. Martin simply told me so.

*

Was I nervous before the concert? Of course I was. No professional can appear in front of a discerning audience, one that includes the critics from the national press, and not feel nervous. But I didn't give way to nerves. My hands didn't shake. Arriving at the piano stool to the anticipatory applause of three hundred people I didn't find myself unable to decipher the dots in front of me, as I'd heard could happen even to seasoned pros when they were least expecting it. Matteo took his seat beside me. He turned to me and gave me a beaming smile. I smiled back at him. That exchange of smiles gave me the courage and the calm I needed. I knew things were going to be OK.

Then Martin walked on. He was no longer the ordinary-looking music professor I knew. Transformed by white tie and tails, his hair neatly brushed, his glasses not required, he seemed to have shed ten years and grown about a foot. He looked what he was – a concert artist of international renown – and he looked more than confident in the role.

Mozart's big violin sonata in A. Beethoven's big sonata in C minor. I'd played them both before, in front of different audiences of critical students and teachers at the college. That stood me in good stead now. And A major, the brightest of keys, followed by the darkest – C minor – went together as well as cherries followed by bitter chocolate. I'd never realised that before. I learnt it now.

I played not a single wrong note in either piece! I put my heart and soul into them. Martin did too. That went without saying. At the end of the first sonata the applause was big. Matteo grinned at me. After the Beethoven the applause was massive. The audience had warmed, had taken to Martin and me in a big way. They might also have been taken with the striking looks of the smiling page-turner, Matteo…

It was the interval, suddenly. We were back in the band room. And there Matteo and I stayed while Martin returned for his unaccompanied piece by Ysaye. Then Matteo and I were back on stage again. But the last bit was child's play. I romped through those Sarasate and Kreisler accompaniments without a care in the world. Time went in a flash. I was standing, bowing – Martin had stood and bowed first then indicated that I should join him. Though this applause was for Martin I still basked in it. I had to resist the urge to haul Matteo to his feet and get him to take a share in the applause; I did know that would have been going too far. I would thank him in my own more intimate way later, privately. But before that time came something else happened for which I would have to thank Matteo.

We were a large group at the restaurant table at that celebratory supper. Nine or ten, I think. Martin had booked us into an Italian place – one of many near the Festival Hall and the rest of the South Bank complex. I was a little worried about how Matteo would react to Italian restaurants in London, and for that reason I hadn't taken him to any till now. I was relieved to find that he seemed quite happy with the experience. Well, after all, as far as this evening was concerned he was only the page-turner.

Martin, meeting Matteo socially for the first time (I had introduced them in passing at the college) was particularly nice to him, and so was his wife, which I appreciated. Of course Matteo was very young and good-looking, which never hurts. Martin actually told an old story about a page-turner.

'The pianist Artur Rubinstein used to tell this story,' he began, while chiselling his way into a pizza. 'I'm not sure if we're supposed to believe it. It's about the great violinist George Enescu...' Martin looked around the table and saw that the name meant nothing to most people. 'Yehudi Menuhin's teacher,' he added helpfully. 'Well, a wealthy friend of Enescu's had a son who played the violin with more confidence than talent, and who one day hired a major concert hall in Paris to give a recital. The boy's father begged Enescu to play the piano accompaniments for him and Enescu agreed, although reluctantly, because – violin virtuoso though he was – he wasn't all that great a pianist.

'Of course Enescu's name on the bill sold tickets and on the night the hall was full. But Enescu got an attack of stage fright as he approached the piano and decided he needed someone to help him turn the pages. Looking round the audience he saw his great friend Alfred Cortot sitting there...' Realising that the name wouldn't mean much to some of the dinner guests Martin went on seamlessly, 'Cortot was probably the greatest player of Chopin in the generation before Rubinstein. Anyway, Enescu beckons Cortot up to the platform and asks him to turn the pages. And everything goes more or less without problem. Until the review comes out in the press in the morning. "An unexpected surprise was enjoyed at last night's recital at the Salle Pleyel. A man who delights us when he plays the violin entertained us, for a change, at the piano. And the greatest French pianist of his generation turned the pages for him. While the violin solos were played by a young man who would have been better employed turning the pages."' There was a little polite laughter. Martin probably didn't tell jokes as well as Rubinstein had.

'I mention this,' Martin went on, 'because you can never tell when you meet a page-turner, what depths he has within him. This young man, I happen to know,' he gestured with his pizza-cutter towards Matteo, 'is blessed with a great talent as a pianist. He's highly thought of by his teachers at the college. That's not to say,' he continued, now pointing his cutlery at me, 'that *this* young man is any less talented. But Ben's talents were on show tonight, Matteo's were not.' Martin turned to my parents. 'You should be proud to have such an asset as an addition to your family.'

I wrote in an earlier chapter that when Matteo came out at his family's dinner table it was as though a rock had fallen through the ceiling. Well, it was exactly the same now. Except that this time the rock had fallen through my parents' ceiling. I could see the shocked looks on both their faces. And yet it was a lucky moment. My parents had met Martin twice before, at college. They'd seen him in his dowdy role as music teacher. Tonight they'd watched him, in white tie and tails, deliver magical dazzling things on a violin in a brightly lit London concert hall, among three hundred rapt people. They'd seen me up there on the same platform, also in white tie and tails, managing not to put a foot wrong with Mozart and Beethoven. For this short time we inhabited a charmed space. Briefly, for this hour only, we probably could do no wrong in their eyes, but carried with us the auras of angels. Matteo too, was shining in the reflected illumination. Though not in white tie, he'd been suited and Chelsea-booted, and shared our auras.

'What exactly...?' began my father haltingly.

'I'm gay, Dad,' I said. 'I always thought you knew that.' (The second bit was a lie, I'm afraid, but sometimes...)

Then I heard Matteo say to my parents, in the firmest voice I'd ever heard from him, 'You've got the most wonderful son in the world in Ben. It's an honour to be his boyfriend.'

'Good heavens!' said my mother, and there were murmurs of surprise from around the table. Not of surprise that Matteo and I were a gay couple, only that this scene should be playing out publicly in front of them.

'Ben,' my father said to me, 'this is going to take your mother and me a bit of getting used to. In the meantime I have to ask you: are you as serious about Matteo as he says he is about you?'

'Yes, Dad,' I said. I was amazed at myself for not breaking down. But I found I didn't even feel like crying.

'In that case,' said my father, 'when we've had a bit of time to get used to the idea ... well, you'll probably be able to expect our blessing.'

'I heard the funniest story the other day,' piped up a woman's voice from the other end of the table. 'Some friends of ours were going to have their house painted...'

We all turned with gratitude towards the speaker and pretended to be riveted while we listened to her jolly story.

*

'I can't believe you did that,' I said to Martin on the pavement afterwards, as we were all separating to go our different ways homeward. I made sure that I was out of earshot, for the moment, of my parents.

'Well, I did,' said Martin. 'I thought I could save you a bit of time and trouble. And it did seem like a good moment.'

'I don't know what to say,' I told him. 'Except thank you.'

'That's probably enough in the circumstances,' said Martin. 'And thank you, Ben, thank you again, for being a superb partner in Mozart and Beethoven this evening. We'll do it again sometime.' My parents were coming towards us. To say their goodnights presumably. They would be taking the underground towards Victoria, Matteo and I the mainline train to Woolwich. 'Just one more thing,' Martin said. 'Before your parents get here. There's a job coming up at the college. One of the junior piano teachers is leaving. I wondered if you'd be interested…'

'I…' I began.

'Good,' said Martin. 'But keep it under your hat for the moment. It isn't yet official. I suppose you can tell Matteo though. But he must keep it under his hat too. The chap in question, the one who's leaving, happens to be Matteo's teacher.' My parents were upon us. 'Phone me,' said Martin quickly. 'Come and see me at the college and we'll talk about it some more.'

Love in Venice

PER SEMPRE

It's nearly Christmas. Matteo and I are flying back to Venice. Easy-Jet from Gatwick. So much has happened in such a short space of time that I feel almost dizzy thinking about it.

I got the job, that's the first thing. I start at the beginning of the new term in January. On the strength of the decent salary this will entail, and of future prospects, Matteo and I are moving into a good-sized flat in Docklands. My parents and Matteo's parents have agreed to pay the first two month's rent for us between them. To help us get started, as they put it. The flat is quite a size, at least its principal room is. It needs to be, in order to accommodate the two full-size grand pianos, both second-hand Bechsteins, that the Dragonetti parents are giving us as a present.

Docklands is nice. It's very handy for Trinity College. You can actually see the top of the college's Christopher Wren gables from one of the windows in the flat we're moving into. It's also pretty well surrounded by water, so Matteo should feel quite at home there.

We have longer-term plans too, though. Matteo and I hope to launch ourselves as a piano duo partnership, giving public recitals at two pianos. People we've talked to about this always laugh and say we'll be a younger, male version of the Labèque Sisters. But why not? we always answer. They've done pretty well out of it. Like them we have the looks as well as the talent and the oomph.

We shall divide our time between London and Venice. London in term-time, Venice during the vacations. Like now. Of course the plans may have to be adapted somewhat when we've got concert engagements…

Matteo says sometimes, aren't we being too optimistic, too naïve in our expectations? After all, the world only has room, each generation, for a few dozen top-flight concert pianists.

You have to aim high, I tell him. Like a pilot. Pull back on the column, head skywards and see where that takes us. After all, if we fall back to earth with a bump we'll still be holding onto each other. For ever, Matteo agrees solemnly. I repeat the words back to him in Italian. *'Per sempre.'*

'I can see the sea now,' says Matteo, squinting into the porthole, leaning against my shoulder. (It's my turn for the window seat this time.)

'Yeah,' I say. For I've seen it too now. The shine of the morning sun on the Adriatic, appearing suddenly like the flash of diamonds when a box of jewellery is opened near a window's light.

We're nearly there. We're dying to see Marco again – and Tonio. We won't see Sol and Alex though – which is a pity. They've got a winter job crewing a film star's yacht around the Caribbean. We've told them to be sure to text us if they get kidnapped.

Love in Venice

In a few days' time my parents will be joining us. Just for a few days over Christmas itself. Christmas in Venice. Routine perhaps for Matteo, but a new experience for me.

Our plane banks steeply and begins the turn that will line it up for the runway at Marco Polo. As we straighten up onto what pilots call finals the lagoon comes flashing and sparkling into sight outside the window. Venice lies on its surface, like a pattern of dark leaves laid flat on a silver salver. There is the main island, there the Canal of the Giudecca, and there the long thin railway bridge that connects the Sea City to the mainland. 'It's beautiful,' I say.

'Take my hand,' says Matteo and he gives it to me. I clasp it. We can't embrace properly. Our seatbelts are fastened and we shall be touching down in ninety seconds or so. For the moment we can't even kiss easily. But Matteo squirms sideways towards me. Our knees touch, and our shoulders, and I feel a motion in Matteo's chest as he somehow presses it sideways against mine.

THE END

****

Adam Wye

Also by Adam Wye: **Boy Next Door**. **Gay in Moscow**.

About the Author

Adam Wye is a pen-name of the British author **Anthony McDonald**. (You can find Anthony McDonald's author page on Amazon, with information about the books he has written under his own name.) Under the name Adam Wye he is creating a new series of Gay Romance novels, light and sexy. **Boy Next Door**, **Love in Venice**, and **Gay in Moscow** are the first three in the series. More to follow in the months and years ahead!

www.anthonymcdonald.co.uk

Printed in Great Britain
by Amazon

The Five Jars

THE FIVE JARS

M.R. JAMES

TUFTS & CO.

The Five Jars
by Montague Rhodes James

First edition: March 2025
Printed and distributed by
Amazon.com, Inc., 1996-2025

TUFTS & CO.
Fair access to culture, fair prices.

'The Five Jars,' was originally published by Longman, Green & Co., New York, in 1922.

© of the photograph: unknown author, 1900
© of this edition: Tufts & Co., 2025
All rights reserved

ISBN: 979-83-13993-59-1

To the best of our knowledge, the following published work is presumed to be in the public domain. Every effort has been made to ascertain and acknowledge its copyright status, but if there's any unwitting oversight on our part, we will be happy to rectify the error. This work has been faithfully transcribed from original sources and early publications, hence its anachronic language which might contain what today's may be considered errors or misspellings. For any issues or concerns, please, feel free to contact us.

No part of this publication may be reproduced, stored in or introduced into a retrieval system, or transmitted, in any form or by any means without the prior written permission of the publisher. This book is sold subject to the condition that it shall not be resold, lent, hired out or otherwise circulated without the express prior consent of the publisher.

Contents

9   Chapter I: The Discovery
19   Chapter II: The First Jar
25   Chapter III: The Second Jar
33   Chapter IV: The Small People
45   Chapter V: Danger to the Jars
59   Chapter VI: The Cat, Wag, Slim and Others
73   Chapter VII: The Bat-Ball
83   Chapter VIII: Wag at Home

Chapter I
The Discovery

MY DEAR JANE,

You remember that you were puzzled when I told you I had heard something from the owls— or if not puzzled (for I know you have some experience of these things), you were at any rate anxious to know exactly how it happened. Perhaps the time has now come for you to be told.

It was really luck, and not any skill of mine, that put me in the way of it; luck, and also being ready to believe more than I could see. I have promised not to put down on paper the name of the wood where it happened: that can keep till we meet; but all the rest I can tell exactly as it came about.

It is a wood with a stream at the edge of it; the water is brown and clear. On the other side of it are flat meadows, and beyond these a hillside quite covered with an oak wood. The stream has alder-trees along it, and is pretty well shaded over; the sun hits it in places and makes flecks of light through the leaves.

The day I am thinking of was a very hot one in early September. I had come across the meadows with some idea of sitting by the stream and reading. The only change in my

The Five Jars

plans that I made was that instead of sitting down I lay down, and instead of reading I went to sleep.

You know how sometimes— but very, very seldom— you see something in a dream which you are quite sure is real. So it was with me this time. I did not dream any story or see any people; I only dreamt of a plant. In the dream no one told me anything about it: I just saw it growing under a tree: a small bit of the tree root came into the picture, an old gnarled root covered with moss, and with three sorts of eyes in it, round holes trimmed with moss— you know the kind. The plant was not one I should have thought much about, though certainly it was not one that I knew: it had no flowers or berries, and grew quite squat in the ground; more like a yellow aconite without the flower than anything else. It seemed to consist of a ring of six leaves spread out pretty flat with nine points on each leaf. As I say, I saw this quite clearly, and remembered it because six times nine makes fifty-four, which happens to be a number which I had a particular reason for remembering at that moment.

Well, there was no more in the dream than that: but, such as it was, it fixed itself in my mind like a photograph, and I was sure that if ever I saw that tree root and that plant, I should know them again. And, though I neither saw nor heard anything more of them than I have told you, it was borne in upon my mind that the plant was worth finding.

When I woke up I still lay, feeling very lazy, on the grass with my head within a foot or two of the edge of the stream and listened to its noise, until in five or six minutes— whether I began to doze off again or not does not much matter— the water-sound became like words, and said, "*Trickle-up, trickle-up,*" an immense number of times. It pleased me, for though in poetry we hear a deal about bab-

bling brooks, and though I am particularly fond of the noise they make, I never was able before to pretend that I could hear any words. And when I did finally get up and shake myself awake I thought I would anyhow pay so much attention to what the water said as to stroll up the stream instead of down. So I did: it took me through the flat meadows, but still along the edge of the wood, and still every now and then I heard the same peculiar noise which sounded like *Trickle-up*.

Not so very long after, I came to a place where another stream ran out of the wood into the one I had been following, and just below the place where the two joined there was— not a bridge, but a pole across, and another pole to serve as a rail, by which you could cross, without trouble. I did cross, not thinking much about it, but with some idea of looking at this new little stream, which went at a very quick pace and seemed to promise small rapids and waterfalls a little higher up. Now when I got to the edge of it, there was no mistake: it was saying "*Trickle-up*," or even "*Track-up*," much plainer than the old one. I stepped across it and went a few yards up the old stream. Before the new one joined it, it was saying nothing of the kind. I went back to the new one: it was talking as plain as print. Of course there were no two words about what must be done now. Here was something quite new, and even if I missed my tea, it had got to be looked into. So I went up the new stream into the wood.

Though I was well on the look-out for unusual things— in particular the plant, which I could not help thinking about— I cannot say there was anything peculiar about the stream or the plants or the insects or the trees (except the words which the water kept saying) so long as I was in the flat part of the wood. But soon I came to a steepish bank—

The Five Jars

the land began to slope up suddenly and the rapids and waterfalls of the brook were very gay and interesting. Then, besides *Track-up*, which was now its word always instead of *Trickle*, I heard every now and then *All right*, which was encouraging and exciting. Still, there was nothing out of the way to be seen, look as I might.

The climb up the slope or bank was fairly long. At the top was a kind of terrace, pretty level and with large old trees growing upon it, mainly oaks. Behind there was a further slope up and still more woodland: but that does not matter now. For the present I was at the end of my wanderings. There was no more stream, and I had found what of all natural things I think pleases me best, a real spring of water quite untouched.

Five or six oaks grew in something like a semicircle, and in the middle of the flat ground in front of them was an almost perfectly round pool, not more than four or five feet across. The bottom of it in the middle was pale sand which was continually rising up in little egg-shaped mounds and falling down again. It was the clearest and strongest spring of the kind I had ever seen, and I could have watched it for hours. I did sit down by it and watch it for some time without thinking of anything but the luck I had had to find it. But then I began to wonder if it would say anything. Naturally I could not expect it to say "*Track-up*" any more, for here I was at the end of it. So I listened with some curiosity. It hardly made so much noise as the stream: the pool was deeper. But I thought it must say something, and I put my head down as close as I could to the surface of the water. If I am not mistaken (and as things turned out I am sure I was right) the words were: *Gather gather, pick pick, or quick quick.*

Now I had not been thinking about the plant for a little time; but, as you may suppose, this brought it back to my mind and I got up and began to look about at the roots of the old oaks which grew just round the spring. No, none of the roots on this side which faced towards the water were like that which I had seen— still, the feeling was strong upon me that this, if any, was the kind of place, and even the very place, where the plant must be. So I walked to the back of the trees, being careful to go from right to left, according to the course of the sun.

Well, I was not mistaken. At the back of the middlemost oak-tree there were the roots I had dreamt of with the moss and the holes like eyes, and between them was the plant. I think the only thing which was new to me in the look of it was that it was so extraordinarily *green*. It seemed to have in it all the greenness that was possible or that would be wanted for a whole field of grass.

I had some scruples about touching it. In fact, I actually went back to the spring and listened, to make sure that it was still saying the same thing. Yes, it was: *"Gather gather, pick."* But there was something else every now and then which I could not for the life of me make out at first. I lay down, put my hand round my ear and held my breath. It might have been *bark tree* or *dark tree* or *cask free*. I got impatient at last and said:

"Well, I'm very sorry, but do what I will I *cannot* make out what you are trying to say."

Instantly a little spirt of water hit me on the ear, and I heard, as clear as possible, what it was: *"Ask tree."*

I got up at once. "I *beg* your pardon," I said, "of course. Thank you very much;" and the water went on saying *"Gather gather, all right, dip dip."*

The Five Jars

After thinking how best to greet it, I went back to the oak, stood in front of it and said (of course baring my head):

"Oak, I humbly desire your good leave to gather the green plant which grows between your roots. If an acorn falls into this my right hand" (which I held out) "I will count it that you answer yes— and give you thanks." The acorn fell straight into the palm of my hand. I said, "I thank you, Oak: good growth to you. I will lay this your acorn in the place whence I gather the plant."

Then very carefully I took hold of the stalk of the plant (which was very short, for, as I said, it grew rather flat on the ground) and pulled, and to my surprise it came up as easily as a mushroom. It had a clean round bulb without any rootlets and left a smooth neat hole in the ground, in which, according to promise, I laid the acorn, and covered it in with earth. I think it very likely that it will turn into a second plant.

Then I remembered the last word of the spring and went back to dip the plant in it. I had a shock when I did so, and it was lucky I was holding it firm, for when it touched the water it struggled in my hand like a fish or a newt and almost slipped out. I dipped it three times and thought I felt it growing smaller in my hand: and indeed when I looked at it I found it had shut up its leaves and curled them in quite close, so that the whole thing was little more than a bulb. As I looked at it I thought the water changed its note and said, *"That'll do, that'll do."*

I thought it was time to thank the spring for all it had done for me, though, as you may suppose, I did not yet know in the least what was to be done with the plant, or what use it was going to be.

So I went over and said in the politest words I could how much I was obliged, and if there was anything I had or could do which would be agreeable, how glad I should be. Then I listened carefully, for it seemed by this time quite natural that I should get some sort of answer. It came. There was a sudden change in the sound, and the water said clearly and rapidly, "*Silver silver silver silver.*" I felt in my pocket. Luckily I had several shillings, sixpences and half-crowns. I thought the best way was to offer them all, so I put them in the palm of my right hand and held it under the water, open, just over the dancing sand. For a few seconds the water ran over the silver without doing anything: only the coins seemed to grow very bright and clean. Then one of the shillings was very neatly and smoothly slid off, and then another and a sixpence. I waited, but no more happened, and the water seemed to draw itself down and away from my hand, and to say "*All right.*" So I got up.

The three coins lay on the bottom of the pool looking brighter than even the newest I have ever seen, and gradually as they lay there they began to appear larger. The shillings looked like half-crowns and the sixpence like a shilling. I thought for a moment that it was because water magnifies, but I soon saw that this could not be the reason, for they went on growing larger, and of course thinner, until they finally spread into a kind of silver film all over the bottom of the pool; and as they did so the water began to take on a musical sound, much like the singing that comes when you wet your finger and draw it round the edge of a finger glass at dessert (which some people's idea of table manners allows them to do). It was a pretty sight and sound, and I listened and looked for a long time.

The Five Jars

But all this time what had become of the plant? Why, when I gave the silver to the spring I had wrapped the plant carefully in a silk handkerchief and put it safe in my breast pocket. I took the handkerchief out now, and for a moment I was afraid the plant was gone; but it was not. It had shrunk to a very small whity-green ball. Now what was to be done with it, or rather what could it do? It was plain to me that it must have a strange and valuable property or virtue, since I had been put on its track in such a remarkable way. I thought I could not do better than ask the spring. I said, "O Spring of water, have I your good leave to ask what I should do with this precious plant to put it to the best use?" The silver lining of the spring made its words much easier to catch when it said anything— for I should tell you that for the most part now it did not speak, or not in any language that I could understand, but rather sang— and it now said, "*Swallow swallow, drink, swallow.*"

Prompt obedience, dear Jane, has always been my motto, as it is doubtless yours, and I at once laid myself down, drank a mouthful of water from the spring, and put the little bulb in my mouth. It instantly grew soft and slipped down my throat. How prosaic! I have no idea what it tasted like.

And again I addressed the spring: "Is there anything more for me to do?"

"*No no, no no, you'll see, you'll see— good-bye, good-bye,*" was the answer which came at once.

Accordingly I once more thanked the spring, wished it clear water, no mud, no tramplings of cattle, and bade it farewell. But, I said, I should hope to visit it again.

Then I turned away and looked about me, wondering whether, now that I had swallowed the mysterious plant, I should see anything different. The only thing I noticed was

due, I suppose, not to the plant, but to the spring; but it was odd enough. All the trees hard by were crowded with little birds of all kinds sitting in rows on the branches as they do on telegraph wires. I have no doubt they were listening to the silver bell in the spring. They were quite still, and did not take any notice when I began to walk away.

I said, you will remember, that the ground I was on was a sort of flat terrace at the top of a steep slope. Now at one end this terrace just went down into the wood, but at the other end there was a little mound or hillock with thick underwood behind it. I felt a curiosity, an inclination, to walk that way: I have very little doubt that the plant was at the bottom of it. As I walked I looked at the ground, and noticed a curious thing: the roots of the plants and grasses seemed to show more than I was accustomed to see them.

It was not a great way to the hillock. When I got to it I wondered why I had gone, for there was nothing odd about it. Still I stepped on to the top, and then I did see something, namely, a square flat stone just in front of my feet. I poked at it with my walking-stick, but somehow I did not seem to touch it, nor was there any scraping noise. This was funny. I tried again, and now I saw that my stick was not touching it at all; there was something in between. I felt with my hands, and they met with what seemed like grass and earth, certainly not like stone. *Then* I understood. The plant was the one which makes you able to see what is under the ground!

I need not tell you all I thought, or how surprising and delightful it was. The first thing was to get at the flat stone and find out what was underneath it.

Accordingly, what with a knife and what with my fingers, I soon had it uncovered: it was four or five inches un-

The Five Jars

der the surface. There were no marks on it; it measured more than a foot each way. I lifted it. It was the cover of a sort of box with bottom and sides each made of a slab just like the lid. In this box was another, made of some dark metal, which I took to be lead. I pulled it out and found that the lid of the box was all of one piece with the rest, like a sardine tin. Evidently I could not open it there and then. It was rather heavy, but I did not care, and I managed without too much inconvenience to carry it home to the place I was lodging in. Of course I put back the stone neatly and covered it up with earth and grass again.

I was late for tea, but I had found what was better than tea.

Chapter II
The First Jar

That night I waited till the moon was up before trying to open the box. I do not well know why, but it seemed the right thing, and I followed my instinct, feeling that it might be the plant that made me think as I did. I drew up the blind and laid the box on a table near the window, where the moon shone full on it, and waited to see if anything else occurred to me. Suddenly I heard a sort of metallic snap. I went and looked at the box. Nothing appeared on the side nearest to me— but when I turned it round I saw that all along the side which the moon had shone upon there was a line along the metal. I turned another side to the moonlight, and another snap came in two or three minutes. Of course I went on. When the moon had made a groove on all four sides, I tried the lid. It would not come off yet, so there was nothing to be done but continue the process. Three times I did it: every side I turned to the moon thrice, and when that was done the lid was free. I lifted it, and what did I see in the box? All this writing would be very little use if I did not tell you, so it must be done.

The Five Jars

There were five compartments in the box: in each of them was a little jar or vase of glass with a round body, a narrow neck, and spreading out a little at the top. The top of each was covered with a plate of metal and on each plate was a word or two in capital letters. On the one in the middle there were the words *unge oculos*, the other jars had one word apiece, *aures, linguam, frontem, pectus.*

Now, years ago, I took great pains to learn the Latin language, and on many occasions I have found it *most useful*, whatever you may see to the contrary in the newspaper: but seldom or never have I found it more useful than now. I saw at once that the words meant *anoint the eyes, the ears, the tongue, the forehead, the chest*. What would be the result of my doing this, of course I knew no more than you: but I was pretty sure that it would not do to try them all at once, and another thing I felt, that it would be better to wait till next day before trying any of them. It was past midnight now, so I went to bed: but first I locked up the box in a cupboard, for I did not want anyone to see it as yet.

Next day I woke bright and early, looked at my watch, found there was no need to think about getting up yet, and, like a wise creature, went to sleep again. I mention this, not merely by way of being jocose, but because after I went to sleep I had a dream which most likely came from the plant and certainly had to do with the box.

I seemed to see a room, or to be in a room about which I only noticed that the floor was paved with mosaic in a pattern mostly red and white, that there were no pictures on the walls and no fireplace, no sashes or indeed panes in the window, and the moon was shining in very bright. There

was a table and a chest. Then I saw an old man, rather badly shaved and bald, in a Roman dress, white for the most part, with a purple stripe somewhere, and sandals. He looked by no means a wicked or designing old man. I was glad of that. He opened the chest, took out my box, and placed it carefully on the table in the moonlight. Then he went to a part of the room I could not see, and I heard a sound of water being poured into a metal basin, and he came into sight again, wiping his hands on a white towel. He opened the box, took out a little silver spoon and one of the jars, took off the lid and dipped the spoon in the jar and touched first his right eye and then his left with it. Then he put the jar and the spoon back, laid the lid on the box and put it back in the chest. After that he went to the window and stood there looking out, and seemed to be very much amused with what he saw. That was all.

"Hints for me," I remember thinking. "Perhaps it will be best not to touch the box before the moon is up to-night, and always with washed hands." I suppose I woke up immediately, for it was all very fresh in my mind when I did.

It was something of a disappointment to have to put off my experiments till the night came round. But it was all for the best, for letters came by the post which I had to attend to: in fact, I was obliged to go to the town a little way off to see someone and to send telegrams and so on. I was a little doubtful about the seeing things underground, but I soon found that unless I— so to say— turned on the tap, and specially wished and tried to use the power, it did not interfere with my ordinary seeing. When I did, it seemed to come forward from the back of my eyes, and was stronger than the day before. I could see rabbits in their burrows and followed the roots of one oak-tree very deep down. Once it

The Five Jars

threatened to be awkward, when I stooped to pick up a silver coin in the street, and grazed my knuckle against a paving stone, under which, of course, it was.

So much for that. By the way, I had taken a look at the box after breakfast, I found (not very much to my surprise) that the lid was as tight on it as when I found it first.

After dinner that evening I put out the light— the moon being now bright— placed the box on the table, washed my hands, opened it and, shutting my eyes, put my hand on one of the jars at random and took it out. As I had rather expected, I heard a little rattle as I did so, and feeling in the compartment, I found a little, a very little, spoon. All was well. Now to see which jar chance or the plant had chosen for my first experiment. I took it to the window: it was the one marked *aures*— ears— and the spoon had on the handle a letter A. I opened the jar. The lid fitted close but not over tightly. I put in the spoon as the old man had done, as near as I could remember. It brought out a very small drop of thick stuff with which I touched first my right ear and then my left. When I had done so I looked at the spoon. It was perfectly dry. I put it and the jar back, closed the box, locked it up, and, not knowing in the least what to expect, went to the open window and put my head out.

For some little time I heard nothing. That was to be expected, and I was not in the least inclined to distrust the jar. Then I was rewarded; a bat flew by, and I, who have not heard a bat even squeak these twenty years, now heard this one say in a whistling angry tone, "Would you, would you, *I've* got you— no, drat, drat." It was not a very exciting remark, but it was enough to show me that a whole new world (as the books say) was open to me.

22

This, of course, was only a beginning. There were some plants and flowering shrubs under the window, and though I could see nothing, I began to hear voices— two voices— talking among them. They sounded young: of course they were anyhow very small, but they seemed to belong to young creatures of their kind.

"Hullo, I say, what have you got there? Do let's look; you might as well."

Then a pause— another voice: "I believe it's a bad one."

Number one: "Taste it."

Number two, after another pause, with a slight sound (very diminutive) of spitting: "Heugh! bad! I should rather think it was. Maggot!"

Number one (after laughing rather longer than I thought kind): "Look here— don't chuck it away— let's give it to the old man. Here— shove the piece in again and rub it over— here he is!" (Very demurely): "O sir, we've got such a nice-looking——" (*I could not catch what it was*) "here; we thought you might perhaps like it, sir. Would you, sir?... Oh no, thank you, sir, we've had plenty, sir, but this was the biggest we found."

A third voice said something; it was a deeper one and less easy to hear.

Number two: "Bitten, sir? Oh no, I don't think so. Do you ——?" (*a name which I did not make out*).

Number one: "Why, how could it be?"

Number three again— angry, I thought.

Number two (rather anxiously): "But, sir, really, sir, I don't much like them... Must I really, sir? O sir, it's got a maggot in it, and I believe they're poison." (*Smack, smack, smack, smack.*)

Two voices, very lamentable: "O *sir*, sir, please sir!"

The Five Jars

A considerable pause, and sniffing. Then *Number two*, in a broken voice: "You silly fool, why did you go laughing like that right under his snout? You might have known he'd cog it." ("Cog." I had not heard the word since 1876.) "There'll be an awful row to-morrow. Look here, I shall go to bed."

The voices died away; I thought *Number one* seemed to be apologizing.

That was all I heard *that* night. After eleven o'clock things seemed to get very still, and I began to feel just a little apprehensive lest something of a less innocent kind should come along. So I went to bed.

Chapter III
The Second Jar

Next day, I must say, was very amusing. I spent the whole of it in the fields just strolling about and sitting down, as the fancy took me, listening to what went on in the trees and hedges. I will not write down yet the kind of thing I heard, for it was only the beginning. I had not yet found out the way of using the new power to the very best advantage. I felt the want of being able to put in a remark or a question of my own every now and then. But I was pretty sure that the jar which had *linguam* on it would manage that.

Very nearly all the talking I heard was done by the birds and animals— especially the birds; but perhaps half a dozen times, as I sat under a tree or walked along the road, I was aware of voices which sounded exactly like those of people (some grown-up and some children) passing by or coming towards me and talking to each other as they went along. Needless to say, there was nothing to be *seen*: no movement of the grass and no track on the dusty road, even when I could tell exactly where the people who owned the voices must be. It interested me more than anything else to guess what sort of creatures they were, and I determined that the

The Five Jars

next jar I tried should be the Eye one. Once, I must tell you, I ventured to say "Good afternoon" when I heard a couple of these voices within a yard of me. I think the owners must nearly have had a fit. They stopped dead: one of them gave a sort of cry of surprise, and then, I believe, they ran or flew away. I felt a little breath of wind on my face, and heard no more. It wasn't (as I know now) that they couldn't see me: but they felt much as you would if a tree or a cow were to say "Good afternoon" to you.

When I was at supper that evening, the cat came in, as she usually did, to see what was going. I had always been accustomed to think that cats talk when they mew, dogs when they bark, and so on. It is not so at all. Their talking is almost all done (except when they are in a great state of mind) in a tone which you cannot possibly hear without help. Mewing is for the most part only shouting without saying any words. Purring is, as we often say, singing.

Well, this cat was an ordinary nice creature, tabby, and in she came, and sat watching me while I had soup. To all appearance she was as innocent as a lamb— but no matter for that. What she was saying was something of this kind:

"Get on with it, do: shove it down, lap it up! Who cares about soup? Get to business. I know there's fish coming."

When the fish actually came, there was a great deal of good feeling shown at first. "Oh, *how* much we have to be thankful for, all of us, have we not? Fish, fish: what a thought! Dear, kind, generous people all around us, all striving to supply us with what is best and pleasantest for us."

Then there was a silence for a short time, then in a somewhat different tone I heard: "Ah dear! the longer I live, the wiser I find it is not to expect too much consideration

from others! Self-love! how few, how terribly few, are really free from it! The nature that knows how to take a hint, how rare it is!"

Another short silence, and then: "There you go— another great bit. I wonder you don't choke or burst! Disgusting! A good scratch all down your horrible fat cheek is what you want, and I know some cats that would give it you. No more notion how to behave than a cockroach."

About this time I rang the bell and the fish was taken away. The cat went too, circling round the maid with trusting and childlike glances, and I heard her saying in the former tone:

"Well, I daresay after all there are *some* kind hearts in the world, some that can feel for a poor weary creature, and know what a deal of strength and nourishment even the least bit of fish can give——" And I lost the rest.

When the time came and the box was open once more, I duly anointed my eyes and went to the window. I knew something of what I might expect to see, but I had not realized at all how much of it there would be. In the first place there were a great many buildings, in fact a regular village, all about the little lawn on which my window looked. They were, of course, not big; perhaps three feet high was the largest size. The roofs seemed to be of tiles, the walls were white, the windows were brightly lighted, and I could see people moving about inside. But there were plenty of people outside, too— people about six inches high— walking about, standing about, talking, running, playing some game which might have been hockey. These were on levelled spaces, for the grass, neatly kept as it was, would have come half-way up their legs; and there were some driving along smooth tracks in carriages drawn by horses of the right size,

The Five Jars

which were really the most charming little animals I ever saw.

You may suppose that I should not soon have got tired of watching them and listening to the little treble buzz of voices that went on, but I was interrupted. Just in front of me I heard what I can only call a snigger. I looked down, and saw four heads supported by four pairs of elbows leaning on the window-sill and looking up at me. They belonged to four boys who were standing on the twigs of a bush that grew up against the wall, and who seemed to be very much amused. Every now and again one of them nudged another and pointed towards me; and then, for some unexplained reason, they sniggered again. I felt my ears growing warm and red.

"Well, young gentlemen," I said, "you seem to be enjoying yourselves." No answer. "I appear to be so fortunate as to afford you some gratification," I went on, in my sarcastic manner. "Perhaps you would do me the honour of stepping into my poor apartment?" Again no answer, but more undisguised amusement. I was thinking out a really withering remark, when one of them said:

"Do look at his nose. I wonder if they know how ridiculous they are. I *should* like to talk to one of them for five minutes."

"Well," I said, "that can be managed very easily, and I assure you I should be equally glad of the opportunity. *My* remarks would deal with the subject of good manners."

Another one spoke this time, but did not answer me. "Oh, I don't know," he said, "I expect they're pretty stupid. They look it— at least this one does."

"Can they talk?" said the third. "I've never heard 'em."

"No, but you can see them moving their jaws and mouths and things. This one did just now."

I saw how it was now, and, becoming cooler, I recognized that these youths were behaving very much as I might have done myself in the presence of someone who I was sure could neither see nor hear me. I even smiled. One of them pointed at me at once:

"Thought of a joke, I s'pose. Don't keep it all to yourself, old chap."

At this moment the fourth, who had not said anything so far, but seemed to have been listening, piped up: "I say! I believe I know what it is that makes that hammering noise: it's something he has got in his clothes."

I could not resist this. "Right again," I said; "it's my watch, and you're very welcome to look at it." And I took it out and put it on the window-sill.

An awful horror and surprise came into their faces. In a second they had dived down like so many ducks. In another second I saw them walking across the grass, and each of them threw his arms round the waist or the neck of one of the elder people who were walking about among the houses. The person so attacked pulled himself up and listened attentively to what the boy was saying. The particular one I was watching looked towards my window and then burst out laughing, slapped the boy on the back, and resumed his walk. The boy went slowly off towards one of the houses. One or two of the other "men" came and stood nearer to the window, looking up. I thought I would venture a bow, and made one rather ceremoniously. It did not produce much effect, and I could not at the moment think of anything I could do that would show them quite clearly that I saw them. They went on looking at me quietly enough, and

The Five Jars

then I heard a deep low bell, seemingly very far off, toll five times. They heard it too, turned sharply round and walked off to the houses. Soon after that the lights in the windows died down and everything became very still. I looked at my watch. It was ten o'clock.

I waited for a while to see if anything would happen, but there was nothing; so I got some books out (which took a few minutes) and before I settled down to them I thought I would just take one more look out of the window. Where were all the little houses? At the first glance I thought they had vanished, but it was not exactly so. I found I could still see the chimneys above the grass, but as I looked they too disappeared. It was done very neatly: there was no hole, the turf closed in upon the roofs as they sank down, just as if it was of india-rubber. There was not a trace left of houses or roads or playgrounds or anything.

I was strongly tempted to go out and walk over the site of the village, but I did not. For one thing I was afraid I might disturb the people of the house, and besides there was a mist coming up over the meadows which sloped away outside the garden. So I stopped where I was.

But what a very odd mist, I began to think. It was not coming in all in one piece as it should. It was more in patches or even pillars of a smoky grey which moved at different rates, some of them occasionally standing still, others even seeming to go to and fro. And now I began to hear something like a hollow whispering coming from their direction. It was not conversation, for it went on quite continuously in the same tone: it sounded more as if something was being recited. I did not like it.

Then I saw what I liked less. Seven of these pillars of mist, each about the size of a man, were standing in a row

just outside the garden fence, and in each I thought I saw two dull red eyes; and the hollow whispering grew louder.

Just then I heard a noise behind me in the room, as if the fire-irons had suddenly fallen down. So they had: and the reason why they had was that an old horseshoe which was on the mantelpiece had, for no reason that I could see, tumbled over and knocked them. Something I had heard came into my mind. I took the horseshoe and laid it on the window-sill. The pillars of mist swayed and quivered as if a sudden gust of wind had struck them, and seemed all at once to go farther off; and the hollow murmur was no longer to be heard. I shut the window and went to bed. But, the last thing, I looked out once again. The meadow was clear of mist and bright beneath the light of the moon.

As I lay in bed I thought and thought over what I had seen last. I was quite sure that the pillars of mist concealed some beings who wished me no good: but why should they have any spite against me? I was also sure that they wanted to get into the house: but again, why? You may think I was slow in the wits, but I must confess that some few minutes passed before I guessed. Of course they wanted to get hold of the box with the five jars. The thought disturbed me so much that I got up, lighted a candle, and went to the cupboard to see if all was safe. Yes, the box was there, but the cupboard door, which I knew I had locked, was unfastened, and when I had to turn the key it became plain that the lock was hampered and useless. How could this have come about? Earlier in the evening it had been perfectly right, and nobody had been in the room since I locked it last.

Whoever had done it, they had made the cupboard no safe place for the box. I took it into the bedroom and after a minute's thought cleared out a space in a suit-case which I

The Five Jars

had brought with me, locked it in that, and put the key on the ring of my watch-chain. Watch and all went under my pillow, and once more I got into bed.

Chapter IV
The Small People

You will have made sure that the next jar I meant to try was the one for the tongue, in hopes that it would help me to speak to some of the creatures. Though I looked forward to the experiment very much, and felt somewhat restless until I had made it, I did get a good deal of amusement out of what I saw and heard the next day. The small people were not to be seen— at least not in the morning. No, I am wrong: I found a bunch of three of them— young ones— asleep in a hollow tree. They woke up and looked at me without much interest, and when I was withdrawing my head they blew kisses to me. I am afraid there is no doubt they did so in derision. But there were others. I passed a cottage garden in which a little dog was barking most furiously. It seemed to be barking at a clothes-line, on which, with a lot of other things, was a print dress with rather a staring pattern of flowers. The dress caught my eye, and so did something red at the top which stuck up above the line. I gave it another glance, and really I had a most dreadful shock. It was a face. I gazed at it in horror, and was just gathering my wits to run and call for help or something, when I saw that it was laugh-

The Five Jars

ing. Then I realized that it could not be an ordinary person, hanging as it was on a thin bit of cord and blowing to and fro in the breeze. I went nearer, staring at it with all my eyes, and made out that it was the face of an old woman, very cheerful and ruddy, and, as I said, laughing and swinging to and fro. Suddenly she seemed to catch my eye and to see that I saw her, and in a flash she was off the line and round the corner of the house, nearly tumbling over the dog as she went. It rushed after her, still very angry, but soon came trotting back, rather out of breath, and *that* incident was over.

I walked on. Among the village people I met, there were one or two whom I didn't think I had seen before— elderly, bright-eyed people they were— who seemed very much surprised when I said "Good morning" to them, and stopped still, looking after me, when I passed on. At last, some little way outside the village, I saw in the distance the same bright-coloured dress that had been on the clothes-line. The person who wore it was going slowly, and looking in the grass and hedges, and sometimes stooping to pick a plant, as it seemed. I quickened my pace and came up with her, and when I was just behind her, I cleared my throat rather loudly and said, "Fine day," or words to that effect.

You should have seen her jump! I was well paid for the fright she had given me just before. However, the startled look cleared away from her face, and she drew herself up and looked at me very calmly.

"Yes," she said, "it's a fine day." Then she actually blushed and went on: "I think I ought to beg your pardon for giving you such a turn just now."

34

"Well," I said, "I certainly was a good deal startled, but no harm was done. The dog took it more to heart than I did."

She gave a short laugh. "Yes," she said. "I hardly know why I was behaving like that. I suppose we all of us feel skittish at times." She paused and said with some little hesitation, "You have them, I suppose?" and at the same time she rapidly touched her ears, eyes and mouth with her forefinger.

I looked at her in some doubt, for I thought, might not she be one of the unknown who wished to get hold of the Five Jars? But her eye was honest, and my instinct was to trust her: so I nodded, and put my finger on my lips.

"Of course," she said. "Well, you are the first since I was a little thing, and that's fourteen hundred years ago." (You may think I opened my eyes.) "Yes, Vitalis was the last, and he lived in the villa— they called it so— down by the stream. You'll find the place some of these days if you look. I heard talk yesterday that someone had got them, and I'm told the mist was about last night. Perhaps you saw it?"

"Yes," I said, "I did, and I guessed what it meant." And I told her all that had happened, and ended by asking if she could kindly advise me what to do.

She thought for a moment, and then handed me a little bunch of the leaves she held in her hand. "Four-leaved clover," she said. "I know nothing better. Lay it on the box itself. You'll hear of them again, be sure."

"Who are *they*?" I asked in a whisper.

She shook her head. "Not allowed," was all she would say. "I must be going"; and she was gone, sure enough. You might suppose (as I did, when I came to think of it) that my new sight ought to have been able to see what became of

The Five Jars

her. I think it would, if she had gone straight away from me; but what I believe she did was to dart round behind me and then go away in a straight line, so that I was left looking in front of me while she was travelling away behind me like a bullet from a gun. You need practice with these things, and I had only been at it a couple of days.

I turned and walked rather quickly homewards, for I thought it would be wise to protect my box as soon as possible now that I had the means. I think it was fortunate that I did.

As I opened the garden gate I saw an old woman coming down the path— an old woman very unlike the last. "Old" was not the word for her face: she might have been born before the history-books begin. As to her expression, if ever you saw a snake with red rims to its eyes and the expression of a parrot, you might have some idea of it. She was hobbling along with a stick, in quite the proper manner, but I felt certain that all that was put on, and that she could have glided as swift as an adder if she pleased. I confess I was afraid of her. I had a feeling that she knew everything and hated everybody.

"And what," I suddenly thought, "has she been up to? If she has got at the box, where am I? and more than that, what mischief will she and her company work among the small people and the birds and beasts?" There would be no mercy for them; a glance at her eye told me that.

It was an immense relief to see that she could not possibly have got the box about her, and another relief when my eye travelled to the door of the house and I saw no fewer than three horseshoes nailed above it. I smiled to myself. Oh, how angry she looked! But she had to act her part, and with feeble curtseys and in a very small hoarse trembling

36

voice she wished me a good day (though I noticed her pointing to the ground with her thumb as she said the words) and would be very obliged if I could tell her the right time. I was going to pull out my watch (and if I had, she would have seen a certain key we know of), when something said suddenly and clearly to my brain, "Look out," and by good luck I heard a clock inside the house strike one before I could answer.

"Just struck one," was my reply accordingly, and I said it as innocently as I could. She drew her breath in hard and quivered all over, and her mouth remained open like a cat's when it is using its worst expressions, and when she eventually thanked me I leave it to you to imagine how gracefully she did it.

Well, she had no more cards to play at the moment, and no excuse for remaining. I stood my ground and watched her out of the gate. A path led down the meadow, and, much against her will no doubt, she had to keep up the pretence and toil painfully along it until she reached another hedge and could reckon on being out of my sight. After that I neither saw nor expected to see anything more of her. I went up to my room and found all safe, and laid the four-leaved clover on the box. At luncheon I took occasion to find out from the maid, without asking her in so many words, whether the old woman had been visible to her; evidently she had not: evidently also, the evil creatures were really on the track of the Five Jars, knew that I had them, and had a very fair idea of where they were kept.

However, if the maid had not seen her, the cat had, and murmured a good deal to herself, and was in a rather nervous state. She sat, with her ears turned different ways, on the window-sill, looking out, and twitching her back uncom-

The Five Jars

fortably, like an old lady who feels a draught. When I was available, she came and sat on my knee (a very uncommon attention on her part) with an air half of wishing to be protected and half of undertaking to protect me.

"If there is fish to-night," I said, "you shall have some." But I was not yet in a position to make myself understood.

"Pussy's been sleepin' on your box all the afternoon, sir," said the maid when I came in to tea. "I couldn't get her to come off; and when I did turn her out of the room, I do believe she climbed up and got in again by the winder."

"I don't mind at all," I said; "let her be there if she likes." And indeed I felt quite grateful to the cat. I don't know that she could have done much if there had been any attempt on the box, but I was sure her intentions were good.

There was fish that evening, and she had a good deal of it. She did not say much that I could follow, but chiefly sang songs without words.

* * *

Not to go over the preliminaries again, I did, when the proper time came, touch my tongue with the contents of the third jar. I found that it worked in this way: I could not hear what I was saying myself, when I was talking to an animal: I only *thought* the remark very clearly, and then I felt my tongue and lips moving in an odd fashion, which I can't describe. But with the small people in human shape it was different. I spoke in the ordinary way to them, and though I dare say my voice went up an octave or two, I can't say I perceived it.

The village was there again to-night, and the life going on in it seemed much the same. I was set upon making acquaintance in a natural sort of way with the people, and as it would not do to run any risk of startling them, I just took my place near the window and made some pretence of playing Patience. I thought it likely that some of the young people would come and watch me, in spite of the fright they had had the night before. And it was not long before I heard a rustling in the shrubs under the window and voices saying:

"Is he in there? Can you see? Oh, I say, *do* look out: you all but had me over that time!"

They were suddenly quiet after this, and apparently one must have, very cautiously, climbed up and looked into the room. When he got down again there was a great fuss.

"No, is he really?" "What d'you say he was doing?" "What sort of charm?" "I say, d'you think we'd better get down?" "No, but what is he really doing?" "Laying out rows of flat things on the table, with marks on them." "I don't believe it." "Well, you go and look yourself." "All right, I shall." "Yes, but, I say, do look out: suppose you get shut in and we're late for the bell?" "Why, you fool, I shan't go into the room, only stop on the window-sill." "Well, I don't know, but I do believe he saw us last night, and my father said he thought so too." "Oh, well, he can't move very quick, anyway, and he's some way off the window. *I* shall go up."

I managed, without altering my position too much, to keep my eye on the window-sill, and, sure enough, in a second or two a small round head came into sight. I went on with my game. At first I could see that the watcher was ready to duck down at the slightest provocation, but as I took no sort of notice, he gained confidence, leant his el-

The Five Jars

bows on the sill, and then actually pulled himself up and sat down on it. He bent over and whispered to the others below, and it was not long before I saw a whole row of heads filling up the window-sill from end to end. There must have been a dozen of them. I thought the time was come, and without moving, and in as careless a tone as I could, I said:

"Come in, gentlemen, come in; don't be shy." There was a rustle, and two or three heads disappeared, but nobody said anything. "Come in, if you like," I said again; "you can hear the bell quite well from here, and I shan't shut the window."

"Promise!" said the one who was sitting on the sill.

"I promise, honour bright," I said, whereupon he made the plunge. First he dropped on to the seat of a chair by the window, and from that to the floor. Then he wandered about the room, keeping at a distance from me at first, and, I have no doubt, watching very anxiously to see whether I had any intention of pouncing on him. The others followed, first one by one and then two or three at a time. Some remained sitting on the window-sill, but most plucked up courage to get down on to the floor and explore.

I had now my first good chance of seeing what they were like. They all wore the same fashion of clothes— a tunic and close-fitting hose and flat caps— seemingly very much what a boy would have worn in Queen Elizabeth's time. The colours were sober— dark blue, dark red, grey, brown— and each one's clothes were of one colour all through. They had some white linen underneath; it showed a little at the neck. There were both fair and dark among them: all were clean and passably good-looking, one or two certainly handsome. The firstcomer was ruddy and auburn-haired and evidently a leader. They called him Wag.

40

I heard whispers from corners of the room, and appeals to Wag to explain what this and that unfamiliar object was, and noticed that he was never at a loss for an answer of some kind, correct or not. The fireplace, which had its summer dressing, was, it appeared, a rock garden; an old letter lying on the floor was a charm ("Better not touch it"); the waste-paper basket (not unnaturally) a prison; the pattern on the carpet was— "Oh, you wouldn't understand it if I was to tell you."

Soon a voice— Wag's voice— came from somewhere near my foot.

"I say, could I get up on the top?" I offered to lift him, but he declined rather hastily and said my leg would be all right if I didn't mind putting it out a bit sloping: and he then ran up it on all fours— he was quite a perceptible weight— and got on to the table from my knee without any difficulty.

Once there, there was a great deal to interest him— books, papers, ink, pens, pipes, matches and cards. He was full of questions about them, and his being so much at his ease encouraged the others to follow him, so that before very long the whole lot were perambulating the table and making me very nervous lest they should fall off, while Wag was standing close up to me and putting me through a catechism.

"What do you have such *little* spears for?" he wanted to know, brandishing a pen at me. "Is that blood on the end? whose blood? Well then, what do you do with it? Let's see— only that?" (when I wrote a word or two). "Well, you can tell me about it another time. Now I want to know what these clubs in the chest are."

The Five Jars

I said, "We make fire with them; if you like I'll show you— but it makes a little noise."

"Go on," said Wag; and I struck a match, rather expecting a stampede. But no, they were quite unmoved, and Wag said, "Beastly row and smell— why don't you do the ordinary way?"

He brushed the palm of his left hand along the tips of the fingers on his right hand, put them to his lips and then to his eyes, and behold! his eyes began to glow from behind with a light which would have been quite bright enough for him to read by. "Quite simple," he said; "don't you know it?" Then he did the same thing in reverse order, touching eyes, lips and hand, and the light was gone. I didn't like to confess that this was beyond me.

"Yes, that's all very well," I said, "but how do you manage about your houses? I am sure I saw lights in the windows."

"Course," he said, "put as many as you want;" and he ran round the table dabbing his hand here and there on the cloth, or on anything that lay on it, and at every place a little round bud or drop of very bright but also soft light came out. "See?" he said, and darted round again, passing his hands over the lights and touching his lips; and they were gone. He came back and said, "It's a *much* better way; it is *really*," as if it were only my native stupidity that prevented me from using it myself.

A smaller one, who looked to me rather a quieter sort than Wag, had come up and was standing by him: he now said in a low voice:

"P'raps they can't."

It seemed a new idea to Wag: he made his eyes very round. "Can't? Oh, rot! it's quite simple."

42

The other shook his head and pointed to my hand which rested on the table. Wag looked at it too, and then at my face.

"Could I see it spread out?" he said.

"Yes, if you'll promise not to spoil it."

He laughed slightly, and then both he and the other— whom he called Slim— bent over and looked closely at the tips of my fingers. "Other side, please," he said after a time, and they subjected my nails to a like examination. The others, who had been at the remoter parts of the table, wandered up and looked over their shoulders. After tapping my nails and lifting up one or more fingers, Wag stood upright and said:

"Well, I s'pose it's true, and you can't. I thought your sort could do anything."

"I thought much the same about you," I said in self-defence. "I always thought you could fly, but you——"

"So we can," said Wag very sharply, and his face grew red.

"Oh," I said, "then why haven't you been doing it to-night?"

He kicked one foot with the other and looked quickly at Slim. The rest said nothing and edged away, humming to themselves.

"Well, we *can* fly perfectly well, only——"

"Only not to-night, I suppose," said I, rather unkindly.

"No, *not* to-night," said Wag; "and you needn't laugh, either— we'll soon show you."

"That *will* be nice," I said; "and when will you show me?"

"Let's see" (he turned to Slim), "two nights more, isn't it? All right then (to me), in two nights more you'll see."

The Five Jars

Just then a moth which flew in caused a welcome diversion— for I could see that somehow I had touched on a sore subject, and that he was feeling awkward— and he first jumped at it and then ran after it. Slim lingered. I raised my eyebrows and pointed at Wag. Slim nodded.

"The fact is," he said in a low voice, "he got us into rather a row yesterday and we're all stopped flying for three nights."

"Oh," said I. "I *see*: you must tell him I am very sorry for being so stupid. May I ask who stopped you?"

"Oh, just the old man, not the owls."

"You do go to the owls for something, then?" I asked, trying to appear intelligent.

"Yes, history and geography."

"To be sure," I said; "of course they've seen a lot, haven't they?"

"So they say," said Slim, "but——"

Just then the low toll of the bell was wafted through the window and there was an instant scurry to the edge of the table, then to the seat of the chair, and up to the window-sill; small arms waved caps at me, the shrubs rustled, and I was left alone.

Chapter V
Danger to the Jars

Now my ears and eyes and tongue had been dealt with, and what remained were the forehead and the chest. I could not guess what would come of treating these with the ointment, but I thought I would try the forehead first. There was still a day or two when the moon would be bright enough for the trial. I hoped that perhaps the effect of these two last jars might be to make me able to go on with my experiences— to keep in touch with the new people I had come across— during the time when she— the moon, I mean— was out of sight.

I had one anxiety. The precious box must be guarded from those who were after it. About this I had a conviction, that if I could keep them off until I had used each of the five jars, the box and I would be safe. Why I felt sure of this I could not say, but my experience had led me to trust these beliefs that came into my head, and I meant to trust this one. It would be best, I thought, if I did not go far from the house— perhaps even if I did not leave it at all till the time of danger was past.

The Five Jars

Several things happened in the course of the morning which confirmed me in my belief. I took up a position at the table by the window of my sitting-room. I had put the box in my suit-case, which I had locked, and I now laid it beside me where I could keep an eye upon it. The view from my window showed me, first, the garden of the cottage, with its lawn and little flower beds, its hedge and back gate, and beyond that a path leading down across a field. More fields, I knew, came after that one, and sloped pretty sharply down to a stream in the valley, which I could not see; but I could see the steep slope of fields, partly pasture, and then clothed with green woods towards the top. There were no other houses in sight: the road was behind me, passing the front of the cottage, and my bedroom looked out that way. I had some writing and reading to do, and I had not long finished breakfast before I settled down to it, and heard the maid "doing out" the bedroom as usual, accompanied every now and then by a slight mew from the cat, who (also as usual) was watching her at work. These mews meant nothing in particular, I may say; they were only intended to be met by an encouraging remark, such as "There you are, then, pussy," or "Don't get in my way, now," or "All in good time." Finally I heard "Come along then, and let's see what we've got for you downstairs," and the door was shut. I mention this because of what happened about a quarter of an hour later.

There was suddenly a fearful crash in the bedroom, a fall, a breaking of glass and crockery and snapping of wood, and then, fainter, sobbings and moans of pain. I started up.

"Goodness!" I thought, "she must have been dusting that heavy shelf high up on the wall with all the china on it, and the whole thing has given way. She must be badly hurt!

46

But why doesn't her mistress come rushing upstairs? and what was that rasping noise just beside me?"

I looked at my suit-case, which lay on the table just inside the open window. Across the new smooth top of it there were three deep scratches running towards the window, which had not been there before. I moved it to the other side of me and sat down. There had been an attempt to decoy me out of the room, and it had failed. Certainly there would be more.

I waited; but everything was quiet in the house: no more noise from the bedroom and no one moving about, upstairs or downstairs; nothing but the pump clanking in the scullery. I turned to my work again.

Half an hour must have gone by, and, though on the look-out, I was not fidgety. Then I was aware of a confused noise from the field outside.

"Help! help! Keep off, you brute! Help, you there!" as well as I could make out, again and again. Towards the far end of the field, which was a pretty large one, a poor old man was trying to get to a gate in the hedge at a staggering run, and striking now and then with his stick at a great deer-hound which was leaping up at him with hollow barks. It seemed as if nothing but the promptest dash to the spot could save him; it seemed, too, as if he had caught sight of me at the window, for he beckoned. How strange the cries sounded! It was as if someone was shouting into an empty jug. My field-glasses were by me on the table, and I thought I would take just one look before I rushed out. I am glad I did; for, do you know, when I had the glasses focused on the dog and the man, all that I could see was a sort of fuzz of dancing vapour, much as if the shimmering air that you see

47

The Five Jars

on the heath on a hot day had been gathered up and rolled into a shape.

"Ha! ha!" I said, as I put down the glasses; and something in the air, about four yards off, made a sharp hissing sound. No doubt there were words, but I could not distinguish them. A second attempt had failed; you may be sure I was well on the alert for the next.

I put away my books now, and sat looking out of the window, and wondering as I watched whether there was anything out of the common to be noticed. For one thing, I thought there were more little birds about than I expected. At first I did not see them, for they were not hopping about on the lawn; but as I stared at the hedge of the garden, and at that of the field, I became aware that these were full of life. On almost every twig that could hold a bird in shelter— not on the top of the hedges— a bird was sitting, quite still, and they were all looking towards the window, as if they were expecting something to happen there. Occasionally one would flutter its wings a little and turn its head towards its neighbour; but this was all they did.

I picked up my glasses and began to study the bottom of the hedges and the bushes, where there was some quantity of dead leaves, and here, too, I could see that there were spectators. A small bright eye or a bit of a nose was visible almost wherever I looked; in short, the mice, and, I don't doubt, some of the rats, hedgehogs, and toads as well, were collected there and were as intently on the watch as the birds. "What a chance for the cat, if only she knew!" I put my head cautiously out of the window, and looking down on the sill of the window below, I could see her head, with the ears pushed forward; she was looking earnestly at the hedge, but she did not move. Only, at the slight noise I

48

made, she turned her face upwards and crowed to me in a modest but encouraging manner.

Time passed on. Luncheon was laid— on another table— and was over, before anything else happened.

The next thing was that I heard the maid saying sharply:

"What business 'ave you got going round to the back? We don't want none of your rubbish here."

A hoarse voice answered inaudibly.

Maid: "No, nor the gentleman don't want none of your stuff neither; and how do you know there's a gentleman here at all I should like to know? What? Don't mean no offence? I dare say. That's more than I know. Well, that's the last word I've got to say."

In a minute more there was a knock at my door, and at the same time a step on the gravel path under my window, and a loud hiss from the cat. As I said "Come in" to the knock, I hastily looked out of the window, but saw nothing. It was the maid who had knocked. She had come to ask if there was anything I should like from the village, or anything I should want before tea-time, because the mistress was going out, and wanted her to go over and fetch something from the shop. I said there was nothing except the letters and perhaps a small parcel from the post office. She lingered a moment before going, and finally said:

"You'll excuse me naming it, sir, but there seems to be some funny people about the roads to-day, if you'd please to be what I mean to say a bit on the look-out, if you're not a-going out yourself."

"Certainly," I said. "No, I don't mean to go out. By the way, who was it came to the door just now?"

"Oh, it was one of these 'awking men, not one I've seen before, and he must be a stranger in this part, I think, be-

The Five Jars

cause he began going round to the garden door, only I stopped him. He'd got these cheap rubbishing 'atpins and what not; leastways, if you understand me, what I thought to myself I shouldn't like to be seen with 'em, whatever others might."

"Yes, I see," I answered; and she went, and I turned to my books once more.

Within a very few minutes I began to suspect that I was getting sleepy. Yes, it was undoubtedly so. What with the warmth of the day, and lunch, and not having been out... There was a curious smell in the room, too, not exactly nasty, like something burning. What did it remind me of? Wood smoke from a cottage fire, that one smells on an autumn evening as one comes bicycling down the hill into a village? Not quite so nice as that; something more like a chemist's shop. I wondered: and as I wondered, my eyes closed and my head went forward.

A sharp pain on the back of my hand, and a crash of glass! Up I jumped, and which of three or four things I realized first I don't know now. But I did realize in a second or two that my hand was bleeding from a scratch all down the back of it, that a pane of the window was broken and that the whole window was darkened with little birds that were bumping their chests against it; that the cat was on the table gazing into my face with intense expression, that a little smoke was drifting into the room, and that my suitcase was on the point of slipping out over the window-sill. A despairing dash at it I made, and managed to clutch it; but for the life of me I could not pull it back. I could see no string or cord, much less any hand that was dragging at it. I hardly dared to take my hand from it to catch up something

50

and hack at the thief I could not see. Besides, there was nothing within reach.

Then I remembered the knife in my pocket. Could I get it out and open it without losing hold? "They hate steel," I thought. Somehow— frantically holding on with one hand— I got out the knife, and opened it, goodness knows how, for it was horribly small and stiff, with my teeth, and sheared and stabbed indiscriminately all round the farther end of the suit-case. Thank goodness, the strain relaxed. I got the thing inside the window, dropped it, and stood on it, craning over the garden path and round the corner of the house. Of course there was nothing to be seen. The birds were gone. The cat was still on the table saying "O you owl! O you owl!" The sole and only clue to what had been happening was a small earthenware saucer that lay on the path immediately below the window, with a little heap of ashes in it, from which a thin column of smoke was coming straight up and curling over when it reached the window level. That, I could not doubt, was the cause of my sudden sleepiness. I dropped a large book straight on to it, and had the satisfaction of hearing it crush to bits and of seeing the smoke go four ways along the ground and vanish.

I was perfectly awake now. I looked at the cat, and showed her the back of my hand. She sat quite still and said:

"Well, what did you expect? I had to do something. I'll lick it if you like, but I'd rather not. No particular ill-feeling, you understand; all the same a hundred years hence."

I was not in a position to answer her, so I shook my head at her, wound up my hand in a handkerchief, and then stroked her. She took it agreeably, jumped off the table, and requested to be let out.

The Five Jars

So the third attack had failed. I sat down and looked out. The hedges were empty; not a bird, not a mouse was left. I took this to mean that the dangerous time was past, and great was the relief. Soon I heard the maid come back from her errands in the village, then the mistress's chaise, then the clock striking five. I felt it would be all right for me to go out after tea.

And so I did; first, however, concealing the suit-case in my bedroom— not that I supposed hiding it would be of much use— and piling upon it poker, tongs, knife, horse-shoe, and anything else I could find which I thought would keep off trespassers. I had, by the way, to explain to the maid that a bird had flown against the window and broken it, and when she said "Stupid, tiresome little things they are," I am afraid I did not contradict her.

I went out by way of the garden and crossed the field, near the middle of which stands a large old oak. I went up to this, for no particular reason, and stood gazing at the trunk. As I did so I became aware that my eyes were beginning to "see through," and behold! a family of owls was inside. As it was near evening, they were getting wakeful, stirring, smacking their beaks and opening their wings a little from time to time. At last one of them said:

"Time's nearly up. Out and about! Out and about!"

"Anyone outside?" said another.

"No harm there," said the first.

This short way of talking, I believe, was due to the owls not being properly awake and consequently sulky. As they brightened up and got their eyes open, they began to be more easy in manner.

"Oop! Oop! Oop! I've had a very good day of it. You have, too, I hope?"

"Sound as a rock, I thank you, except when they were carrying on at the cottage."

"Oh goodness! I forgot! They didn't bring it off, I hope."

"Not they; the watch was too well set, but it was wanted. I had a leaf about it a few minutes after, and it seems they got him asleep."

"Well! I never heard anyone bring a leaf."

"I dare say not, but I was expecting it; pigeon dropped it. There it is, on that child's back."

I saw the hen-owl stoop and examine a dead chestnut leaf which lay, as the other had said, on an owlet's back.

"Fa-a-ther!" said this owlet suddenly, in a shrill voice, "mayn't I go out to-night?"

But all that Father did was to clasp its head in his claw and push it to and fro several times. When he let go, the owlet made no sound, but crept away and hid its face in a corner, and heaved as if with sobs. Father closed his eyes slowly and opened them slowly— amused, I thought. The mother had been reading the leaf all the time.

"Dear me! *very* interesting!" she said. "I suppose now the worst of it is over."

"All's quiet for to-night, anyhow," said Father, "but I wish he could see someone about to-morrow; that's their last chance, and they *may*——" He ruffled up his feathers, lifted first one foot and then the other. "The awkwardness is," he went on, "if I say too much and they do get the jars, there's one risk; and if there's no warning and they get them, there's another risk."

"But if there *is* a warning and they *don't* get them," said she, very sensibly.

The Five Jars

"Well, to be sure, that would be better, even though we don't know much about him."

"But where do you suppose he is, and whom ought he to see?" (It was just what I wanted to know, and I thanked her.)

"Why, as to the first, I suspect he's outside; there is someone there, and why they should stop there all this time unless they're listening, I don't know."

"Good gracious! listening to our private conversation! and me with my feathers all anyhow!" She began to peck at herself vigorously; but this was straying from the point, and annoyed me. However, Father went slowly on:

"As to that, I don't much care whether he's listening or not. As to whom he ought to see, that's rather more difficult. If he's got as far as talking to any of the Right People (he said this as if they had capital letters), they'd know, of course; and some of them down about the village, they'd know; and the Old Mother knows, and——"

"What about the boys?" said she, pausing in the middle of her toilet and poking her head up at him. He wholly disdained to answer, and merely butted at her with his head, so that she slipped down off her ledge several inches, with a great scrabbling. "Oh, *don't*!" she said peevishly, as she climbed back. "I'm all untidy again."

"Well then, don't ask such ridiculous questions. I shall buffle you with both wings next time. And now, as soon as the coast is clear, I shall be out and about."

I took the hint and moved off, for I had learnt as much perhaps as I could expect, even if all was not yet plain; and before I had gone many paces I was aware of the pair both sailing smoothly off in the opposite direction.

I was "seeing through" a good deal that evening; it is surprising what a lot of coppers people drop, even on a field path; surprising, too, in how many places there lie, unsuspected, bones of men. Some things I saw which were ugly and sad, like that, but more that were amusing and even exciting. There is one spot I could show where four gold cups stand round what was once a book, but the book is no more than earth now. That, however, I did not see on this particular evening.

What I remember best is a family of young rabbits huddled round their parents in a burrow, and the mother telling a story: "And so then he went a little farther and found a dandelion, and stopped and sat up and began to eat it. And when he had eaten two large leaves and one little one, he saw a fly on it— no, two flies; and then he thought he had had enough of that dandelion, and he went a little farther and found another dandelion..." And so it went on interminably, and entirely stupid, like everything else I ever heard a rabbit say, for they have forgotten all about their ancestor, Brer Rabbit. However, the children were absorbed in the story, so much so that they never heard a stoat making its way down the burrow. But I heard it, and by stamping and driving my stick in I was able to make it turn tail and go off, cursing. All stoats, weasels, ferrets, polecats, are of the wrong people, as you may imagine, and so are most rats and bats.

At last I left off seeing through, by trying not to do so, and went back to the house, where I found all safe and quiet.

I ought to say that I had not as yet tried speaking to any animal, even to the cat when she scratched me, but I thought I would try it now. So when she came in at dinner-

The Five Jars

time and circled about, with what I may call pious aspirations about fish and other such things, I summoned up my courage and said (using my voice in the way I described, or rather did not describe, before):

"I used to be told, 'If you are hungry, you can eat dry bread.'"

She was certainly horribly startled. At first I thought she would have dashed up the chimney or out of the window; but she recovered pretty quickly and sat down, still looking at me with intense surprise.

"I suppose I might have guessed," she said; "but dear! what a turn you did give me! I feel quite faint; and gracious! what a day it has been! When I found you dozing off like a great—— Well, no one wants to be rude, do they? but I can tell you I had more than half a mind to go at your face."

"I am glad you didn't," I said; "and really, you know, it wasn't my fault: it was that stuff they were burning on the path."

"I know that well enough," she said; "but to come back to the point, all this anxiety has made me as empty in myself as a clean saucer."

"Just what I was saying; if you are hungry, you can——"

"Say that again, say it just once more," she said, and her eyes grew narrow as she said it, "and I shall——"

"What shall you do?" I asked, for she stopped suddenly.

She calmed herself. "Oh, you know how it is when one's been all excited-like and worked up; we all say more than we mean. But that about dry bread! Well, there! I simply can't bear it. It's a wicked, cruel untruth, that's what it is; and besides, you *can't* be going to eat all the whole of what she's put down for you." Excitement was coming on again, and she ended with a loud ill-tempered mew.

Well, I gave her what she seemed to want, and shortly after, worn out doubtless with the fatigues of the day, she went to sleep on a chair, not even caring to follow the maid downstairs when things were cleared away.

Chapter VI
The Cat, Wag, Slim and Others

I got out my precious casket. I sat by the window and watched. The moon shone out, the lid of the box loosened in due course, and I touched my forehead with the ointment. But neither at once nor for some little time after did I notice any fresh power coming to me.

With the moon, up came also the little town, and no sooner were the doors of the houses level with the grass than the boys were out of them and running in some numbers towards my window; in fact, some slipped out of their own windows, not waiting for the doors to be available. Wag was the first. Slim, more sedate, came among the crowd that followed. These were still the only two who felt no hesitation about talking to me. The others were all fully occupied in exploring the room.

"To-morrow," I said (after some sort of how-do-you-do's had been exchanged), "you'll be flying all over the place, I suppose."

"Yes," said Wag, shortly. "But I want to know— I say, Slim, what was it we wanted first?"

"Wasn't there a message from your father?" said Slim.

The Five Jars

"Oh, yes, of course. 'If they're about the house,' he said, 'give them horseshoes; if there's a bat-ball, squirt at it': he thinks there's a squirt in the tool-house— Oh, there's the cat; I must——" After delivering all this in one sentence, he rushed to the edge of the table and took a kind of header into the midst of the unfortunate animal, who, however, only moaned or crowed without waking, and turned partly over on her back.

Slim remained sitting on a book and gazing soberly at me.

"Well," I said, "it's very kind of Wag's father to send me a message, but I must say I can't make much of it."

Slim nodded. "So he said, and he said you'd see when the time came; of course I don't know, myself; I've never seen a bat-ball. Wag says he has, but you never know with Wag."

"Well, I must do the best I can, I suppose; but look here, Slim, I wish you could tell me one or two things. What *are* you? What do they call you?"

"They call me Slim: and the whole of us they call the Right People," said Slim; "but it's no good asking us much, because we don't know, and besides, it isn't good for us."

"How do you mean?"

"Why, you see, our job is to keep the little things right, and if we do more than that, or if we try to find out much more, then we burst."

"And is that the end of you?"

"Oh, no!" he said cheerfully, "but that's one of the things it's no good asking."

"And if you don't do your job, what then?"

"Oh, then they get smaller and have no sense." (He said *they*, not *we*, I noticed.)

60

"I see. Well now, you go to school, don't you?" He nodded. "What for? Isn't that likely to be bad for you?" (I hardly liked to say "make you burst.")

"No," he said; "you see, it's to learn our job. We have to be told what used to go on, so as we can put things right, or keep them right. And the owls, you see, they remember a long way back, but they don't know any more than we do about the swell things."

I was very shy about putting the next question I had in mind, but I felt I must. "Now do you know how old you are, or how long it takes you to grow up, or how— how long you go on when you *are* grown up!"

He pressed his hands to his head, and I was dreadfully afraid for the moment that it might be swelling and would burst; but it was not so bad as that. After a few seconds he looked up and said:

"I think it's seven times seven moons since I went to school and seven times seven times seven moons before I grow up; and the rest is no good asking. But it's all right"; upon which he smiled.

And this, I may say, was the most part of what I ventured to ask any of them about themselves. But at other times I gathered that as long as they "did their job" nothing could injure them; and they were regularly measured— all of them— to see if they were getting smaller, and a careful record kept. But if anyone lost as much as a quarter of his height, he was doomed, and he crept off out of the settlement. Whether such a one ever came back I could not be sure; most of the failures (and they were not common) went and lived in hollow trees or by brooks, and were happy enough, but in a feeble way, not remembering much, nor able to make anything; and it was supposed that very slowly

The Five Jars

they shrunk to the size of a pin's point, and probably to nothing. All the same, it was believed that they *could* recover. Many other things that *you* would have asked, I did not, being anxious to avoid giving trouble.

But this time, anyhow, I felt I had catechized Slim long enough, so I broke off and said:

"What can Wag be doing all this while?"

"There's no knowing," said Slim. "But he's very quiet for him; either he's doing something awful, or he's asleep."

"I saw him with the cat last," I said; "you might go and look at her."

He walked to the edge of the table, and said, "Why, he *is* asleep!" And so he was, with his head on the cat's chest, under her chin, which she had turned up; and she had put her front paws together over the top of his head. As for the others, I descried them sitting in a circle in a corner of the room, also very quiet. (I imagine they were a little afraid of doing much without Wag, and also of waking him.) But I could not make out what they were doing, so I asked Slim.

"Racing earwigs, I should think," he said, with something of contempt.

"Well, I hope they won't leave them about when they go. I don't like earwigs."

"Who does?" he said; "but they'll take them away all right; they're prize ones, some of them."

I went over and looked at the racing for a little. The course was neatly marked out with small lights sprouting out of the boards, and the circle was at the winning-post, the starters being at the other end, some six feet away. I watched one heat. The earwigs seemed to me neither very speedy nor very intelligent, and all except one were apt to

62

stop in mid-course and engage in personal encounters with each other.

I was beginning to wonder how long this would go on, when Wag woke up. Like most of us, he was not willing to allow that he had been asleep.

"I thought I'd just lie down a bit," he said, "and then I didn't want to bustle your cat, so I stopped there. And now I want to know— Slim, I say, what was it you were asking me?"

"Me asking you? I don't know."

"Oh, yes, you do; what he was doing the other time before we came in."

"I didn't ask you that; you asked me."

"Well, it doesn't matter who asked." (Turning to me): "What *were* you doing?"

"I don't know," I said. "Was it these things I was using" (taking up a pack of cards), "or something like this?" (I held up a book.)

"Yes, that one. What were you doing with it? What's it for?"

"We call it reading a book," and I tried to explain what the idea was, and read out a few lines; it happened to be *Pickwick*. They were absorbed. Slim said, half to himself, "Something like a glass," which I thought quite meaningless at the time. Then I showed them a picture in another book. That they made out very quickly.

"But when's it going to move on?" said Slim.

"Never," I said. "Ours stop just like that always. Do yours move on?"

"Of course they do; look here." He lay down on the tablecloth and pressed his forehead on it, but evidently could make nothing of it. "It's all rough," he said. I gave him a

sheet of paper. "That's better;" and he lay down again in the same posture for a few seconds. Then he got up and began rubbing the paper all over with the palms of his hands. As he did so a coloured picture came out pretty quickly, and when it was finished he drew aside to let me see, and said, somewhat bashfully, "I don't think I've got it *quite* right, but I meant it for what happened the other evening." He had certainly not got it right as far as I was concerned. It was a view of the window of the house, seen from outside by moonlight, and there was a back view of a row of figures with their elbows on the sill. So far, so good; but inside the open window was standing a figure which was plainly— much too plainly, I thought— meant for me; far too short and fat, far too red-faced, and with an owlish expression which I am sure I never wear. This person was now seen to move his hand— a very poor hand, with only about three fingers— to his side, and pull, apparently, out of his body, a round object more or less like a watch (at any rate it was white on one side with black marks, and yellow on the oth- er) and lay it down in front of him. At this the figures at the window-sill threw up their arms in all directions and fell or slid down like so many dolls. Then the picture began to get fainter, and disappeared from the paper. Slim looked at me expectantly.

"Well," I said, "it's very interesting to see how you do it, but is that the best likeness of me that you can make?"

"What's wrong with it?" said he. "Isn't it handsome enough or something?"

I heard Wag throw himself down on the table, and, look- ing at him, I saw that he had got both hands pressed over his mouth.

"May I ask what the joke is?" I said rather dryly (for it is surprising how touchy one can be over one's personal appearance, even at my time of life). He looked up for an instant at me, and then gasped and hid his face again. Slim went up to him and kicked him in the ribs.

"Where's your manners?" he said in a loud whisper. Wag rolled over and sat up, wiping his eyes.

"I'm very sorry," he said. "I'm sure I don't know what I was laughing for." Slim whistled. "Well," said Wag, "what *was* I?"

"Him, of course, and you know perfectly well!"

"Oh, was I? Well, perhaps you'll tell me what there is to laugh at about him?" said Wag, rather basely, I thought; so, as Slim put his finger to his lip and looked unhappy, I interrupted.

"Get up a minute, Wag," I said. "I want to see something."

"What?" said he, jumping up at once.

"Stand back to back with Slim, if you don't mind. That's it. Dear me! I thought you were taller than that— you looked to me taller last night. My mistake, I dare say. All right, thanks." But there they stood, gazing at each other with horror, and I felt I had been trifling with a most serious subject, so I laughed and said, "Don't disturb yourselves. I was only chaffing you, Wag, because you seemed to be doing something of the kind to me."

Slim understood, and heaved a sigh of relief. Wag sat down on a book and looked reproachfully upon me. Neither said a word. I was very much ashamed, and begged their pardon as nicely as I knew how. Luckily Wag was soon convinced that I was not in earnest, and he recovered his spirits directly.

The Five Jars

"All *right*," he said, nodding at me; "did I hear you say you didn't like earwigs? That's worth remembering, Slim."

This reduced me at once; I tried to point out that he had begun it, and that it would be a mean revenge, and very hard on the earwigs, if he filled my room with them, for I should be obliged to kill all I could.

"Why," he said, "they needn't be real earwigs; my own tickle every bit as much as real ones."

This was no better for me, and I tried to make more appeals to his better feelings. He did not seem to be listening very attentively, though his eyes were fixed on me.

"What's that on your neck?" he said suddenly, and at the same moment I felt a procession of legs walking over my skin. I brushed at it hastily, and something seemed to fall on the table. "No, the other side I mean," said he, and again I felt the same horrid tickling and went through the same exercises, with a face, I've no doubt, contorted with terror. Anyhow, it seemed to amuse them very much; Wag, in fact, was quite unable to speak, and could only point. It was dull of me not to have realized at once that these were "his" earwigs and not real ones. But now I did, and though I still felt the tickling, I did not move, but sat down and gazed severely at him. Soon he got the better of his mirth and said, "I think we are quits now." Then, with sudden alarm, "I say, what's become of the others? The bell hasn't gone, has it?"

"How should I know?" I said. "If you hadn't been making all this disturbance, perhaps we might have heard it."

He took a flying leap— an extraordinary feat it was— from the edge of the table to a chair in the window, scrambled up to the sill, and gazed out. "It's all right," he said, in a faint voice of infinite relief; let himself down limply to the floor, and climbed slowly up my leg to his former place.

66

"Well," I said, "the bell hasn't gone, it seems, but where are the rest? I've hardly seen anything of them."

"Oh, *you* go and find 'em, Slim; I'm worn out with all these frights."

Slim went to the farther end of the table, prospected, and returned. He reported them "all right, but they're having rather a slow time of it, I think." I, too, got up, walked round, and looked; they were seated in a solemn circle on the floor round the cat, who was now curled up and fast asleep on a round footstool. Not a word was being said by anybody. I thought I had better address them, so I said:

"Gentlemen, I'm afraid I've been very inattentive to you this evening. Isn't there anything I can do to amuse you? Won't you come up on the table? You're welcome to walk up my leg if you find that convenient."

I was almost sorry I had spoken the moment after, for they made but one rush at my legs as I stood by the table, and the sensation was rather like that, I imagine, of a swarm of rats climbing up one's trousers. However, it was over in a few seconds, and all of them— over a dozen— were with Wag and Slim on the table, except one, who, whether by mistake or on purpose, went on climbing me by way of my waistcoat buttons, rather deliberately, until he reached my shoulder. I didn't object, of course, but I turned round (which made him catch at my ear) and went back to my chair, seated in which I felt rather as if I was presiding at a meeting. The one on my shoulder sat down and, I thought, folded his arms and looked at his friends with some triumph. Wag evidently took this to be a liberty.

"My word!" he said, "what do you mean by it, Wisp? Come off it!"

The Five Jars

Wisp was a little daunted, as I judged by his fidgeting somewhat, but put a bold face on it and said, "Why should I come off?"

I put in a word: "I don't mind his being here."

"I dare say not; that's not the point," said Wag. "Are you coming down?"

"No," said Wisp, "not for you." But his tone was rather blustering than brave.

"Very well, don't then," said Wag; and I expected him to run up and pull Wisp down by the legs, but he didn't do that. He took something out of the breast of his tunic, put it in his mouth, lay down on his stomach, and, with his eyes on Wisp, puffed out his cheeks. Two or three seconds passed, during which I felt Wisp shifting about on his perch, and breathing quickly. Then he gave a sharp shriek, which went right through my head, slipped rapidly down my chest and legs and on to the floor, where he continued to squeal and to run about like a mad thing, to the great amusement of everyone on the table.

Then I saw what was the matter. All round his head were a multitude of little sparks, which flew about him like a swarm of bees, every now and then settling and coming off again, and, I suppose, burning him every time; if he beat them off, they attacked his hands, so he was in a bad way. After watching him for about a minute from the edge of the table, Wag called out:

"Do you apologize?"

"Yes!" he screamed.

"All right," said Wag; "stand still! stand still, you bat! How can I get 'em back if you don't?" Wag was back to me and I couldn't see what he did, but Wisp sat down on the carpet free of sparks, and wiped his face and neck with his

68

handkerchief for some time, while the rest gradually recovered from their laughter. "You can come up again now," said Wag; and so he did, though he was slow and shy about it.

"Why didn't he send sparks at Wag?" said I to Slim.

"He hasn't got 'em to send," was the answer. "It's only the Captain of the moon."

"Well now, what about a little peace and quiet?" I said. "And, you know, I've never been introduced to you all properly. Wouldn't it be a good idea to do that, before the bell goes?"

"Very well," said Wag. "We'll *do* it properly. You bring 'em up one at a time, Slim, and" (to me) "you put your sun-hand out on the table."

I: "Sun-hand?"

Wag: "Yes, sun-hand; don't you know?" He held up his right hand, then his left: "Sun-hand, Moon-hand, Day-hand, Night-hand, Star-hand, Cloud-hand, and so on."

I: "Thank you."

This was done, and meanwhile Slim formed the troop into a queue and beckoned them up one by one. Wag stood on a book on the right and proclaimed the name of each. First he had made me arrange my right hand edgeways on the table, with the forefinger out. Then "Gold!" said Wag. Gold stepped forward and made a lovely bow, which I returned with an inclination of my head, then took as much of my forefinger top joint in his right hand as he could manage, bent over it and shook it or tried to, and then took up a position on the left and watched the next comer. The ceremony was the same for everyone, but not all the bows were equally elegant; some of the boys were jocular, and shook my finger with both hands and a great display of effort.

The Five Jars

These were frowned upon by Wag. The names (I need not set them all down now) were all of the same kind as you have heard; there was Red, Wise, Dart, Sprat, and so on. After Wisp, who came last and was rather humble, Wag called out Slim, and, after him, descended and presented himself in the same form.

"And now," he said, "perhaps you'll tell us *your* name."

I did so (one is always a little shamefaced about it, I don't know why) in full. He whistled.

"Too much," he said; "what's the easiest you can do?"

After some thought I said, "What about M or N?"

"Much better! If M's all right for you, it'll do for us." So M was agreed upon.

I was still rather afraid that the rank and file had been passing a dull evening and would not come again, and I tried to express as much to them. But they said:

"Dull? Oh no, M; why we've found out all sorts of things!"

"Really? What sort of things?"

"Well, inside the wall in that corner there's the biggest spider I've ever seen, for one thing."

"Good gracious!" I said. "I hate 'em. I hope it can't get out?"

"It would have to-night if we hadn't stopped up the hole. Something's been helping it to gnaw through."

"Has it?" said Wag. "My word! that looks bad. What was it made the hole?"

Some called out, "A bat," and some "A rat."

"It doesn't matter much for that," said Slim, "so long as it's safe now. Where is it?"

"Gone down to the bottom and saying awful things," Red answered.

70

"Well, I *am* obliged to you," I said. "Anything else?"

"There's a lot of this stuff under the floor," said Dart, pointing with his foot at a half-crown which lay on the table.

"Is there? Whereabouts?" said I. "Oh, but I was forgetting; I can look after that myself."

"Yes, of course you can," they said; "and lots of things happened here before you came. We were watching. The old man and the woman, they were the worst, weren't they, Red?"

"Do you mean you've been here before?" I asked.

"No, no, but to-night we were looking at them, like we do at school."

This was beyond me, and I thought it would be of no use to ask for more explanations. Besides, just at this moment we heard the bell. They all clambered down either me or the chairs or the tablecloth. Slim lingered a moment to say, "You'll look out, won't you?" and then followed the rest on to the window-sill, where, taking the time from Captain Wag, they all stood in a row, bowed with their caps off, straightened up again, each sang one note, which combined into a wonderful chord, faced round and disappeared. I followed them to the window and saw the inhabitants of the house separating and going to their homes with the young ones capering round them. One or two of the elders— Wag's father in particular— looked up at me, paused in their walk, and bowed gravely, which courtesy I returned. I went on gazing until the lawn was a blank once more, and then, closing and fastening the sitting-room window, I betook myself to the bedroom.

Chapter VII
The Bat-Ball

It had certainly been an eventful day and evening, and I felt that my adventures could not be quite at an end yet, for I had still to find out what new power or sense the Fourth Jar had brought me. I stood and thought, and tried quite vainly to detect some difference in myself. And then I went to the window and drew the curtain aside and looked out on the road, and within a few minutes I began to understand.

There came walking rapidly along the road a young man, and he turned in at the garden gate and came straight up the path to the house door. I began to be surprised, not at his coming, for it was not so very late, but at the look of him. He was young, as I said, rather red-faced, but not bad-looking; of the class of a farmer, I thought. He wore biggish brown whiskers— which is not common nowadays— and his hair was rather long at the back— which also is not common with young men who want to look smart— but his hat, and his clothes generally, were the really odd part of him. The hat was a sort of low top-hat, with a curved brim; it spread out at the top and it was brushed rough instead of smooth. His coat was a blue swallow-tail with brass buttons.

The Five Jars

He had a broad tie wound round and round his neck, and a Gladstone collar. His trousers were tight all the way down and had straps under his feet. To put it in the dullest, shortest way, he was "dressed in the fashion of eighty or ninety years ago," as we read in the ghost stories. Evidently he knew his way about very well. He came straight up to the front door and, as far as I could tell, into the house, but I did not hear the door open or shut or any steps on the stairs. He must, I thought, be in my landlady's parlour downstairs.

I turned away from the window, and there was the next surprise. It was as if there was no wall between me and the sitting-room. I saw straight into it. There was a fire in the grate, and by it were sitting face to face an old man and an old woman. I thought at once of what one of the boys had said, and I looked curiously at them. They were, you would have said, as fine specimens of an old-fashioned yeoman and his wife as anyone could wish to see. The man was hale and red-faced, with grey whiskers, smiling as he sat bolt upright in his arm-chair. The old lady was rosy and smiling too, with a smart silk dress and a smart cap, and tidy ringlets on each side of her face— a regular picture of wholesome old age; and yet I hated them both. The young man, their son, I suppose, was in the room standing at the door with his hat in his hand, looking timidly at them. The old man turned half round in his chair, looked at him, turned down the corners of his mouth, looked across at the old lady, and they both smiled as if they were amused. The son came farther into the room, put his hat down, leaned with both hands on the table, and began to speak (though nothing could be heard) with an earnestness that was painful to see, because I could be certain his pleading would be of no use; sometimes he spread out his hands and shook them, every now and

74

again he brushed his eyes. He was very much moved, and so was I, merely watching him. The old people were not; they leaned forward a little in their chairs and sometimes smiled at each other— again as if they were amused. At last he had done, and stood with his hands before him, quivering all over. His father and mother leaned back in their chairs and looked at each other. I think they said not a single word. The son caught up his hat, turned round, and went quickly out of the room. Then the old man threw back his head and laughed, and the old lady laughed too, not so boisterously.

I turned back to the window. It was as I expected. Outside the garden gate, in the road, a young slight girl in a large poke-bonnet and shawl and rather short-skirted dress was waiting, in great anxiety, as I could see by the way she held to the railings. Her face I could not see. The young man came out; she clasped her hands, he shook his head; they went off together slowly up the road, he with bowed shoulders, supporting her, she, I dare say, crying. Again I looked round to the sitting-room. The wall hid it now.

It sounds a dull ordinary scene enough, but I can assure you it was horribly disturbing to watch, and the cruel calm way in which the father and mother, who looked so nice and worthy and were so abominable, treated their son, was like nothing I had ever seen.

Of course I know now what the effect of the Fourth Jar was; it made me able to see what had happened in any place. I did not yet know how far back the memories would go, or whether I was obliged to see them if I did not want to. But it was clear to me that the boys were sometimes taught in this way. "We were watching them like we do at school," one of them said, and though the grammar was poor, the meaning was plain, and I would ask Slim about it when we next met.

The Five Jars

Meanwhile I must say I hoped the gift would not go on working instead of letting me go to sleep. It did not.

Next day I met my landlady employing herself in the garden, and asked her about the people who had formerly lived in the house.

"Oh yes," said she. "I can tell you about them, for my father he remembered old Mr. and Mrs. Eld quite well when he was a slip of a lad. They wasn't liked in the place, neither of them, partly through bein' so hard-like to their workpeople, and partly from them treating their only son so bad— I mean to say turning him right off because he married without asking permission. Well, no doubt, that's what he shouldn't have done, but my father said it was a very nice respectable young girl he married, and it do seem hard for them never to say a word of kindness all those years and leave every penny away from the young people. What become of them, do you say, sir? Why, I believe they emigrated away to the United States of America and never was heard of again, but the old people they lived on here, and I never heard but what they was easy in their minds right up to the day of their death. Nice-looking old people they was too, my father used to say; seemed as if butter wouldn't melt in their mouths, as the saying is. Now I don't know when I've thought of them last, but I recollect my father speaking of them as well, and the way they're spoke of on their stone that lays just to the right-hand side as you go up the churchyard path— well, you'd think there never was such people. But I believe that was put up by them that got the property; now what was that name again?"

But about that time I thought I must be getting on. I also thought (as before) that it would be well for me not to go very far away from the house.

As I strolled up the road I pondered over the message which Wag's father had been so good as to send me. "If they're about the house, give them horseshoes; if there's a bat-ball, squirt at it. I think there's a squirt in the tool-house." All very well, no doubt. I had one horseshoe, but that was not much, and I could explore the tool-house and borrow the garden squirt. But more horseshoes?

At that moment I heard a squeak and a rustle in the hedge, and could not help poking my stick into it to see what had made the noise. The stick clinked against something with its iron ferrule. An old horseshoe!— evidently shown to me on purpose by a friendly creature. I picked it up, and, not to make a long story of it, I was helped by much the same devices to increase my collection to four. And now I felt it would be wise to turn back.

As I turned into the back garden and came in sight of the little potting-shed or tool-house or whatever it was, I started. Someone was just coming out of it. I gave a loud cough. The party turned round hastily; it was an old man in a sleeved waistcoat, made up, I thought, to look like an "odd man." He touched his hat civilly enough, and showed no surprise; but, oh, horror! he held in his hand the garden squirt.

"Morning," I said; "going to do a bit of watering?" He grinned. "Just stepped up to borrer this off the lady; there's a lot of fly gets on the plants this weather."

"I dare say there is. By the way, what a lot of horseshoes you people leave about. How many do you think I picked up this morning just along the road? Look here!" and I held one out to him, and his hand came slowly out to meet it, as though he could not keep it back.

The Five Jars

His face wrinkled up into a horrible scowl, and what he was going to say I don't know, but just then his hand clutched the horseshoe and he gave a shout of pain, dropped the squirt and the horseshoe, whipped round as quick as any young man could, and was off round the corner of the shed before I had really taken in what was happening. Before I tried to see what had become of him, I snatched up the squirt and the horseshoe, and almost dropped them again. Both were pretty hot— the squirt much the hotter of the two; but both of them cooled down in a few seconds. By that time my old man was completely out of sight. And I should not wonder if he was away some time; for perhaps you know, and perhaps you don't know, the effect of an old horseshoe on that sort of people. Not only is it of iron, which they can't abide, but when they see or, still more, touch the shoe, they have to go over all the ground that the shoe went over since it was last in the blacksmith's hands. Only I doubt if the same shoe will work for more than one witch or wizard. Anyway, I put that one aside when I went indoors. And then I sat and wondered what would come next, and how I could best prepare for it. It occurred to me that it would do no harm to put one of the shoes where it couldn't be seen at once, and it also struck me that under the rug just inside the bedroom door would not be a bad place. So there I put it, and then fell to smoking and reading.

A knock at the door.

"Come in," said I, a little curious; but no, it was only the maid. As she passed me (which she did quickly) I heard her mutter something about "'ankerchieves for the wash," and I thought there was something not quite usual about the voice. So I looked round. She was back to me, but the dress

and the height and the hair was what I was accustomed to see. Into the bedroom she hurried, and the next thing was a scream like that of at least two cats in agony! I could just see her leap into the air, come down again on the rug, scream again, and then bundle, hopping, limping— I don't know what— out of the room and down the stairs. I did catch sight of her feet, though; they were bare, they were greenish, and they were webbed, and I think there were some large white blisters on the soles of them. You would have thought that the commotion would have brought the household about my ears; but it did not, and I can only suppose that they heard no more of it than they did of the things which the birds and so on say to each other.

"Next, please!" said I, as I lighted a pipe; but if you will believe it, there was no next. Lunch, the afternoon, tea, all passed by, and I was completely undisturbed. "They must be saving up for the bat-ball," I thought. "What in the world can it be?"

As candle-time came on, and the moon began to make herself felt, I took up my old position at the window, with the garden squirt at hand and two full jugs of water on the floor— plenty more to be got from the bathroom if wanted. The leaden box of the Five Jars was in the right place for the moonbeams to fall on it... But no moonbeams would touch it to-night! Why was this? There were no clouds. Yet, between the orb of the moon and my box, there was some obstruction. High up in the sky was a dancing film, thick enough to cast a shadow on the area of the window; and ever, as the moon rode higher in the heavens, this obstruction became more solid. It seemed gradually to get its bearings and settle into the place where it would shut off the light from the box most completely. I began to guess. It was

The Five Jars

the bat-ball; neither more nor less than a dense cloud of bats, gradually forming itself into a solid ball, and coming lower, and nearer to my window. Soon they were only about thirty feet off, and I felt that the moment was come.

I have never much liked bats or desired their company, and now, as I studied them through the glass, and saw their horrid little wicked faces and winking wings, I felt justified in trying to make things as unpleasant for them as I could. I charged the squirt and let fly, and again, and again, as quick as I could fill it. The water spread a bit before it reached the ball, but not too much to spoil the effect; and the effect was almost alarming. Some hundreds of bats all shrieking out at once, and shrieking with rage and fear (not merely from the excitement of chasing flies, as they generally do). Dozens of them dropping away, with wings too soaked to fly, some on to the grass, where they hopped and fluttered and rolled in ecstasies of passion, some into bushes, one or two plumb on to the path, where they lay motionless; that was the first tableau. Then came a new feature. From both sides there darted into the heart of the ball two squadrons of figures flying at great speed (though without wings) and perfectly horizontal, with arms joined and straight out in front of them, and almost at the same instant seven or eight more plunged into the ball from above, as if taking headers. The boys were out.

I stopped squirting, for I did not know whether the water would fell them as it felled the bats; but a shrill cry rose from below:

"Go on, M! go on, M!"

So I aimed again, and it was time, for a knot of bats just then detached itself from the main body and flew full-face towards me. My shot caught the middle one on the snout,

80

and as I swung the squirt to left and right, it disabled four or five others, and discouraged the rest. Meanwhile the ball was cloven again and again by the arms of the flying squadrons, which shot through it from side to side and from top to bottom (though never, as appeared later, quite through the middle), and though it kept closing up again, it was plainly growing smaller as more and more of the bats outside, which were exposed to the squirt, dropped away.

I suddenly felt something alight on my shoulder, and a voice said in my ear, "Wag says if you *could* throw a shoe into the middle now, he believes it would finish them. Can you?" It was, I think, Dart who had been sent with the message.

"Horseshoes, I suppose he means," I said. "I'll try."

"Wait till we're out of the way," said Dart, and was off.

In a moment more I heard— not what I was rather expecting, a horn of Elf-land, but two strokes on the bell. I saw the figures of the boys shoot up and away to left and right, leaving the bat-ball clear, and the bats shrieked aloud, I dare say in triumph at the enemy's retreat.

There were two horseshoes left. I had no idea how they would fly, and I had not much confidence in my power of aiming; but it must be tried, and I threw them edgeways, like quoits. The first skimmed the top of the ball, the second went straight through the middle. Something which the bats in the very centre were holding— something soft— was pierced by it, and burst. I think it must have been a globe of jelly-like stuff in a thin skin. The contents spurted out on to some of the bats, and seemed to scald the fur off them in an instant and singe up all the membranes of their wings. They fell down at once, with broken screams. The rest darted off in every direction, and the ball was gone.

The Five Jars

"Now don't be long," said a voice from the window-sill.

I thought I knew what was meant, and looked to the leaden casket. As if to make up for lost time, the moonbeam had already made an opening all round the part on which it shone, and I had but to turn the other side towards it— not even very slowly— to get the whole lid free. After cleansing my hands in the water, I made trial of the Fifth Jar, and, as I replaced it, a chorus of applause and cheering came up from below.

The Jars were mine.

Chapter VIII
Wag at Home

There was no scrambling up to the window-sill this time. My visitors shot in like so many arrows, and "brought up" on their hands on the tablecloth, or lit on their feet on the top rail of a chair-back or on my shoulder, as the fancy took them. It would be tedious to go through all the congratulations and thanks which I offered, and indeed received, for it was important to them that the Jars should not get into wrong hands.

"Father says," said Wag, who was sitting on a book, as usual— "Oh, what fun it is to be able to fly again!" And he darted straight and level and butted head first into the back of— Sprat, was it?— who was standing near the edge of the table. Sprat was merely propelled into the air a foot or two off, and remained standing, but, of course, turned round and told Wag what he thought of him. Wag returned contentedly to his book. "Father says," he resumed, "he hopes you'll come and see us now. He says you did all right, and he's very glad the stuff got spilt, because they'll take moons and moons to get as much of it together again. He says they meant to squirt some of it on you when they got near

The Five Jars

enough, and while you were trying to get it off they'd have got hold of——" He pointed to the box of jars; there was a shyness about mentioning it.

"Your father's very kind," I said, "and I hope you'll thank him from me; but I don't quite see how I'm to get into your house."

"Fancy you not knowing that!" said Wag. "I'll tell him you'll come." And he was out of the window. As usual, I had recourse to Slim.

"Why, you did put some on your chest, didn't you?" was Slim's question.

"Yes, but nothing came of it."

"Well, I believe you can go pretty well anywhere with that, if you think you can."

"Can I fly, then?"

"No, I should say not; I mean, if you couldn't fly before, you can't now."

"How do you fly? I don't see any wings."

"No, we never have wings, and I'm rather glad we don't; the things that have them are always going wrong somehow. We just work it in the proper way with our backs, and there you are; like this." He made a slight movement of his shoulders, and was standing in the air an inch off the table. "You never tried that, I suppose?" he went on.

"No," I said, "only in dreams," which evidently meant nothing to him. "Well now," I said, "do you tell me that if I went to Wag's house now, I could get inside it? Look at the size I am!"

"It doesn't look as if you could," he agreed, "but my father said just the same as Wag's father about it."

Here Wag shot on to my shoulder. "Are you coming?"

"Yes, if I knew how."

84

M. R. James

"Well, come and try, anyhow."

"Very well, as you please; anything to oblige."

I picked up a hat and went downstairs. All the rest followed, if you can call it following, when there was at least as much flying up steps and in and out of banisters as going down. When we were out on the path, Wag said with more seriousness than usual:

"Now you do mean to come into our house, don't you?"

"Certainly I do, if you wish me to."

"Then that's all right. This way. There's Father."

We were on the grass now, and very long it was, and nice and wet I thought I should be with all the dew. As I looked up to see the elder Wag I very nearly fell over a large log which it was very careless of anyone to have left about. But here was Mr. Wag within a yard of me, and to my extreme surprise he was quite a sizeable man of middle height, with a sensible, good-humoured face, in which I could see a strong likeness to his son. We both bowed, and then shook hands, and Mr. Wag was very complimentary and pleasant about the occurrences of the evening.

"We've pretty well got the mess cleared up, you see. Yes, don't be alarmed," he went on, and took hold of my elbow, for he had, no doubt, seen a bewildered look in my eyes. The fact was, as I suppose you have made out, not that he had grown to my size, but that I had come down to his. "Things right themselves; you'll have no difficulty about getting back when the time comes. But come in, won't you?"

You will expect me to describe the house and the furniture. I shall not, further than to say that it seemed to me to be of a piece with the fashion in which the boys were dressed; that is, it was like my idea of a good citizen's house

85

The Five Jars

in Queen Elizabeth's time; and I shall not describe Mrs. Wag's costume. She did not wear a ruff, anyhow.

Wag, who had been darting about in the air while we walked to his home, followed us in on foot. He now reached up to my shoulder. Slim, who came in too, was shorter.

"Haven't you got any sisters?" I took occasion to say to Wag.

"Of course," said he; "don't you see 'em? Oh! I forgot. Come out, you sillies!"

Upon which there came forward three nice little girls, each of whom was putting away something into a kind of locket which she wore round her neck. No, it is no use asking me what *their* dresses were like; none at all. All I know is that they curtsied to me very nicely, and that when we all sat down the youngest came and put herself on my knee as if it was a matter of course.

"Why didn't I see you before?" I asked her.

"I suppose because the flowers were in our hair."

"Show him what you mean, my dear," said her father. "He doesn't know our ways yet."

Accordingly she opened her locket and took out of it a small blue flower, looking as if it was made of enamel, and stuck it in her hair over her forehead. As she did so she vanished, but I could still feel the weight of her on my knee. When she took it out again (as no doubt she did) she became visible, put it back in the locket, and smiled agreeably at me. Naturally, I had a good many questions to ask about this, but you will hardly expect me to put them all down. Becoming invisible in this way was a privilege which the girls always had till they were grown up, and I suppose I may say "came out." Of course, if they presumed on it, the lockets were taken away for the time being— just in the

86

same way as the boys were sometimes stopped from flying, as we have seen. But their own families could always see them, or at any rate the flowers in their hair, and they could always see each other.

But dear me! how much am I to tell of the conversation of that evening? One part at least: I remembered to ask about the pictures of the things that had happened in former times in places where I chanced to be. Was I obliged to see them, whether they were pleasant or horrible? "Oh no," they said; if you shut your eyes from below— that meant pushing up the lower eyelids— you would be rid of them; and you would only begin seeing them, either if you wanted to, or else if you left your mind quite blank, and were thinking of nothing in particular. Then they would begin to come, and there was no knowing how old they might be; that depended on how angry or excited or happy or sad the people had been to whom they happened.

And that reminds me of another thing. Wag had got rather fidgety while we were talking, and was flying up to the ceiling and down again, and walking on his hands, and so forth, when his mother said:

"Dear, do be quiet. Why don't you take a glass and amuse yourself with it? Here's the key of the cupboard."

She threw it to him and he caught it and ran to a tall bureau opposite and unlocked it. After humming and flitting about in front of it for a little time, he pulled a thing like a slate off a shelf where there were a large number of them.

"What have you got?" said his mother.

"The one I didn't get to the end of yesterday, about the dragon."

"Oh, that's a very good one," said she. "I used to be very fond of that."

The Five Jars

"I liked it awfully as far as I got," he said, and was betaking himself to a settle on the other side of the room when I asked if I might see it, and he brought it to me.

It was just like a small looking-glass in a frame, and the frame had one or two buttons or little knobs on it. Wag put it into my hand and then got behind me and put his chin on my shoulder.

"That's where I'd got to," he said; "he's just going out through the forest."

I thought at the first glance that I was looking at a very good copy of a picture. It was a knight on horseback, in plate-armour, and the armour looked as if it had really seen service. The horse was a massive white beast, rather of the cart-horse type, but not so "hairy in the hoof"; the background was a wood, chiefly of oak-trees; but the undergrowth was wonderfully painted. I felt that if I looked into it I should see every blade of grass and every bramble-leaf.

"Ready?" said Wag, and reached over and moved one of the knobs. The knight shook his rein, and the horse began to move at a foot-pace.

"Well, but he can't *hear* anything, Wag," said his father.

"I thought you wanted to be quiet," said Wag, "but we'll have it aloud if you like."

He slid aside another knob, and I began to hear the tread of the horse and the creaking of the saddle and the chink of the armour, as well as a rising breeze which now came sighing through the wood. Like a cinema, you will say, of course. Well, it was; but there was colour and sound, and you could hold it in your hand, and it wasn't a photograph, but the live thing which you could stop at pleasure, and look into every detail of it.

Well, I went on reading, as you may say, this glass. In a theatre, you know, if you saw a knight riding through a forest, the effect would be managed by making the scenery slide backwards past him; and in a cinema it could all be shortened up by increasing the pace or leaving out part of the film. Here it was not like that; we seemed to be keeping pace and going along with the knight. Presently he began to sing. He had a loud voice and uttered his words crisply, so that I had no difficulty in making out the song. It was about a lady who was very proud and haughty to him and would have nothing to say to his suit, and it declared that the only thing left for him was to lay himself down under a tree. But he seemed quite cheerful about it, and indeed neither his complexion nor the glance of his eye gave any sign that he was suffering the pangs of hopeless love.

Suddenly his horse stopped short and snorted uneasily. The knight left off singing in the middle of a verse, looked earnestly into the wood at the back of the picture, and then out towards us, and then behind him. He patted his horse's neck, and then, humming to himself, put on his gauntlets, which were hanging at his saddle bow, managed somehow to latch or bolt the fastenings of them, slipped down his visor, and took the hilt of his sword in one hand and the sheath in the other and loosened the blade in the sheath. He had hardly done this when the horse shied violently and reared; and out of the thicket on the near side of the road (I suppose) something shot up in front of him on the saddle. We all drew in our breath.

"Don't be frightened, dear," said Mrs. Wag to the youngest girl, who had given a sort of jump. "He's quite safe this time."

The Five Jars

I must say it did not look like it. The beast that had leapt on to the saddle was tearing with its claws, drawing back its head and driving it forward again with horrid force against the visor, and was at such close quarters that the knight could not possibly either draw or use his sword. It was a horrible beast, too; evidently a young dragon. As it sat on the saddle-bow, its head was just about on a level with the knight's. It had four short legs with long toes and claws. It clung to the saddle with the hind feet and tore with the fore feet, as I said. Its head was rather long, and had two pointed ears and two small sharp horns. Besides, it had bat wings, with which it buffeted the knight, but its tail was short. I don't know whether it had been bitten or cut off in some previous fight. It was all of a mustard-yellow colour. The knight was for the moment having a bad time of it, for the horse was plunging and the dragon doing its very worst. The crisis was not long, though. The knight took hold of the right wing with both hands and tore the membrane upwards to the root, like parchment. It bled yellow blood, and the dragon gave a grating scream. Then he clutched it hard by the neck and managed to wrench it away from its hold on the saddle; and when it was in the air, he whirled its body, heavy as it was, first over his back and then forwards again, and its neck-bone, I suppose, broke, for it was quite limp when he cast it down. He looked down at it for a little, and seeing it stir, he got off, with the rein over his arm, drew his sword, cut the head off, and kicked it away some yards. The next thing he did was to push up his visor, look upward, mutter something I could not well hear, and cross himself; after which he said aloud, "Where man finds one of a brood, he may look for more," mounted, turned his horse's head and galloped off the way he had come.

90

We had not followed him far through the wood when—

"Bother!" said Wag, "there's the bell"; and he reached over and slid back the knobs in the frame, and the knight stopped.

I was full of questions, but there was no time to put them. Good-nights had to be said quickly, and Father Wag saw me out of the front door.

I set out on what seemed a considerable walk across the rough grass towards the enormous building in which I lived. I suppose I did not really take many minutes about getting to the path; and as I stepped on to it— rather carefully, for it was a longish way down— why, without any shock or any odd feeling, I was my own size again. And I went to bed pondering much upon the events of the day.

Well, I began this communication by saying that I was going to explain to you how it was that I "heard something from the owls," and I think I have explained how it is that I am able to say that I have done so. Exactly what it was that you and I were talking about when I mentioned the owls, I dare say neither of us remembers. As you can see, I have had more exciting experiences than merely conversing with them— interesting, and, I think, unusual as that is. I have not, of course, told you nearly all there is to tell, but perhaps I have said enough for the present. More, if you should wish it, another time.

As to present conditions. To-day there is a slight coolness between Wisp and the cat. He made his way into a mouse-hole which she was watching, and enticed her close up to it by scratchings and other sounds, and then, when she came quite near (taking great trouble, of course, to make

The Five Jars

no noise whatever), he put his head out and blew in her face, which affronted her very much. However, I believe I have persuaded her that he meant no harm.

The room is rather full of them to-night. Wag and most of the rest are rehearsing a play which they mean to present before I go. Slim, who happens not to be wanted for a time, is manœuvring on the table, facing me, and is trying to produce a portrait of me which shall be a little less libellous than his first effort. He has just now shown me the final production, with which he is greatly pleased. I am not.

Farewell. I am, with the usual expressions of regard,

Yours, M (or N).

Printed in Dunstable, United Kingdom